Praise for *The Chalet*

'I didn't know who to trust in this twisting, turning
thriller. Pure adrenaline, from the killer first page to
the chilling last line.'
ERIN KELLY

'I was gripped by *The Chalet* from start to finish and
absolutely loved the vivid setting. A cracking read.'
CASS GREEN

'I LOVED this fun, fast-paced murder mystery. Luxurious
surroundings, great characters and deep, dark secrets. Can't
think of a more perfect book to take a stay-cation with!'
SUZY K QUINN

'I could feel the icy chill blowing through the pages in
The Chalet, and this wasn't just down to the
ominous snow storms. This is a thrilling read that
I just couldn't put down.'
MICHELLE FRANCES, author of *The Girlfriend*

'A chilling and atmospheric thriller full of dark secrets
and addictive twists.'
ROZ WATKINS

'A cleverly plotted thriller set almost entirely in the French
Alps. The descriptions of the snow and the cold brought
back nostalgic memories and m
there. I loved the action on the s
into the world of s
ALLIE REYNOLDS, a

D1506384

Catherine Cooper is a journalist specialising in travel, hotels, and skiing who writes regularly for the *Telegraph* and the *Guardian* among others. She lives near the Pyrenees in the South of France with her husband and two teenage children, and is a keen skier. *The Chalet* is her debut novel.

www.catherinecooperauthor.com

🐦 @catherinecooper
📷 @catherinecooperjournalist

The Chalet

CATHERINE COOPER

HarperCollins*Publishers*

HarperCollins*Publishers*
1 London Bridge Street
London, SE1 9GF

www.harpercollins.co.uk

HarperCollins*Publishers*
1st Floor, Watermarque Building, Ringsend Road
Dublin 4, Ireland

Published by HarperCollins*Publishers* 2020

A catalogue record for this book
is available from the British Library

ISBN: 978-0-00-840022-4

This novel is entirely a work of fiction.
The names, characters and incidents portrayed in it are
the work of the author's imagination. Any resemblance to
actual persons, living or dead, events or localities is
entirely coincidental.

Set in Sabon LT Std by Palimpsest Book Production Limited,
Falkirk, Stirlingshire

Printed and bound in the UK using 100% Renewable Electricity at CPI Group (UK) Ltd

MIX
Paper from
responsible sources
FSC™ C007454

This book is produced from independently certified FSC™ paper
to ensure responsible forest management.

For more information visit: www.harpercollins.co.uk/green

Dedicated to my Mum, much loved and greatly missed xxx

PART ONE

PART ONE

Press Association

18 January 2020

BREAKING NEWS: A British national is reported to have died at the ski resort of La Madière, France. Details are as yet unclear. *More to follow.*

ENDS

1

December 1998, La Madière, France

I hate these kind of people. They come out here on holiday once a year with their brand shiny new Salomon this and K2 that and think they know it all. They're so annoying. They know nothing compared to me.

'So we want some virgin tracks today. Back country. Somewhere no one else goes. Somewhere a bit challenging. Know what I mean?' says one, his accent plummy and entitled.

Yes, I know what you mean. You think you're it, just because you went on a few trips with your posh school and now your smart City job or whatever pays enough for you to come out skiing once or twice a year. Well, let me tell you, you're not. That's why you have to pay someone like me who actually knows what they're doing

5

to come with you as soon as you venture off-piste. For all your flash gear and trying to use the right lingo, you know nothing about the mountains. Nothing.

But of course I don't say that. These are my clients, after all. Instead I say: 'Yup, no problem. I know exactly the place.'

I smile, rictus-like, and answer their pointless, predictable questions as we take the various lifts up to the very top. Yes, it's fun living in a ski resort. Yes, I live here all year round. I lie about how long I've been here – I always do – that's none of their business. No, I don't have any plans to go back to the UK, etc., etc., etc. I love the mountains. They are my home. And my job would be almost perfect – if only I didn't have to deal with clients.

It must be around a Force 8 wind as we get out at the top. The less confident of the two – I can't be bothered to learn their names – pulls a face as the wind slams into us. 'Bloody hell, it's freezing!' he yelps. The other one, maybe a few years older, but it's difficult to tell the way they are so swaddled up in scarves, claps him on the back and booms, 'Don't be such a girl! This is what it's all about!'

I snap my goggles on, pull my hat down over my ears and click my boots into my skis. My two clients are still faffing around with their gloves. Hurry up! I scream inwardly. I'm freezing.

'Hey,' shouts someone in a logoed jacket, one of the annoying tour reps who seem to change pretty much

6

every year, schussing to a stop next to me. 'You taking these guys down the couloir?'

'That's the plan,' I reply, *not that it's any of his business.*

He pulls a face. 'I hope they know what they're doing.' *And I hope you know what you're doing, is what he actually means.*

I roll my eyes – he can't tell as I am wearing my goggles. 'I wouldn't be taking them if I didn't think they were up to it,' *I snap.* 'I've done the risk assessment and they've signed all the correct forms.'

'Hmm. Well, they're my clients too and it's a lot of paperwork and hassle for me if there's an accident,' *he warns. Like I care about his paperwork.*

'Guys!' *the rep, I think he's called Richard, calls to his clients, who are finally putting on their skis, thank Christ.* 'You be careful down there, OK?'

'Right-ho!' *the older one yells.* 'We ready for the off?'

Just then, my business partner Andy turns up. Not for the first time, I wish I'd set up Skitastic on my own.

'Why are you here?' *I ask. Checking up on me, no doubt.*

'My clients have decided to call it a day. Too cold, for them, apparently. Shall I come along with you?'

I'd much rather go on my own – I don't want Andy babysitting me and picking holes in the way I do things – but even I know I can't say that and still look like a

7

reasonable person. So I shrug and say: 'If you like. Makes no difference to me.'

And off we go.

The visibility is appalling. It was bad enough at the top, but once we're over the back, the wind blasts directly into our faces. As I predicted, my two charges are barely up to the task. They both ticked boxes saying 'confident black-run skiers' on the forms – yeah right. It's already clear that that isn't true. I told them this was back country, but it isn't really, luckily for them. I knew they wouldn't be able to cope with anything properly hard-core. 'Couloir Noir', as it's called, isn't actually a couloir at all, it's just a steep, narrow slope. Officially it's off-piste, but it's about as vanilla as off-piste can get. As long as you know where you're going, like I do, you start at the top of the chairlift and you pop right back out at the bottom of the chairlift, no major deal. No hiking, no putting on skins. Nothing much to be alarmed about at all. But because it's at the top of the glacier, these losers can boast about how they went 'down a couloir off the back of the glacier' when they get back to their pathetic little offices or university or wherever it is they go when they're back at home, which is all they want. I know their type.

It's no surprise to me that they don't look like they're enjoying it in any way. Andy has hung back a bit, saying 'I'll pick up any stragglers' and left me leading the clients. As one of them snowploughs and picks their way down,

8

the other one bolts past me, thinking he's something special because he can go fast, whereas in reality he's simply out of control. It's not big or clever, it's downright dangerous. Andy races past me and I shout, 'Make that guy wait! He doesn't know where he's going!' but my voice disappears into the howling wind.

'This is trickier than I expected,' says the slower one.

He's trying to sound confident, but I can hear a wobble in his voice. I know I should say 'You're doing great,' but I can't bring myself to do that, because, well, he isn't. Being nice is Andy's remit, not mine. That's the only reason I have a business partner, I'm not that good at the being friendly bit, while Andy is. I'm just here for the mountains; as far as I'm concerned, the clients are a necessary evil. Andy does the client stuff: the showing them Mont Blanc, the boasting about how the mountains are our office, the going on about how we have the best job in the world and all that. So instead of offering the struggling skier some platitude like Andy would (or lying, if you will), I turn away and simply say: 'Follow my trail. Stay close.'

We catch up with the other guy, who has mercifully had the sense to wait, but after a brief chat about the importance of skiing within your limits I set off again, faster than I would normally like to in these conditions, to make sure I stay ahead of him. He is not going to out-ski me – I am clearly the better skier here by a mile, as well as being in charge. They should be behind me, following my trail, like I told them. Why would they book me if they're not going to do as they're told?

Totally unhelpfully, Andy has disappeared again, who knows how far down the slope. I make a few more turns, faster this time to make sure the clients can't overtake me again, and then look back to see where they are.

And by the time I do that, they've both disappeared.

2

January 2020, La Madière, France

Ria

'Champagne?' says the devastatingly pretty girl in a discreetly logoed polo shirt, holding out a tray of silver flutes. I smile and take one.

'Thank you.'

'How was your trip?' she chirrups, and then surprises me by actually waiting for an answer.

'Oh. It was fine. Thank you.'

'I'm Millie. I'm your chalet girl for the week, and if there's anything I can do to make your stay more comfortable or enjoyable, you only need to ask.'

There's a whoosh of cold air as Hugo comes through the door and puts a proprietorial hand on my waist. I flinch.

'Champagne, sir?' the girl asks, proffering the tray. 'I'm Millie. I'm here to make your stay as comfortable as possible,' she repeats.

'Lovely stuff,' he says.

'Would you like to take a seat by the fire while Matt brings your things in?' Millie continues. 'And I'll bring you some canapés. The others are due in the next hour or so, so I thought we'd wait for them before we start dinner?' With a small nod, she turns and disappears through a wooden door into what I assume must be the kitchen.

Hugo and I sit down on one of the two huge sofas by the roaring fire. I take a swig of my champagne as Hugo slowly sips his. 'It's quite a place, huh?' he says.

It is. An entire side of the building is plate glass – it's dark now, but even so the view of twinkling lights across the valley is amazing – I bet it's even more impressive during the day. The ceiling is double-height, the walls are made of stone, there's a large granite dining table and expensive-looking fur throws everywhere. Real flambeaux were burning outside when we arrived. 'It's quite a place,' I agree. Before I met Hugo, I'd never been anywhere like this.

'It was a good idea of yours, coming here,' he says.

'I knew you'd like it,' I say, blandly.

'I'm sure Simon will love it too,' he adds. 'Very . . . suitable.'

'*Suitable?*' I say, trying and failing to keep the

sarcasm out of my voice. 'Really?' He looks moment-arily hurt, and for a split second, I feel bad. Hugo can be annoying, but he means well. And this week is important to him, I know that. 'What is he, royalty or something?'

'Well, maybe "suitable" was the wrong word,' he mumbles. 'But if Simon has a good week, I've got a much better chance of him buying into the company. You know how these things go.'

I nod, wondering if I'm imagining a subtext of 'so make sure you behave yourself then and don't do anything to embarrass me'.

He takes my hand. 'Are you glad you came along too now?'

I turn to him and smile. 'Yes,' I lie.

Simon arrives around an hour later and is exactly as I expected him to be – overweight, red-faced, and with a booming voice. His comb-over looks distinctly Grecian 2000-ed. Conversely, his wife Cass isn't what I expected at all – she's about twenty years younger than the rest of us – easily young enough to be Simon's daughter – with immaculate blond hair and, most surprisingly, a tiny baby in her arms. Hugo didn't mention that. They are trailed by another young woman, in her very early twenties like Cass, who I guess must be the child's nanny.

After a round of shoulder-slapping and mild insults (Hugo and Simon) and air-kisses and fussing over the baby

(Cass and I – totally insincere on my part), the nanny, Sarah, whisks baby Inigo away and we all sit down for dinner around an enormous table.

Dinner is exquisite. More champagne and dainty amuse-bouches are followed by an incredibly light soufflé, then quail with dauphinoise potatoes, and a platter of desserts. And lots of wine, of course.

I thought it was traditional for chalet girls to eat with their guests, but it turns out this isn't that kind of chalet. I should have guessed. In fact, I should have known, being the one who booked it. Millie moves efficiently between the table and the kitchen, bringing dishes, clearing plates, pouring more wine and water, so no one's glass ever runs dry. Simon is booming away about something – I'm not really listening – and every now and then Hugo laughs or agrees sycophantically. I feel a stab of hatred for him, and then feel guilty. I knew what I was getting into when I married him. It isn't his fault.

Cass and I make polite conversation during dinner. She is sweet but dull. I ask her about the baby even though there is probably no one in the world less interested in babies than me, and she answers politely but somewhat uninterestedly. Before Inigo's birth she worked in catering; she hasn't decided if she's going back to work yet but probably not; Simon is keen she stays at home. She's not very forthcoming. I talk a bit about my work and mine and Hugo's wedding and she smiles and nods, her eyes glazing.

14

I'm beginning to wish I had tried harder to persuade Hugo I didn't need to come along this week.

Millie returns with a tray of coffees and herbal teas and places it gently on the table. 'Unless you need anything else, I'll say goodnight?' she says, tactfully phrasing it as a question. She must be desperate to leave by now. 'I'll see you all in the morning. What time would you like breakfast?'

'Eight o'clock please!' Simon says, without as much as catching anyone else's eye for agreement. 'We want to be out on the first lift tomorrow, don't we, Hugo?'

'Absolutely!' he agrees, as I knew he would. Whatever Simon says goes this week.

'Ladies?' Simon adds. 'I've taken the liberty of booking you an instructor – I hope you don't mind.'

I open my mouth to object – I don't want to get up at eight o'clock and nor do I want a ski lesson. But Hugo shoots me a look and I close my mouth again, silently fuming.

'Sounds great,' says Hugo.

'If you'll excuse me, I think I'm going to go to bed,' I say, yawning theatrically and picking up a mug of herbal tea. 'I'm going to have this in our room.'

'Be there in a minute, darling,' Hugo calls. My skin prickles, and I pretend I haven't heard.

Our room is almost as impressive as the living room. The enormous bed has crisp white linen enclosing an incredibly puffy duvet which is practically obscured by

15

various furry throws and rugs. I stroke one of the throws. Real fur.

There are exposed stone walls and wood panelling everywhere, like downstairs. A huge sliding door rolls back to reveal a freestanding bath for two in the enormous bathroom and there's also a massive marble tile-lined shower. I kick my boots off to feel the heated floors which can be controlled by a touch panel on the wall.

The room is immaculate because all our things from our matching Mulberry luggage (a wedding present from Hugo's mother) have already been unpacked and put away. That's one of those services that these kind of places always offer which I hate – I don't want other people touching my things. I check that my purse and iPad are still in place in my handbag, not that I suppose for one moment they would have been stolen.

I turn the taps on in the enormous bath and tip the entire contents of one of the little green Hermès bottles in. Hermès – very nice. I strip off and throw my clothes on the floor. The mess will annoy Hugo, but I don't care. I sink back into the bubbles, turn off the taps, and close my eyes. Only seven more days to go.

'Ria?' Hugo's voice is sharp and too loud. I open my eyes. The water is lukewarm – I must have fallen asleep. 'Have you seen my book?' He gives me a look – I can't quite work out if it's reproachful or sympathetic. 'You shouldn't fall asleep in the bath. It's dangerous.'

I haul myself up and Hugo hands me a robe, but not before his gaze flicks up and down my naked body. Ugh. 'I know,' I say. 'I'm exhausted though. It's been a long day.'

He trails his fingers lightly down from my neck across my breasts and down to my waist. 'Too tired to . . .' he asks.

I kiss him chastely on the cheek and say: 'Why don't you have a quick shower and then we'll see?' knowing full well that I will pretend to be asleep by the time he gets into bed.

I keep my eyes closed and breathe slowly and evenly as I feel Hugo lie down beside me. He gently kisses the back of my shoulder and I think I hear him sigh as he rolls away and turns the light off.

It feels like the middle of the night when there is a knock on the door. 'Morning! I have tea for you. Can I come in?' Millie calls softly through the door. I press my face into the pillow, ignoring Hugo's erection which is jabbing into my back.

'Come in, we're decent!' Hugo mumbles, flicking the light on.

'I'll leave it here for you,' Millie says as she puts the tray down on the desk, discreetly averting her eyes from the bed. 'Breakfast will be ready for you at eight, but there's no rush if you'd rather have a lie-in.'

I catch a whiff of Hugo's morning breath as he

stretches and yawns while the door clicks quietly shut behind Millie. 'No chance of that,' he says. 'Not if Simon has anything to do with it. Come on,' he throws back the covers exuberantly, 'up you get!'

I sit up blearily. 'Did Simon say something about a ski lesson? Do I honestly have to do that?'

'It would help me massively if you did,' Hugo shouts from the bathroom. 'I'd like you to spend some time with Cass so you can find out what Simon's plans are.'

'Plans?'

He pushes the door open and pulls his toothbrush out of his mouth, rolling his eyes. 'For the business! Is he planning to buy in? What might it take to impress him? What can I do to persuade him? That sort of thing.' He wraps a big white towel around his waist and starts shaving. 'It's no big deal, is it? Cass has skied before, but she's lost her confidence since the baby was born, according to Simon. It's not like you're only going to be on the nursery slopes or anything. Simon just thought she'd be happier with an instructor. I think it's rather sweet. Thoughtful of him.'

I sigh and throw back the duvet. 'Fine. But if it's too boring, I'm going to make my excuses and leave.'

I pad into the shower and switch it on, enjoying the powerful torrent of slightly too hot water from the huge rainhead on my skin. Much as I'd prefer not to be here, I have to admit the luxurious surroundings are pretty fantastic.

Once Hugo has finished shaving, he drops his towel

18

and takes it upon himself to join me in the shower. It is absolutely the last thing I can be bothered with right now, but I can't think of an excuse to get him out.

3

December 1998, La Madière, France

Where are they? I go to call out to them but then remember I don't know their names. Andy will probably know. 'You all right there?' I yell. Silence. The wind is picking up and the visibility is worse than ever. 'Guys? You there?'

Andy finally hones into view further down the slope as I slowly traverse my way down.

'Where were you?' I fume as I stop, deliberately spraying snow at the fucker. 'I've lost the clients!' A panicky feeling is rising inside me even though this is not my fault. It isn't. The clients shouldn't have lied to me. They shouldn't have told me they were much better skiers than they actually are. What if I'd taken them down the kind of terrain they were actually asking for?

What if we'd tried something steeper and more gnarly? Then where would we be?

'I thought you had them,' Andy says.

'You should have been watching!' I explode.

'Bloody hell, calm down, Cameron! They'll be fine. They must have gone ahead of us – you can't see where anyone is when it's like this.'

'I would have seen them if they'd gone past me,' I counter.

'Yeah, right, whatever. Either way, standing here isn't going to achieve anything. Best we can do is carry on down and see if we catch up with them. If we get down and we still haven't seen then, then we'll think about what to do next.'

Andy sets off down the slope without waiting for me to reply, almost instantly disappearing out of sight because the visibility is so bad. I race after, furiously. No one is beating me down the slope just to prove they're the better skier! After a few seconds I whizz past the twat, down, down, down. I can barely see a thing but it doesn't matter, I know this slope so well I could ski it with my eyes closed. Which I might as well be doing, given the conditions right now.

I'm so focused on beating Andy down that it's only when I get to the bottom I remember the missing clients. Argh! Where are they?

I stare up at the slope, but there's no one in sight. A few seconds later, Andy appears. 'I thought we were meant to be looking for the clients? Why'd you race off like that?'

22

'Seeing if I could catch them up if they were ahead,' I lie. 'Don't want them deciding to fuck off home because we've left them standing in the cold too long.' Where are they? 'You didn't see them?' I ask Andy.

'No.' There's a pause. 'D'you think we should call someone? Let someone know they've gone AWOL?'

In spite of the freezing wind I feel a bead of sweat run down my back inside my jacket. 'It's a bit early for that, isn't it? I bet they're fine. Let's head up on the lift and ski down again, properly slowly this time. We'll probably pick them up second time around. You'll give me a hand, won't you?' I ask, even though it almost kills me to say it.

Andy gives me a strange look. 'Yeah. I will. It's dangerous for them out there on their own in these conditions. Let's get going.'

Back on the lift, it is even colder and windier than before. I pull my scarf tighter around my neck and dig my chin into the top of my jacket. I peer downwards through the blizzard in case the clients have somehow made it back on to the piste – it's possible from the couloir, though only really if you know the way – but I can barely see a thing. Even the piste appears to be deserted – anyone sensible has already called it a day.

The lift shudders to a halt about halfway up, leaving us swinging as the wind continues to roar around us. We sit in silence, huddled into our jackets, faces down against the wind. After a few minutes which pass more *like hours, there is a squeal and the lift starts moving again. Thank God. 'Can't wait to get off this mountain,' Andy says. 'It's freezing. God knows why these poor saps come out in this weather.'*

The chairlift stops again just as the lift station comes into sight. Someone has fallen over getting off and is for some reason taking forever to get themselves back upright, despite the lift guy hauling them up. There's something purple in the snow by their feet – a hat or scarf. I watch as they bend to pick it up and drop their pole.

'Hurry up!' I mutter, through clenched teeth. My fingers hurt, they're dug so far into my hands now. Andy looks at me sideways and says: 'It'll be OK. You need to calm down.'

'I am calm!' I snap, but I'm lying. I'm not. The lift finally starts moving again and we slide off onto the snow.

'OK – I'll take the left side, you take the right,' I say. 'We need to go down really slowly. Both of us,' I emphasize. I feel like I'm going to be sick. The trail is narrow and what I want to say is, 'We need to check over the edges too,' but I can't quite bring myself to. The weather is still closing in and it's going to be impossible to see anything anyway. Andy nods solemnly. My unspoken words are hanging in the air.

I feel worse and worse as we ski down in near silence. I try to peer over the edges but it's impossible. We call out periodically – 'Hey! You there? You OK?' but I can

tell it's pointless – I can't even hear myself over the wind.
We get to the bottom and look at each other.

   I am so cold and stressed I can barely get my words
out. 'What do we do now?'

4

January 2020, La Madière, France

Ria

I didn't want to come this week, for many reasons, but even so, it feels good to be in the mountains. The sun is out, the sky is blue and the air is clear. I went out this morning with every intention of playing the dutiful wife and skiing with Cass like Hugo wanted me to, but in the end I found that, after a few runs, I just couldn't be bothered. Sorry, Hugo. Cass is young and boring and once I've asked about the baby which I'm not interested in and her former catering business (ditto) we don't really have anything to say to each other.

I head back to the chalet hoping that no one will be there so I can spend some time in the hot tub on my own. But as soon as I open the door I can hear that someone else is here. Millie appears at the top of the stairs, straightens her logoed polo shirt and rearranges her face into its usual fixed smile.

'Hello, Ria. I wasn't expecting you back so early – I understood Simon had booked you an instructor for the whole day.' Her forehead creases. 'I hope everything's OK?'

'Yes, everything's fine – just thought I'd spend some time in the hot tub.' It comes out snappier than I'd intended, so I smile to try to soften it. Sometimes I forget how to play the part of the dutiful corporate wife. Or it's not so much that I forget, it's more that I simply don't want to. 'It's a while since I've skied and my legs are already aching. Is it OK if I use the hot tub? I don't want to get in your way.'

'Yes of course!' she gushes. 'Whatever you like. I'll go and take the cover off for you now if you want to go up and get changed? I've finished doing the rooms up here. Would you like me to bring you anything out there – a glass of bubbly maybe? Or some water?'

I shake my head. 'No, that's fine, thank you.'

Millie nods discreetly, comes down the stairs and goes out to the large terrace where I see steam rise from the hot tub as she pulls back the cover. After changing, I spend the afternoon alternating between the hot tub and the terrace, where Millie brings me a heated blanket for my lounger. I decide to take her up on her offer of a glass of champagne or two after all. It is blissful.

* * *

It's amazing what a difference an afternoon all to myself makes to my mood – by the early evening I'm almost glad to be here. Almost. The fire is lit in the double-height living room, the stars are out, and the champagne is ice-cold. I guess things could be a lot worse.

'Ria – may I introduce Matt please?' Millie says as she offers me a tray of hors d'oeuvres. Matt is in the same polo shirt as Millie and very much in the same mould although older – immaculately groomed and with a fixed smile.

'I'm the rep for Snow Snow within the resort,' he says, shaking my hand. 'We have five chalets here, as you may know, twenty throughout the Alps, but we like to pride ourselves on individual service. Is the chalet to your liking?'

'Yes – it's lovely,' I say. 'It's even better in the flesh than in the pictures.' I feel myself redden. I'm not sure why.

'We're particularly proud of this one – our most luxurious, even if it is one of the smaller ones,' Matt says. 'So how was your day today – did you get out on the slopes?'

'I did for a while – it was very nice. And I enjoyed the hot tub too.'

His eyes almost imperceptibly flick up and down my body and I wonder if he is imagining me naked. Hugo comes over and puts his arm around my shoulders, but I shrug him off, pretending I'm reaching for a canapé.

'Matt, this is Hugo,' I say, deliberately not introducing

29

him as my husband. Hugo shakes Matt's hand and then starts boring on about the runs he and Simon did today, the specifications of his skis, the importance of various bits of kit and loads of other stuff that Matt no doubt has no desire to hear about.

I tune out for a while and when I turn my attention back to the conversation a few seconds (or minutes? Who knows?) later, the conversation has turned to how long Matt has worked in the resort and his plans for the future.

Eventually we sit down to dinner. I make sure I sit next to Matt – not because I particularly fancy him, but at least flirting with him will provide me with a distraction.

Dinner is amazing, again, and the wine is fabulous. I drink more than I should. Hugo won't like me getting drunk, especially in front of a potential investor like Simon, but, well, whatever. I feel like drinking tonight and so I will. Getting drunk is the only way I'm going to get through the week, plus it'll give me a good excuse to stay in bed tomorrow morning and not go to my boring ski lesson with boring Cass and listen to her bore on about her boring baby. Hugo is being pathetically sycophantic, laughing at Simon's crap jokes in between glaring angrily at me when he thinks no one is looking.

Millie reappears at the table and Hugo puts his hand over my wine glass. 'I think you've had enough, don't you, darling?' he says with a fake smile. He almost never does stuff like that – dares to tell me what to do. He's obviously desperate to impress Simon.

But as far as I'm concerned, that doesn't mean I can't have a drink if I want to. 'No, I don't think I have,' I say, flicking his hand off my glass and turning towards Millie. 'More of the delicious red, please – thank you.'

Millie hesitates and then pours me a small glass. I feel a twinge of pity for her – it's not fair to involve her in my rage towards Hugo. I resolve to leave her a huge tip when we leave. 'In fact,' I state, slurring slightly and, I admit, deliberately, riled by Hugo's attempt to make me feel guilty, 'I think we should play a drinking game. Who's up for it?'

'Always up for a drinking game!' Simon practically shouts. 'Quite the filly you've got there, Hugo!' he adds, raising his glass to him across the table. Hugo glances at me and I grin.

'How about "I have never"?' booms Simon.

'Yes! I'll start,' I yelp. 'I have never . . . had a three-some.'

Simon roars with laughter. Hugo looks at me in horror. Matt raises his glass and drinks, smirking.

'Matt!' Simon bellows. 'You dirty dog. Now that's a story I'd like to hear. OK, you go.'

Cass stands up abruptly. 'Will you all excuse me?' She pulls the sleeves of her somewhat frumpy cardigan down over her hands and casts a nervous glance towards her boorish husband. 'I'm going to check on Inigo and then go to bed. I'll see you in the morning.'

31

Without waiting for a response, she smiles tightly and leaves the table. Simon doesn't even look at her. 'Come on, come on . . .' he prompts Matt.

Matt clears his throat. 'I have never . . . been to Zimbabwe.'

'Oh please!' Simon shouts. 'You don't need to go all polite and poncey just because we're clients. Although,' he drains his glass, 'I'll drink to that obviously – and you too Hugo, you girl.' Hugo obediently empties his glass and winces. He's never been a big drinker. 'Do another.'

Matt grins. 'OK . . . I have never . . . had a same-sex sexual encounter.'

Hugo reddens and Simon looks expectant as I slowly drain my glass and slam it down.

Simon slaps his hand on the table. 'Ha! Brilliant. That's an image that . . . anyway, Ria – your go.'

'I have never . . .' the words 'been in love' force themselves into my mind but instead I say, 'been arrested.'

Nobody drinks. I put my hand on the inside of Matt's thigh. He doesn't push it away.

A few rounds later, Hugo, who is quite clearly furious with me for not adequately playing the part of the corporate wife, says he's going to bed and Millie also takes her leave. By now my hand has reached Matt's crotch and I can feel he's hard. I wish Simon would go to bed but he's pouring himself another glass of wine and wants to move on to Fuzzy Duck.

32

Suddenly tiredness overwhelms me in the way it some-times does when I'm too drunk. I retrieve my hand, stand up and say: 'I can't drink any more. I'm off to bed. Night all.'

Matt looks at me aghast – obviously thought his luck was in. Maybe it is. Maybe another night.

I stumble up the stairs into our room, expecting it to be in darkness, but Hugo is sitting up in bed, jaw clenched, pretending to read. He puts his book down and stares at me.

'How dare you embarrass me like that,' he hisses.

I wave my hand at him and lurch into the bathroom. ''S fine. Simon loved it. And you're here to impress Simon, as am I, apparently. If anything, I've done you a favour.' I lean in towards the mirror and beam at myself. 'He thinks I'm *great*.'

'Well, I don't,' Hugo says, prissily, now at the bath-room door in his Hugo Boss boxer shorts instead of the horrible old Y-fronts he used to wear. One of the many minor adjustments I've persuaded him into since we got married. 'And the way you were flirting with Matt too – God! What did I do to deserve that?'

I look at him blearily. 'Nothing, darling,' I say, I can't be bothered with being told off by Hugo. But I know the best way to end this, and as I'm so drunk the idea doesn't seem too unbearable. I wobble over to him and put my hand down his boxers. He makes a pathetic attempt to pull away huffily, but I know he can never resist me. Thankfully, it doesn't take too long.

5

December 1998, La Madière, France

'We're going to have to phone it in,' Andy says. 'Make it official.'

I feel sick. 'Don't you think it's too soon? Maybe they made their own way down and are chugging vin chaud in a bar as we speak?' I suggest.

There's a pause. 'D'you think?'

Argh. 'I don't know!' I shout. 'Either way, we're in serious trouble.'

I know we're both thinking the same thing. If we call out search and rescue and it turns out the men are fine, we've still lost two clients in bad weather. Word gets round about that kind of thing very quickly and no one will ever book us again. And if the clients aren't in the bar, if they're really lost, then . . .

'We can't do nothing, Cameron!' Andy snaps, clearly thinking the same as me and starting to panic too. 'We need to think. Do something. What's the best thing to do? How about we check if they're back at their chalet?'

'For fuck's sake!' I explode. I take a deep breath. Calm down. Calm down. 'OK. Here's the plan,' I say. 'You whizz back to the office and call the chalet. I'll go back up and check the route again. You radio me as soon as you've called them, and I'll radio you if I find them before you're back. If we still haven't found them, then we're going to have to phone it in.'

Andy doesn't say anything.

'Agreed?' I prompt. 'It'll take you max twenty minutes to get back. We don't want to mess everything up for no reason when everything's probably fine. Yeah?'

Andy nods. 'Yeah. I'll go down and we'll speak in twenty. But everyone can hear us on the radio, so I'll say "all good" if it's OK or, um, I don't know, "nothing here" if not. You do the same.'

I watch Andy disappear off down the slope and get back on the lift, bracing myself against the wind. The thought of 'if not' hangs ominously in the air.

6

January 2020, La Madière, France

Ria

There is a gentle knocking at the door and Millie comes in with our morning tea. I keep my eyes tightly shut. My head hurts and my mouth is dry. I don't want to have to deal with Hugo's disapproving looks and I don't want to listen to a lecture about how I need to behave better if he wants to get Simon on board. I simply don't care. I shouldn't have come here. Maybe I shouldn't have even married Hugo.

I hear the door close softly and Hugo prods me in the back. Thankfully this morning it is with his hand. 'Ria? You awake?'

I mumble something incoherent which I hope makes

37

me sound like I'm still asleep. Hugo sighs, gets out of bed and goes into the shower. I carry on pretending to sleep while he gets dressed and he doesn't try to wake me. I guess he's still annoyed about how I behaved last night. Once he's left the room, I manage to fall back to sleep for real.

What feels like seconds later, Hugo slams open the door and says, far too loudly, 'Ria! Wake up! Now!'

I open my eyes and look at him grumpily. 'What? Why can't you let me sleep? Do I have to go skiing each and every day with bloody Cass? I thought this was supposed to be a holiday, for me at least, not just some giant schmoozefest. Why can't I stay in bed if I want to?'

'God, Ria, it's always about *you*, isn't it?' Hugo says, uncharacteristically snappy. 'I don't care if you're too hungover to ski. Serves you right after your appalling display last night. Anyway, you need to get up. Cass has gone missing and we need to help look for her.'

I sit up and rub my eyes. 'What? Why do we need to look for her? She's a grown woman. She's probably gone for a walk or something.'

Hugo sighs. 'You may well be right, but Simon is beside himself. It seems she's been suffering with post-natal depression and he's worried she might hurt herself or something. He says she wouldn't go out without the baby and without telling anyone.'

I sigh and sink back onto the pillows. 'Yes she would

– the baby's always with the nanny. Cass barely seems to spend any time with it at all.'

Hugo strides over to the bed and hauls the covers back. I turn over on to my front, feeling strangely exposed. 'It doesn't matter what you or I think,' he says in a low voice. 'I'm sure she's fine too. But I want us to look like we're being helpful. Like we care – which I do, even if you don't. So get yourself out of bed and get dressed, OK?'

Once I've had a quick shower, some paracetamol and two Berocca to try to wake myself up, I go downstairs to the living room.

Simon is sitting on the leather sofa, holding the baby and staring into space. Matt is on the phone speaking French and gesticulating, and Millie is standing anxiously and awkwardly by the sofa, patting Simon's shoulder.

'Simon?' Hugo says. 'What can we do to help? Should we go and walk around the resort? See if we can see her?'

I look out the window and see that it is snowing. Really quite hard. *Please say no*, I plead inwardly.

Simon ignores Hugo's question, gets up from the sofa and distractedly hands Hugo the baby. Hugo makes a coochy-coo noise at Inigo and Inigo giggles. 'Who's a gorgeous boy?' Hugo says in that stupid high-pitched voice everyone seems to use to talk to babies.

Simon gives Hugo a despairing look, runs his hand through his thinning hair and paces up and down by the enormous glass wall. Hugo turns his attention back to Simon, pulling a sympathetic face while gently rocking the baby.

'It's all my fault,' Simon says, his voice strained and strangulated. 'I shouldn't have stayed up last night. I shouldn't have got drunk. I should have been in bed with Cass, looking after my wife and my baby. It's all my fault. She's so vulnerable at the moment. I shouldn't have brought her here. If anything's happened to her . . .'

Millie pats his shoulder again.

'I'm sure she's fine, Simon,' I say, in what I think is my best sympathetic voice. Hugo will be impressed. 'She's probably gone out to clear her head or something.'

Matt gets off the phone. 'Well I've called the gendarmes and they say they'll keep an eye out for her, but it's too early to do anything yet as she's an adult and she's only been missing a maximum of a few hours. I've also called the tourist office and the *mairie*, but there's not . . .'

'The hospitals!' Simon almost shouts, stopping his pacing. 'Shouldn't we call the hospitals?'

Matt and Millie exchange a look. Sarah, who has just come in with Inigo's blanket, subtly rolls her eyes at me and I hold in a smirk. She reaches her arms out towards Hugo to take the baby and Hugo kisses Inigo's head before he hands him over. Ugh.

'Shall we wait a little and see if Cass turns up first?' Matt says tentatively. 'After all, we've no real evidence that anything is wrong yet.'

Simon slumps down onto the sofa and sinks his head back into his hands. 'I'd like it if you would call the local hospitals, please,' he says quietly, without looking up. 'I would do it, but I don't speak any French.'

'Of course,' Matt says, in a professional tone of voice, no doubt hiding his irritation. 'I'll do it now.'

'I'll go and have a walk around the resort,' Hugo says. 'She's got to be somewhere.' He looks at me meaningfully. I say nothing. But then I glance at Simon again and he seems so pitiful that I can't help but say: 'I'll go too, soon as I've changed into something warmer.'

Hugo and I agree that we will cover the ground more quickly if we split up. The chalet is piste-side on the very edge of the village, so once we've walked down the tree-lined driveway to the main road at the top of the village, he sets off to the left while I say I will walk around to the right. If I was Cass, who has no doubt slipped out for some quiet time by herself, I'd be really annoyed to be found. So I put my head round the door in most of the cafés and shops I pass for the first hundred metres or so and then stop for a café au lait in one which has a particularly nice open fire.

About an hour later I wander back to the chalet. Nothing much seems to have changed except that Matt has gone and Simon has moved over to the huge glass wall where he is staring miserably out over the valley. Hugo isn't there, and I wonder briefly if I should have stayed out longer pretending to look for Cass.

'No news?' I ask. Millie smiles sympathetically and shakes her head.

'Not yet,' she says.

'I don't understand where she could have gone,' Simon says hoarsely, banging his fist against the glass. 'If anything's happened to her, I'll never forgive myself.'

7

December 1998, La Madière, France

I take the chairlift back up again. The wind is now blowing even harder and it is absolutely freezing. The lift keeps stopping, no doubt as the few fools who are still out braving this weather fall over as they fight to get off and stay upright at the top with the wind buffeting them. If the wind gets any stronger, they'll probably have to close these upper lifts. Which means I might only have one more go at checking the run before . . . I must find them this time, I think. I must. It's so hard to see in this weather. They've got to be there somewhere.

As the lift gets to the top, my radio crackles. My hands are so frozen that I struggle to pull my gloves off and unzip my breast pocket. Is it Andy? 'Hello?' I shout. The lift station looms into view through the mist and I

43

wrestle against the wind to force the safety bar up. 'Hello?' I shout again into the radio as the wind catches the bar and throws it back down, bumping my arm and jolting the radio from my frozen fingers.

'Fuck!' I shout as I watch the radio fall, quickly enveloped by the mist. I throw the bar up and slide off the lift onto the snow.

Now what? Were they back at the chalet or not? Was that even Andy on the radio? I'll have one more check of the slope and then I'll have to head back to the office, check in with Andy and see if they've been found.

I ski as slowly as I ever have, traversing wide, unable to see beyond about a metre in front of me, calling all the time. 'Hello? Anyone there?' It's deserted. Anyone with any sense has gone back to their cosy chalets and apartments by now.

I get to the bottom; there's no sign. Feeling like I might be sick, I head back to the office.

If Andy hasn't found them, we're going to have to make a decision. Although chances are, if they really are in trouble, anything we do will already be too late.

44

8

January 2018, London

Hugo

I'd always thought that someone like Ria would be totally out of my league.

I'm not exactly ugly or anything, I'm more what you'd call nondescript. No one remembers me. Even my mum struggles to pick me out in old school photos.

So I absolutely couldn't believe it when Ria approached me at the party. It was a work party, and I hadn't wanted to go, even though it was a party thrown by my company so, by extension, a party hosted by me – not that I had any hand in organizing it beyond signing the cheques. I'm not very good at events, but my brilliant PA Olivia says that, as the owner of the company, I have to go to these things. I don't really see why – I think if anything, my social ineptitude is likely to put people off using my company rather than encourage them to do so. Olivia is beautiful and clever and always knows what to say, so personally I think it would be better if she did all the socializing for me, but no. That's not how it works. Not according to Olivia, anyway.

'Clients like the fact that we're a small company with a real face – your face,' she says. 'When they book a holiday through you, they feel they're getting personal service.'

'But I don't have anything to do with the clients. I certainly don't book their holidays for them. Most of them do it online now, anyway.'

She tuts and rolls her eyes. 'Stop being so literal. You know what I mean.'

I don't, but experience has taught me there's no point arguing with Olivia.

My driver takes us to the party – this one is at the Natural History Museum. At least if I get stuck for something to talk about with the clients, I can comment on the exhibits. Everyone likes the big blue whale, but many liked the dinosaur better. I wonder if Olivia had that in mind when she booked the place – a ready-made conversation piece. She knows I am useless socially and makes allowances for me. I don't know what I'd do without her.

The party starts at eight and we arrive at half past. I'm grateful that Olivia no longer makes me be present at our parties from the outset to greet everyone as they arrive, like she used to when she first started working for me. Luckily, she soon saw how awkward that was for all concerned. In some ways, walking into a huge room full of people is harder, but in other ways it's much easier. If I arrive later, everyone has a drink in their hand and has usually found an old colleague or friend to talk to, so most of them are less bothered about talking to me. Some come along to try to do business with me in a very direct way, which always appals me as I never know how to react. But it seems to me that for most of the people who come, these events are really about the free champagne. It costs the company a fortune but, according to Olivia, the PR people, and the accountants who know more about these things than me, these twice-yearly events are worth it for the 'goodwill', whatever that means. So I take them at their word and grin and bear it. Or bear it, anyway.

The car draws up outside the museum and the driver gets out and opens the door for us.

'Ready?' Olivia says.

I groan. 'As I'll ever be.'

'It's two hours of your life. Maximum three. Try and enjoy it.'

'You know I won't. I never do.' I arrange my face into a fixed smile. 'Better?' I ask.

She sighs. 'Kind of. Come on, let's get inside.'

As soon as we're through the door, a wall of noise hits me. How can anyone enjoy this? A couple of sweaty-looking men in cheap suits and name badges approach me straight away and shake my hand. One of them starts talking at me about some hotel his group has acquired and how it would be a brilliant fit for us. I am looking at him, smiling and nodding occasionally but I'm not listening. I hate all this and I'm no good at it. I'm much happier doing business by email – even a phone call somewhat fills me with dread. I want to go home.

'Do you think it could be of interest?' he pushes.

'Possibly,' I say vaguely, having absolutely no idea because I have no clue what he said. I stopped listening before the end of his first sentence, and I can't stand being put on the spot like this anyway. I pass him my card. 'Can you email my secretary and we'll have a look? As I'm sure you understand, these decisions aren't made in an instant. Or, in all honesty, by me usually. I just sign them off.' I have rehearsed this line. Olivia came up with it for me.

Olivia looks at me in the way that a proud mother might look at a four-year-old performing in his first nativity play – in that 'see, I know you can do it!' way. I should probably feel patronized by her, but I don't – I couldn't manage without her. My palms are sweating. I don't want to talk to these people.

'It was lovely to meet you, but I'd better circulate. I'll look out for your email,' I add, which is a total lie. I've already forgotten the guy's name and who he works for.

'Of course, of course!' he says, whipping out his card and pressing it into my hand. I immediately give it to Olivia, who pulls a face and it's only then I remember that she's told me before that that looks rude. 'I'm giving it to Olivia for safekeeping,' I bluster, no doubt making an already awkward situation worse.

'I'll email your secretary tomorrow,' says the hotel man as he backs away.

Olivia gives me an exasperated look.

'What?' I ask.

'You know what,' she mutters, rolling her eyes. 'Come on, let's get you a drink.'

I wonder about reminding her that she should be more polite to me as I'm paying her salary, but I remember that last time I did that she threatened to resign. And I don't want that. It would be a disaster.

Olivia lifts two glasses from a tray carried by a skinny girl in a black dress which is so tight you can see her nipples. I remind myself that you are not allowed to notice things like that these days and keep my eyes firmly on her face. Olivia hands a glass to me and says: 'Right. Half an hour of mingling, then a short speech. Another half an hour of mingling, and then you can go and get back to your computer games or whatever it is you do in your spare time. OK?'

'Yup.'

A woman in a suit bustles up to Olivia and starts babbling about some issue with the canapés. I am wondering if it's OK to wait for the canapés woman to

49

finish so that Olivia can continue to circulate with me, but then the canapés woman strides off with Olivia teetering after her, so I'm left on my own.

A panicky feeling rises in me as I glance around the huge room full of what looks like tight-knit groups laughing and joking together – how can I possibly march up to one of them and start talking? I might be paying for the party but that doesn't make it any easier to join a group of people I don't know and think of something to say. Now that everyone has had a glass or two and become reacquainted with their industry mates, they've probably forgotten that their whole reason for being here is meant to be to suck up to me.

I down my champagne and abandon the glass on a nearby table. I'm about to head off to the gents for a pee to give me something to do when a woman with sleek dark hair wearing a tight emerald-green dress appears in front of me. My first thought is that she looks like a mermaid.

'Mr Redbush?' She tilts her head to one side and hands me a glass of champagne.

'Hugo, please,' I say, as Olivia said I should in almost all situations. 'And you are?'

'Ria. I run an events company, it's called, um, Ria Events.'

I laugh, even though it isn't funny. 'Good name.'

'Thanks,' she says, blushing. 'Sometimes we book locations and hotels through Redbush Holidays, which is why I'm . . .'

'It's very kind of you to come,' I say. 'I hope you are enjoying the evening?'

I sound like some kind of Victorian gentleman or Montgomery Burns from *The Simpsons*. I am always rubbish at speaking to women. I look over Ria's shoulder to see if I can spot Olivia.

'It's lovely here,' she says, circling her finger around the top of her champagne glass. 'I mean, it's a lovely venue. I haven't been here before.'

'You never came to the museum as a child?' I ask.

'No.' She pauses. 'My childhood was rather odd. But you don't want to hear about that now.'

I do actually, but feel it would now be impolite to ask.

Ria looks up at me through long, dark lashes. 'In all honesty, I'm not much good at parties. I always find events like this intimidating. I feel I have to come for the sake of networking and the like but, honestly, I'd rather be in a quiet bar chatting one-to-one with someone.'

I smile. 'I know exactly how you feel.'

She takes a strand of her almost-black hair and twirls it around her finger. I feel a stirring of lust in my groin and panic – is she about to walk off?

'All these people,' she continues. 'So exhausting. In many ways, I think I'm in the wrong line of work. I make my living organizing parties and events, but I'd rather gouge my eyes out than actually go to one. In many ways, I'm just not that good with people.'

I smile. 'I'm totally with you there. I'm not supposed

51

to admit this, but these parties fill me with dread. I'm much happier talking one-to-one too.' Argh. Does that sound too cheesy? Like a bad pick-up line?

Olivia reappears at my side. 'Right. All sorted. Now then . . .'

'Olivia – this is Ria. She runs Ria Events and books locations through Redbush sometimes.' Making an introduction. Giving them both some information about each other. Olivia will be impressed – it's what she's always trying to drill into me. I don't want Olivia to whisk me off to talk to more boring men in shiny suits – I want to stay here and talk to Ria. She's the only woman who's spoken to me all evening, and definitely the only person I've met here, or anywhere recently for that matter, who I'd actually like to spend more time with.

Olivia extends her hand. 'Ria. Lovely to meet you. Thank you for coming. I hope you're enjoying the evening? I'm so sorry, but I'll need you to excuse Hugo, he has to give a speech . . .'

'It was lovely to meet you, Ria. I'd love to continue our conversation later,' I say. I feel myself blush. I'm terrible at this. Was that too direct? Am I going to scare her away? Am I supposed to pretend I'm not bothered in case she thinks I'm a potential stalker? Might she even think I'm harassing her? Am I being inappropriate as she's a client? Would she feel like she had to come for a drink with me if I asked? It's such a minefield talking to women these days. 'I mean, only if you'd like to . . .' I bluster.

Olivia looks at her watch, clearly embarrassed for me. 'Hugo, we need to—'

'I'd love to,' Ria says, to my utter amazement.

Olivia's mouth drops open. I clap my hands together, and then silently admonish myself for doing so. 'Great! Well, I'll get my presentation out the way, then we can go somewhere quieter. Nicer. Just you and me. Like we were talking about a minute ago.'

She smiles shyly. 'Yeah. That would be lovely.'

Olivia takes me by the arm and smiles tightly at Ria. 'Will you excuse us, please?'

'I'll see you by the stage in twenty minutes,' I call behind me to Ria as Olivia bustles me away.

'What was that about?' Olivia hisses.

'What? Can't I ask a girl out if I want to? I mean, ask a woman out?'

Olivia rolls her eyes. 'Well of course you can, but this is hardly the time or the place. You're supposed to be networking, not asking out the first female who thrusts her tits at you. You're the boss here – there's no need to be so *grateful*.'

I am mildly shocked – Olivia never speaks to me like that. Or rather, she does but I've never heard her say anything like 'tits' before. She sighs, stops marching me towards the stage and turns to face me.

'Sorry. Who you do or don't ask out is none of my business – it's up to you, of course. I just don't want to see you . . . taken advantage of.'

I don't entirely understand what she means. I get

53

that some women are going to find my money attractive but that doesn't mean I can't take anyone out for a drink, does it? Sometimes I think that's why I'm still on my own. It's easy for me to assume women who want to spend time with me are only after my money. Sometimes they are. But I like to think I can spot those women a mile off. Besides, even if I include the so-called gold-diggers, I'm hardly beating off women with a stick.

'Thank you for your concern, but I'm a big boy, Olivia, I can make my own decisions,' I say primly. 'Now, shall we get this presentation out of the way?'

The presentation is mortifying as usual but I read the words on the autocue and everyone claps politely, no doubt counting the minutes until they can get back to drinking their champagne. I can't concentrate properly, wondering if Ria will be waiting for me like she said or if she's already gone off to giggle with her friends about how dorky I was when we spoke. Perhaps she was only talking to me as part of a bet or dare. It's not like that's never happened before, though admittedly not for a good few years (or not that I know of, at least). Do grown-ups do that kind of thing? I don't really know.

I step down off the stage and Ria is there at the front, right where I suggested she wait. I grin. Maybe I didn't mess things up too badly this time. 'Ready?' I ask.

She smiles back. 'Ready.'

I ignore Olivia, who is frantically trying to tell me

that I need to stay at the party and network some more. Business can wait this time.

We go to my club, though I'm not sure it's quite the right place to take someone like Ria. While it's quiet and exclusive, it's not exactly what you might call hip. But as I almost never go out socially, I can't think of anywhere else to go.

We sit on a low sofa, facing each other and holding those enormous gin and tonics with peppercorns and rosemary they serve there. I don't consider myself the most interesting of people, but Ria is easy to talk to and laughs at my feeble jokes. She keeps touching my arm to make her point and, after a few more drinks, her leg is pressed up against my leg. Despite my lack of confidence when it comes to these things, a couple of hours later when I ask her if she'd like to come home with me and she says yes, I'm not really that surprised.

9

January 2020, La Madière, France

Ria

In the time it takes me to go upstairs and get changed into some dry clothes, Cass arrives back. I hear a small commotion while I'm getting dressed and by the time I go downstairs she's sitting on one of the enormous sofas with Inigo fidgeting in her lap while Sarah hovers nearby. Cass's eyes are shiny and she's pulled her oversized cardigan down over her hands again in that nervous way she always does. If I didn't know better, I'd probably assume Cass was the nanny and Sarah the spoilt young wife. Cass somehow looks out of place and uncomfortable in these luxurious surroundings, making even her high-end designer clothes look cheap and

57

ill-fitting. Sarah, however, seems completely unfazed by it all. Perhaps she has nannied for rich families before.

'Ria!' Cass calls as I come in, unnaturally bright. 'I'm so sorry you went out looking for me unnecessarily. I woke up early, went out for a walk and forgot to take my phone – it didn't occur to me that anyone would be worried.' She looks vague and spacey and I wonder if she's on antidepressants. Didn't Hugo say something about postnatal depression earlier?

'Because why would it?' Simon says, snippily. His 'devoted and worried husband' mode of earlier appears to have disappeared. 'We've wasted Matt's entire morning, making him call the hospitals and the police, and Hugo and Ria have been all over the resort looking for you. In fact, Hugo is still out there in the cold for all I know – I can't get hold of him to let him know you're back.'

'It's not a problem for me. Don't worry at all,' Matt says. 'That's what I'm here for.' He glances at his watch. 'That said, I'm a bit behind now with a few other things, so since Cass is safely back perhaps you wouldn't mind if I . . .'

'No! No, of course not,' Simon says, clapping Matt on the back effusively. 'I'm only sorry my *wife* has wasted your time in this way.' He emphasizes wife in a way which couldn't have sounded more sneering if he'd tried – he might as well have said 'stupid little wife' and be done with it.

Cass is fussing over Inigo and pretending she isn't

58

listening, but I see her redden and tears brim at Simon's words.

'It's honestly fine,' Matt reiterates magnanimously. 'I'll pop by for a drink later in case there's anything you need.'

As soon as Matt is out of the door, Simon's face darkens. 'Right. Well, now you're back, Cass, I should go and find Hugo and tell him the *good news* that you're here. Can't have him tramping around in this weather for no good reason.' Simon gives Cass a final disparaging look – she is still dandling Inigo on her knee and pretends not to notice – before he storms out of the chalet, banging the door behind him.

Cass looks up at me. 'I'm sorry if I worried you, Ria.' She looks back at the baby and I see the tears which were brimming fill her eyes and roll slowly down her cheeks.

I sit down next to her. Though I barely know Cass at all, right at this moment I feel sorry for her. Anyone would.

'Are you OK?' I say, lamely. 'Can I get you anything?'

She shakes her head. 'I'm fine. I'm sorry for causing a fuss. All I wanted was a bit of time to myself.'

She hands the baby back to Sarah, who takes him and stands over by the window as if she's looking out at the view. I wonder if she is listening to our conversation. I pat Cass gently on the knee and say 'I understand', though it's not true because I don't understand at all. Sarah seems to have Inigo most of the time so I'm not sure what the problem is for Cass or why she feels she needs time to herself. Perhaps she means time away from Simon – that I *can* understand.

Another couple of fat tears roll down her cheeks and she swipes them away with the heels of her hands. 'It's weird being here,' she almost whispers, her voice hoarse. 'Simon came here a long time ago with an old girlfriend. I know it's silly, but . . . I hate things like that. I keep wondering if he had a better time with her than he's having now with me and Inigo.' She looks down, as if embarrassed by her outburst, having suddenly confided in me, unbidden. She wipes her face again.

I touch her arm gently, thinking to myself that she's being a bit of a bunny boiler. I mean, who cares if Simon has been here before with someone else? But I guess postnatal depression probably does weird things to you.

'Don't be silly,' I say, in my best sympathetic voice. 'He's with you now and you have a baby together! You're his world. You should have seen how worried he was when he didn't know where you were this morning.'

She sniffs and looks up at me. 'Really?'

I tilt my head to one side. 'Yeah. Honestly, you've got nothing to worry about. He adores you.'

She smiles weakly. 'Thanks. Yes. I guess I'm being silly. It's just, with the baby and everything . . . I don't feel like myself at the moment. It makes me think about things I don't want to and brings back bad memories. Makes me think about . . . well. You know.'

We both sit in silence for a few seconds while I

absentmindedly pat her arm. I have no idea what she's on about but telling her so isn't going to help either of us.

'I think I'll go and lie down for a while, if you'll excuse me?' she says, standing up, suddenly brisk. 'I hope Simon manages to find Hugo quickly. It's not a nice day to be outside. And please . . . you won't say anything to Simon about what I said, will you? I wouldn't want him to know I'm being so silly and jealous. I'm sure it's just me being all hormonal. I know Simon loves me. I shouldn't have said anything. Shouldn't have bothered you with my stupid thoughts.'

She does that thing with her cardigan sleeves again and looks down at the floor. I can see she has gone red.

'Of course,' I say. 'And don't worry about Hugo – he won't mind at all, I'm sure. He loves both being out in the snow and playing the hero.' Anything that helps him suck up to Simon is good news as far as he's concerned, I add to myself silently.

After Cass has retreated upstairs, Sarah comes over with Inigo and sits down on the sofa next to me. She lies him down in her lap and he grins up at her.

'Poor Cass,' I venture. 'Seems like she's finding motherhood a little tricky.'

Sarah tickles Inigo and he squeals in delight. He's a big round football of a baby and I can see that if you're into that kind of thing, he's probably quite sweet.

'Yeah,' Sarah says. 'She's very . . . nice and it's clear she wants to be a good mum but I can't help wondering how she'd manage if I wasn't here. Even with my help, it seems like she's struggling.' She looks up at me. 'Shit, sorry, it's not my place to say that, is it?' Her brow furrows. 'You won't tell her, will you?'

I smile. 'Of course not,' I say, though I am mildly shocked. Sarah is Cass's (or at least Simon's) employee, after all, and I am a virtual stranger. It seems out of order that she'd speak about her like that to me. I decide it's best to change the subject.

'Have you been a nanny long?' I ask.

She wiggles Inigo's hands above his head and he giggles. She seems like a natural with babies.

'Not that long,' she says, still looking at Inigo rather than me, pulling faces and making him laugh. 'Cass is only the second mum I've looked after. But I've got a lot of younger brothers and sisters, so I've always been used to babies.'

'And where were you working before?' I ask, struggling to place her accent. Bristol? London? Difficult to tell.

Sarah picks up Inigo and stands abruptly. 'Dubai,' she says. 'With another English family. Look, I'm sorry to be rude, but I think I'd better go and see if Cass is OK. It's been lovely chatting though.'

Sarah heads up the stairs before I can say another word, as if she can't get away from me fast enough.

The coffee I had while I was pretending to look for Cass has made my hangover worse, so I go up to our room to lie down too.

I pick up my iPad to read the news, but it opens on my emails page. My stomach lurches and my heart starts beating faster – I know I didn't leave it like that.

I hear the chalet door bang, heavy footsteps on the stairs and then the door bursts open. 'Cass is back!' Hugo exclaims.

'Yeah, I know. We had a chat. I feel sorry for her – she seems like she's in quite a state. Personally, I think Simon could have been more sympathetic. Plus the nanny is a bit of a bitch, as it turns out. But listen, Hugo, have you been using my iPad?'

He frowns. 'No. Why d'you ask?'

'So you haven't been looking at my emails or in my contacts or anything?'

He kisses me on the forehead. The minor drama of Cass going briefly missing seems to have enlivened him to the point he's forgotten that he was annoyed about me getting drunk last night. 'Of course not! Why would I do that?'

I shrug. 'Dunno,' I say, tugging the pillows from Hugo's side of the bed so I can sit myself up straighter as I start to feel sick again. Hugo is flinging open cupboards and drawers, taking off his clothes and pulling out others. 'What are you doing?' I ask.

'Getting changed! Simon and I are going skiing. We've wasted enough of the day already.'

I glance out the window, where the snow is blowing almost horizontally across the glass. 'Skiing? In this weather? Rather you than me.'

'It'll be great! Fresh snow! Can't come all this way and not ski because of a bit of bad weather. Plus, Simon is hardly going to be impressed if I wuss out of skiing because there are a few snowflakes blowing around, is he?'

I shrug. 'Up to you. I hope you both know what you're doing.'

Hugo hauls on his salopettes, leaps off the bed and kisses me full on the mouth. 'It'll be fine – Simon has booked a guide, so we can do some proper off-piste. You get a couple of hours' rest and we'll do some baby-making later, OK? That app told me it's your most fertile day today.'

I cringe – I hate the way he follows my cycle – it makes me feel like a prize cow. I should have never let him download the app. But I can't be bothered to start a row so instead I smile weakly and say, 'Yeah. I'll be here. See you later. Have fun.'

10

December 1998, La Madière, France

I head back to the lift, but the lift operator wags a finger at me. 'Trop de vent,' he says. Too windy. I feel like I'm going to explode. This is it. No more looking for the clients. If Andy hasn't found them, we have to do something. We can't put it off any longer – we probably shouldn't have left it as long as we have. I wonder about asking the lift guy if I can borrow his radio to try to speak to Andy, but that would mean going public with this as almost anyone can listen in. And what's the point of ruining our reputation if the clients are already safely stuffing their mouths with cake in their chalet?

Part of me knows the good, responsible thing to do would be to alert rescue, just in case, but what are they going to do anyway? You can't get a helicopter out in this weather, and it's going to get dark soon. This could barely be worse.

'It's fine,' I mutter to myself. 'It's fine. Andy will have got hold of them. They'll be in a bar somewhere, showing off to their mates about skiing the couloir in these conditions. It's all fine. Fine.'

My breathing slows. I'm not going to mess up the good name of my company for a couple of arseholes who made out they were better skiers than they actually are and who I'm 99 per cent sure are fine. They're fine. I'm fine. We're all fine. It's all going to be fine.

I head off down the lower slope, which is by now almost deserted, and join a queue for the lift which will get me back to the office and back to news of whether or not we're in deep shit. Because of the wind, the lift is moving slowly and stopping often. The snow bites at my face. It would almost have been quicker to put on skins and hike. By the time I finally get to the top, they are no longer allowing people on any lifts, even down here – the wind is too strong. I ski down the short run back to the office and fling open the door.

'Why the hell aren't you answering your radio!?' Andy yells.

'I dropped it!' I shout back. 'Did you find them or not?'

'No. I found the forms they filled in with their details – you've got to get this office more organized, by the way; it took me forever.'

'Did you call the chalet?' I ask impatiently. Now is hardly the time to be hassling me about housekeeping.

'No! I was waiting for you! I didn't want to broadcast the fact that we've – you've – lost them, when for all I know you might have found them.'

'Well I didn't,' I say tightly. 'Which chalet are they in?'

Andy glances at the form. 'They didn't mark it. Which you would already know if you could stop shouting at me for five minutes! I'm trying to help you here! They're your clients – not mine!'

'They're our clients. Our ski school. We're in this together.'

'They were out with you,' Andy says coldly.

I take a deep breath. This isn't the time. And I need to keep Andy on side. 'We both need to calm down. They're here with Powder Puff – that annoying rep passed by as we were setting off and said they were his clients, remember? Where's their chalet?'

'Powder Puff have loads of chalets. We'll have to call their office. Do you have the number?'

'Somewhere.' I rifle through the piles of paper on my desk and feel Andy's impatience growing until eventually the unhelpful twat shouts, 'Come on!'

'You're not helping!' I shout back. 'Look, it's here. Richard, the rep's name is,' I say, as I pick up the phone and dial.

'Richard? Hi. It's Cameron from Skitastic. We were skiing with a couple of your clients this afternoon and they've gone AWOL. Yeah, the ones you saw me with. No, not long – they're probably fine but could you call *whichever chalet they're in and check if they're back? They didn't mark which one they're in on the . . . I KNOW! I'm not exactly pleased either . . . Look, we're all on the same side here, aren't we? Yeah. Yeah. OK – call me once you've spoken to the chalet girl. I'm in the office. Appreciate it, mate, yeah.'*

Andy sits down, head in hands. 'This is bad.'

'They might be at the chalet,' I say, hearing the desperation even in my own voice.

'And if they're not?'

'They might be in one of the bars,' I offer, though I'm already fearing the worst.

'How are we going to know, though? There are masses of bars! They could be anywhere!'

'If they're down, they should have let us know they're safe, shouldn't they?' I persist. I sound pathetic even to my own ears.

'They should have, but you know what punters are like – they don't think. And it's getting dark now.'

'I think we should give it till six,' I say.

'And if they're not back by then?'

'Well then, I guess . . . I guess we have to call rescue.'

'Who won't be able to do anything in this weather.' There's a pause. 'If they're not back, they don't stand a chance.'

The phone rings.

11

2018, London

Hugo

After Ria spent that first night with me, she never really moved out again. I couldn't believe my luck. I don't remember asking her to move in – it happened by degrees. I cleared a drawer out for her stuff because she was staying so often, then a cupboard, then her letters started arriving there 'because it's easier as I'm here the whole time anyway'. I didn't mind in the slightest; I'd never lived with a woman before and seeing her stuff around the place made it feel like a proper home, rather than somewhere I just came to play X-Box and sleep after work.

After a month or so she said she thought it was

pointless her paying rent on her flat, so would it be OK if she brought the rest of her stuff over? It was only then I realized I'd never been to her flat. I asked her why.

Her face fell. 'My weird flatmate's always there. Plus I'm too embarrassed for you to see it. It's a hole.'

I took her hand. 'Why would you be embarrassed? London is expensive, you're running your own business in tricky times – there's no shame in finding things a bit of a struggle.'

'Yeah but you've got all this.' She cast her hand around the flat, indicating my glass wall overlooking Tower Bridge, my state-of-the-art Bang and Olufsen speakers, and the early Damian Hirst that I'd bought last Christmas for the exposed-brick wall above the reclaimed fireplace. 'I'd feel like the poor relation, taking you to mine. I used to have my own little place, which was nice enough – nothing like this, obviously – but . . . well, I had to sell it.'

I nodded, assuming she couldn't keep up with the mortgage payments. It's not exactly uncommon. I took her in my arms, squeezed her tight and then let her go, feeling a stab of love for her as I saw that tears were brimming in her eyes.

'I inherited the money to buy this flat, and the business, from my father, as you know,' I said. 'I work hard, but all this was pretty much handed to me on a plate. And I doubt I'd have managed to hang on to it if it wasn't for Olivia and the other people around me who are much better at all this stuff than I am.' I put an arm around her again and kissed her forehead. 'You're building your business up from scratch. In my book, that's much more impressive than having a smart place to live.'

She smiled weakly. 'I love you,' she said, burrowing her head into my chest.

I grinned. It was the first time she'd said it. 'I love you too,' I replied. I'd been dying to tell her for ages.

After that, things between Ria and me moved quickly. Olivia disapproved – there were a lot of sly references to gold-digging and the like – but I was in love and Ria loved me, I was sure of it. And even if she didn't, as far as I could see, Ria was as good as I was ever going to get. For me, that was enough. I loved her. I'd be a good husband to her, she would be a good wife to me and . . . well, that's about everything you could want in a marriage, isn't it? I'd never been as happy as I had since Ria came into my life and there was no way I wanted things to go back to how they were before. I wanted to marry Ria, have children with her, buy her things, and make her happy. That was what I wanted from life and it was none of Olivia's business.

I was nearly forty by then, Ria almost the same age, so if we wanted children, there was no time to waste. Six weeks after we met, I took her to Paris and proposed at the top of the Eiffel Tower. It might not have been the most original idea, but she said yes, which was all that mattered.

Three months later we got married in Las Vegas – just us, no friends, or family. Ria didn't want a traditional wedding and I didn't mind what we did as long as she was happy. She agreed to stop taking the pill and we had lots of sex. For the first few months at least.

Her events planning business went from strength to strength, following a cash injection from me. Meantime, several terrorist events in a row and currency changes meant that things weren't so good for Redbush Holidays. Which is why I so desperately need Simon to invest – I wish Ria would take that on board and stop behaving so badly.

12

January 2020, La Madière, France

Ria

With Hugo and Simon out skiing, I settle down on the sofa with my iPad to read. When everyone else is out, it's actually pretty nice here. The leather sofa I'm lounging on, covered in cosy throws and furry cushions, is one of the most comfortable I've ever experienced. The rugs are deep and sumptuous and the view is exquisite, Millie has lit the fire and it's crackling away. It's a far cry from the caravan holidays I was used to in my childhood, but very much the kind of thing I've enjoyed since I met Hugo. My jumper is Brora and my cashmere socks are from The White Company. It would be difficult to feel more cosy and snug, so I'm not remotely tempted to go

73

out skiing in this terrible weather. If only I could stay here alone and not feel like I had to chat to boring Cass, suck up to sad sack Simon, and fend off Hugo's advances, it would all be pretty sweet.

Half an hour later, there's a knock at the door. It's Matt. Arse. If I'd known he was coming round I'd have put some make-up on at least. I smooth my hair and smile. 'Hey.'

He smiles back. 'Hi, Ria. I thought I'd pop by and check everything's OK after all that . . . business with Cass this morning? Is she all right?'

'Come in!' I usher him inside, frowning at the blizzard blowing outside. He stamps his feet on the mat and comes in. 'Sit down,' I say, indicating the fabulous sofa. I might find out what brand it is and see if I can persuade Hugo to get us one for home. 'Yes, I think Cass is fine,' I continue. 'She's in her room. Probably having a nap.'

Matt nods and sits down at one end of the enormous sofa. I sit down at the opposite end, tucking my feet under me. His eyes travel down my body and then back up to my face. I smirk subtly at him.

'So . . . um,' he says, reddening. 'I saw the boys heading off skiing as I arrived. Simon said they'd booked a guide I think and were hoping to get off-piste?'

'Yup,' I say. 'Wouldn't catch me out there in this weather.'

'I went out this morning but didn't stay long,' he says. 'Not fun when it's like this.'

'Nooo', I agree.

There's a pause. I guess he's wondering if I remember coming on to him last night or if I was too drunk and have forgotten. I'll let him wonder for now.

'So what are your plans for today if you're not skiing?' he asks.

'I thought I'd hang out here for a while. It's such a lovely chalet, it's nice to spend some time in it. I'm really enjoying myself.'

'It is a lovely chalet,' he agrees. He looks across to the huge window. 'One of my favourites. Did you choose it for the view?'

'Kind of. I work in events management and I've had my eye on it as a venue for a while.' This is not the entire truth, but it's near enough – it's also the version I've told Hugo. 'Then Hugo was looking for somewhere to bring Simon to impress him – he's hoping he'll invest in his company – so I suggested here and . . . well, here we are.'

Matt nods. There is an awkward silence, filled with sexual tension. We both know what is happening here. But we are at opposite ends of the sofa and I am Matt's married client, so neither of us really know how to move things forward, not now that we are sober. 'Good choice,' Matt ventures.

'But then it turns out that Simon came here with an old girlfriend,' I continue, 'and Cass is feeling insecure about it. I think that was part of the reason for her solo walk which worried everyone so much.'

75

'Ah! Poor Cass. I guess having a new baby can make things . . .' he tails off, realizing this isn't a good conversational route to go down for many reasons. 'I hope she's OK. She seems . . .'

He clears his throat. 'Well, anyway, none of my business. Changing the subject entirely, if the weather improves tomorrow, perhaps I could take you out skiing – show you the resort? With Cass, and the boys too, if they're interested,' he adds, quite clearly as an afterthought. 'It's all part of our service. I have to take my company jacket off so as not to tread on the local instructors' toes but, being a small company, we like to—'

'Sounds great,' I interrupt, cutting him off because I don't want him to go back into corporate mode and I'm already wondering how I can make sure none of the others want to come with us. 'Why don't I meet you at the Schuss Café at ten?'

Matt grins. 'Sounds perfect. I believe I'm due here for dinner tonight, so we can firm things up then. And if there's anything you need in the meantime, give me a shout. Send my regards to Cass, I won't disturb her if she's tired.'

'I will.'

'And I hope the boys have a successful day skiing.'

'I'll pass that on.'

We both get up and move towards the door. 'Well then,' he says. I lean in, inviting him to kiss me on the cheek. He reddens slightly, unsure what to do. I put my

76

hand on his arm and do the *bise*, two kisses French style, as if I do that all the time, which I don't, but I want to touch him.

I squeeze his hand briefly. 'See you tomorrow.'

13

December 1998, La Madière, France

'Hello? Richard. Right. OK. Thanks . . . Yeah, I will. I don't think we've got any option now that . . . Look, now is hardly the time, is it? Yeah. I'll keep you posted. Bye.'

'So?' Andy asks, stupidly. Isn't it obvious?

'They're not there.'

'So what do we do? How long have they been missing now?'

I look at my watch, and then out of the window. It's getting dark, the wind sounds like a jet engine and it's still snowing.

'We don't know that they're missing!' I snap. 'We just don't know where they are.' I am pacing about the office, but it's too small and I feel claustrophobic.

Andy picks up the phone. 'Isn't that the same thing? We have to call rescue now. We can't sit back and do nothing. Something's obviously wrong.'

'But . . .' I say, uselessly. 'We said we'd give it till six. They might have gone to the bar like we said and be boring some poor sod with how they lost their guides and found their way down like heroes and—'

'Apart from anything else, rep-boy Richard knows now. So if they don't turn up . . .'

'And if they do, everyone will think we're incapable idiots anyway,' I counter.

Andy holds up the phone towards me. 'So what do you want me to do?'

'Make the call.'

14

Daily Mail

29 December, 1998

Two British men have gone missing in the French Alpine ski resort of La Madière.

The two men, brothers aged 22 and 24, who have not yet been named, were skiing off-piste with local guides when they went missing in bad weather.

A search team was launched immediately, but so far no trace of either man has been found.

The young men are believed to have been staying in a Powder Puff holiday chalet with their girlfriends, who remain in the resort anxiously awaiting news.

A spokesman for Powder Puff holidays said:

'Obviously we are all deeply worried about the missing men and hoping they will turn up safe and sound. In the meantime, we are supporting the rest of their party as well as we are able.'

15

January 2020, La Madière, France

Ria

Millie appears with a freshly-made cake and a tray of steaming mugs of hot chocolate with mini marshmallows in a dish at almost exactly the same time as Hugo and Simon stomp up the stairs from the boot room.

'Good afternoon!' Millie says as she places the tray carefully down on the granite table. 'How was your day?'

'Cold, windy, fucking amazing,' says Simon, tearing off his too-tight Porsche ski jacket and flinging it down on a chair.

'Hugo?' I ask, slightly naughtily. I know he isn't a

particularly confident skier and is unlikely to have enjoyed the day at all, not that he'd ever be likely to admit that even to me. But there's no way he'd have even considered going out in conditions like today's if he wasn't so desperate to suck up to Simon.

'Yeah, it was good,' he says tightly, also taking off his jacket (Black Crows – chosen by me) and handing it to Millie. I notice it is soaking wet – he's probably had a few falls. 'Looking forward to tomorrow,' Hugo adds. 'We've booked the same guide to take us out. He was great.'

I let my face fall. 'Oh, what a shame. I thought I'd ski with you tomorrow, Hugo, but I've arranged to meet Matt at ten in the Schuss – he said he'd show me around the resort. Is that OK?'

Hugo's face hardens – he won't want me skiing with Matt alone after accusing me of flirting with him the other night, which, to be fair, I was – but I also know he won't say anything in front of Simon. 'Yes, of course,' Hugo says lightly. 'Perhaps we can all meet up for lunch?'

'What a good idea!' I trill. 'That would be *lovely*.'

I turn back to my iPad, quite certain that a lift will close, I'll get lost or something else will make me miss my lunch date. 'Cass could come with us too if she'd like,' I add, making a mental note to make sure that, one way or another, she won't want to. Judging by the ski lesson I joined her for briefly, she doesn't enjoy skiing much, so I don't think it will be difficult. I might book her a nice spa day as a 'treat' to make sure.

Millie cuts the cake, places a slice on each plate and hands them round. 'Hugo, Simon, I understand from head office that you were both keen to meet Cameron, the owner of this chalet and some of the others in the resort. He's planning to come for dinner this evening – assuming it suits you, that is. Would that work for you all?'

Simon nods, stuffing his face full of cake. 'Fine,' he mumbles, crumbs unpleasantly falling out of his mouth as he does so. He swallows the huge mouthful with a large gulp and belches. ''S'cuse me. Looking forward to meeting him.'

'Great!' Millie says. 'I'll let him know. Now, if you have everything you need, I'll go and get on with preparing dinner.'

'Better be a good one if the boss is coming, eh?' Simon quips.

'Absolutely. Although I hope all the meals I prepare are equally as good?'

'You've got no worries there. We're only going to say nice things about you,' Simon adds, staring at Millie's ample boobs. He may as well have smacked her on the bum. I don't know how she puts up with it.

'Thank you. I'll be in the kitchen if you need any-thing else, otherwise I'll see you for canapés at about eight?'

'That sounds lovely, Millie, thank you,' I say, to

avoid giving Simon the chance to say anything suggestive.

Hugo turns to look out of the enormous window. 'It's really coming down now,' he says.

Simon claps him on the back. 'Great!' he roars. 'Imagine the powder tomorrow!'

16

December 1998, La Madière, France

'The most important thing is that we get our stories straight,' I tell Andy as soon as I put the phone down.

'What do you mean? I haven't done anything wrong. I'm not getting involved.'

'You're already involved. You were with me when we lost them. You helped me search.'

'And that's bad because . . .'

'It's not!' I hiss. 'But not only have we lost two men, in retrospect, we probably should have alerted the authorities earlier. Given the conditions.' I wipe my hand over my face. 'This is serious stuff, Andy.'

'But you're the boss, as you never tire of telling me.'

I pull Andy closer to me so that our faces are almost touching. 'You were with me – I didn't hear you saying *we should call rescue out,' I growl. 'Both of us skied too fast at times, we didn't always put the clients' needs first. Either of us. We are in this together. OK? I go down, so do you. Neither of us have covered ourselves in glory here. The way we dealt with things wasn't exactly textbook, was it? Richard saw both of us with the clients. You and I are both on all the business documents, even though I put in pretty much all the money. So you are as liable as me. Understood?'*

Andy violently wrenches out of my grasp. 'Let go of me, OK? Fine. Let's get our stories straight then.'

17

Daily Mail

30 December, 1998

One of two men missing in La Madière in the French Alps has been found alive following an extensive search. The British man in his twenties was airlifted to Grenoble Hospital yesterday, where he remains in a critical condition.

Another man, believed to be his brother, is still missing. François Delpont, leading the rescue said: 'We have a large team of experts searching the mountain where the brothers were skiing, but local weather conditions are making the search difficult. We are delighted to have found one man alive and will continue to search for the other as long as is appropriate and the weather conditions allow.

'The two men were skiing with local guides who are helping our officers to ascertain what happened. No arrests have been made and currently there is nothing to indicate that this was anything other than a tragic accident.'

18

December 1998, La Madière, France

The police interview room is stifling. It's early in the morning and I've been here through the night, stewing, while they find an officer who can speak English to interview me. I'm too stressed to attempt it in French and I need to be 100 per cent clear on what I'm saying.

Officially, it seems I don't have to stay to be interviewed, but if I say I can't be bothered to wait around to talk about how two men came to go missing it isn't going to look good, is it? Eventually, the door opens and a bleary-eyed uniformed man comes in.

I stand up and he offers his hand. I shake it and we both sit down.

'Thank you for coming in,' he says. 'I'm sorry we kept you waiting.'

'That's fine. It's been a long day though and I'm very tired. If you could ask your questions, perhaps we can all get to bed.'

That sounded tetchier than I'd intended. Stay calm. Stick to what we planned, I remind myself.

'You will have heard the news that one of the men has been found,' the officer says.

A whoosh of relief shoots through me, very quickly followed by one of panic. Is he alive? Conscious? Is he going to know that we were too slow to alert rescue? Where was he? Did he see us? What did he tell them? Did he say we skied too fast? Is this some kind of trick?

'No, I didn't know that!' I almost shout. 'Why didn't someone tell me?'

'I must apologize,' the officer says, covering his eyes momentarily and then looking at me again. 'As you say, it's been a long night and we have been very busy. The fact that you hadn't yet been told that he'd been found must have been an oversight.'

Yeah, right. Mind games, more like. 'So is he . . .' A surge of adrenaline pulses through me and for a second I think I'm going to be sick. He's dead. He's dead. He's going to tell me he's dead. I'm sure of it.

'He is on his way to hospital. The last I heard he had not yet woken up. The medics will be doing all they can, but for now his future is uncertain.'

I nod. Panic continues to course through me. What if he dies? Or if the other one turns up dead? Would

92

that be manslaughter in France? Would I go to prison? Why do I not already know this? Why didn't I check when I – we – set up the business? It's not my fault, I remind myself. Not my fault.

'And the other man?'

He pulls a face. 'They continue to search, as much as the weather allows, but I fear his chances are now slim, would you not say?'

I shake my head and then nod. I don't know what to say. My palms are sweating; I wipe them on my trousers.

'Can you please tell us in your own words what happened from the time you met the two men to the time you called the emergency services?' the officer asks.

I swallow hard. 'Right. Um, I met the two men at three. The weather wasn't great even at that point, but they were – are – only here for a week, so like most punters they wanted to ski even so.'

He nods. 'OK. And had you met the men before? Had they filled in any paperwork?'

The paperwork! There's a disclaimer! They'll have ticked the disclaimer! Suddenly I feel a lot lighter. Thank Christ for the French love of paperwork.

'Of course,' I say, though this hadn't occurred to me until that very second. 'They'd come by the office earlier to fill in our standard form – you know: name, address, level of skiing, the standard disclaimer about skiing at their own risk, contact details . . .' I drop in the disclaimer as if it's unimportant, but I see the officer

make a note. While remaining poker-faced on the outside, inwardly I smile.

'I see. And was there anything unusual about that?'

'No, nothing unusual, except that they'd both marked themselves as expert skiers when it turned out that wasn't really the case.'

'I see. So at what point did it become clear they weren't expert skiers?'

'Almost as soon as we set off.'

'Right. So what did you do then?'

'Well, they said they wanted to go into the back country, but I could see they wouldn't be capable – well, more that it wasn't the best idea, given their level of experience and the conditions.' *I add this to make out I was erring on the side of caution when the truth is I couldn't be bothered to try to coax them down something they were going to be incredibly slow on in blizzard conditions.*

'So instead I took them down Couloir Noir – you know the one?' *He nods.* 'Officially it's off-piste, but it starts and ends at the lift and isn't too hairy, so I figured it was a compromise between keeping the clients safe and giving them what they want.'

Argh, I shouldn't have said that. Because I didn't keep them safe, did I? Not my fault. Not my fault.

'I understand. So at what point did you realize the men had gone missing?'

'They started going down the track quite slowly with me leading at first – off-piste, I generally think that's* *safer, especially in bad weather. There was a bit of an issue because one of them turned out to be a speed merchant and kept overtaking me, with his brother racing behind him too so as not to be outdone.'*

Good one. Put some blame on the clients. Not my fault.

'To begin with it was OK though. The weather was getting worse, but they seemed to be getting more confident, turning better, stopping less, definitely going faster though, however much I urged them to slow down and follow me. Then we came to that bend – you know the one? They'd gone ahead again, and by the time I got round it, a few seconds behind them, I couldn't see them.'

I wipe my palms again. I wish I knew where the man had been found. I'm not sure exactly what happened and when, who was in front and behind and at what point – I can't remember any of that now. But I can't say that.

'So I knew they'd been in front of me, and I figured the best thing would be to ski down and catch up with them. Most people wait for you after a while. But the clients were – are – brothers and they seemed a bit competitive as I said, so they might have been trying to race to the bottom, something like that, I don't know. My colleague Andy was also there, assisting me, even though they'd only booked one guide.' I don't mention about Andy tearing off ahead, obviously, or about me trying to overtake so as not to lose face. I'll have to hope that the guy in the hospital bed doesn't remember

too many details about who was where and when – I certainly don't. Assuming the poor sap wakes up, that is. I take a sip of water from the plastic cup in front of me and notice my hands are shaking. Calm down. Calm down.

The officer nods. 'I see. Did you do anything else?'

Anything else? Like what? What else was I meant to do? I swallow the panic down. What is he looking for me to say?

'Well, obviously we called out, stuff like that.'

'And when did you decide to call the emergency services?'

'Once I got to the bottom, given the bad weather, I asked my colleague to go to the office to call their chalet, see if anyone knew where they were. They hadn't noted which chalet they were staying in on the forms, so we had to call the tour company rep first, which meant we lost some time doing that.' *The clients' fault that time was lost. Not ours.* 'Meanwhile, I went back up to check the track again, see if I could spot them, in spite of the worsening weather.'

Making myself out to be a bit of a hero there.

The officer nods again. 'I see. And how long did all this take?'

'Um – for my colleague to get back to the office? Twenty minutes?' *Way longer than that by the time we'd dithered about what to do.* 'It's hard to say,' I continue, 'I was more focused on finding the men than on what time it was. Besides, with the weather so bad it would* have been difficult to look at my watch anyway . . .' Stupid thing to say. Think. Calm down.

'Richard from Powder Puff said he couldn't be exact, but he thinks he received a call from you at around five.'

I swallow hard. 'Yes, that sounds about right. The men were a few minutes late for our meeting, we had to get up the mountain, then they spent ages at the top fiddling with their goggles and boot buckles – you know how punters do – and then they were very slow at the top of the slope so . . . yes, that would make sense.'

Big risk. If the guy in hospital wakes up, he'll know that they weren't late – if anything, we left a little early – they weren't that slow and Andy and I spent a good forty-five minutes faffing around before I alerted rescue. Quite possibly longer. Forty-five minutes to an hour when the pisteurs and snowcats could have been out searching for these two missing men. Before the weather worsened. Vital minutes which could have made all the difference. Life-or-death minutes, literally. I swallow hard.

The officer puts his pen down and leans back in his chair. 'OK. Obviously, we will need to see the paperwork and we will be checking the phone records when they arrive.'

'That's fine. Of course. I'm happy to help in any way I can.'

Thank Christ for the disclaimer.

19

Ria

I am feeling so refreshed and relaxed after another hot tub session that I let Hugo have sex with me before dinner without even trying to come up with an excuse to get out of it.

'I hope this is the one,' he sighs as he rolls off me.

'The one what?'

'The one where it works. You know, the one where you get pregnant.'

He props himself up on his elbow and gestures towards the window. 'Look at that – snow falling outside, here in this beautiful room, what an amazing place it

99

would be to conceive a child! What a lovely story to be able to tell her. We could call her Snowy.'

'Ewww. No child wants to hear about their conception. And Snowy?' I laugh. 'That's a kitten's name.'

He traces his finger down my stomach. 'OK. Not Snowy. A name that means snow. Or winter or something. What about calling her Winter? You get kids called Summer. Is Winter a good name for a girl?' He reaches over me for my iPad and starts browsing. I feel a lurch of alarm.

'I thought you said you didn't touch my iPad?' I ask.

'I didn't the other day,' he says distractedly, 'I'm just looking for wintery names now, and mine is downstairs. Here – Neve – that's nice. Noelle – hmm, not sure. Alaska. Christmas. Crystal. Maybe not.'

I snatch my iPad back, pretending I am looking at the names but really I don't want him holding it. 'Maybe we could call her Elsa, like in *Frozen*,' I suggest, trying to shut this conversation down. 'Anyway, how do you know it would be a girl?'

He snuggles his face into my shoulder. 'I don't. I just hope it would be so that she would be like you.'

I stroke his hair and at that moment, I almost feel sorry for him.

20

January 2020, La Madière, France

Hugo

Whatever Millie said about hoping that all her meals were equally as good as each other, you can see she's gone all out for dinner this evening with her boss here. We have oysters for canapés, three-cheese soufflé starters, some kind of bird within a bird within a bird like you might imagine Henry VIII eating at a banquet when he wants to impress foreign kings, and then a very light homemade ice cream thing topped with elaborate spun sugar creations.

I sometimes wish I could bring Olivia on these trips. I'm hopeless at schmoozing. I wonder if that's partly why the business isn't doing so well at the moment –

being able to do small talk seems so much more important now than it used to be. I could really do with some
of the Snow Snow chalets in my stable, and also I need
Simon to feel like I'm the kind of person he wants to
do business with. So there's a lot at stake, but I know
I'm rubbish when it comes to this aspect of the business
and it makes me uncomfortable. And much as I love
Ria, I can't always trust her to behave herself like Olivia
would. Ria seems to be behaving especially obstreper-
ously this week. She always likes a drink and to be
sociable, but she doesn't usually get so wasted. She's not
her usual self at the moment and I don't understand
why.

On top of that, this evening is not being made any
easier by the fact that chalet-owner Cameron is a total
arse. He isn't what I was expecting at all. In all honesty,
I thought he'd be a bit like me – public-school-educated,
maybe someone who'd inherited the family business and
built it up over the years, or made some money in the
City or something like that and then decided to invest
in ski chalets.

But no, it turns out he built up the company from
scratch. Not that there's anything wrong with that –
clearly, it's something to be admired – but does he need
to wang on about it so much? On and on with his self-
congratulatory spiel about how hard he's worked and
how well he's done, along with how much he knows
about the industry, about the mountains, and about
pretty much everything else as far as I can tell.

I realize I haven't heard a word Cameron's said for the last few minutes, partly because Millie is being especially attentive about topping up everyone's glasses this evening, but mainly because he is such a bore.

'. . . So I knew from the start that what I wanted to offer was properly luxurious chalets, not those mass market ones aimed at people who like to pretend they're richer than they really are,' he is postulating. 'I started off with one chalet – broke my balls to get the finance to rent it for the season and did pretty much everything myself, from airport transfers to cleaning and cooking. The punters lap up that kind personal service, nothing being too much trouble, so that's what I've tried to build on. It's difficult to find the right staff – no one is as dedicated to it as me, obviously, but there you go, that's how it is as a business owner. Fortunately there are good people out there if you have a rigorous inter-view process and pay a decent wage as I do, and I certainly got lucky with Millie here.'

Millie fills his glass and smiles tightly.

'I hope she's been looking after you well,' Cameron adds.

'She's fabulous! I wouldn't mind one like her at home myself!' Simon leers. I cringe. Cass fiddles with something on her plate, her face going crimson as she pretends not to be bothered by Simon's comment. Simon needs someone like Olivia to keep him in line. Remarks like that will land him in trouble if he's not careful.

'How many chalets do you have now, Cameron?' I

ask, remembering what Ria said about Cass feeling insecure and wanting to move the conversation on and away from Millie.

'Five in La Madière – this is where I started and it's still my favourite resort – and a total of twenty chalets across the Alps. All high-end and luxurious, but very different in style. Some modern, some retro, some huge, some tiny – or "intimate" as we say in the biz – but all offering top levels of service.'

'Well we're certainly enjoying our week here,' I say. 'It was my wife Ria who suggested we come here – I believe she's organized events in some of your chalets before?'

'Yup,' Ria slurs, holding her glass out for Millie to top up, despite the fact she's clearly had more than enough already. 'Events. Some reeeaaallly nice events.'

I shoot her a disdainful look, but she is leaning in towards Matt and whispering something in his ear. After how she was upstairs, before dinner, when I'd felt closer to her than I had for a very long time, I thought things might be starting to change. I thought she might at least make an effort, given that Cameron is here and he could be important to the business. But no, here she is getting embarrassingly drunk and flirting with the rep. My face feels hot and I have a sudden need to be outside. I stand up too quickly, bumping the table and at least four glasses tip over, red wine spilling on to the pristine white tablecloth.

'Shit! I mean, argh, I'm so sorry.' I right the glasses

as Millie dashes over with kitchen roll and cloths and starts dabbing at the mess.

'It's no problem, don't worry at all,' she says. 'If everyone's finished, it might be easiest if I simply clear things away? Perhaps you'd like some more wine or digestifs in the living room?'

'That's my girl, Millie,' Cameron says. 'Hugo,' he claps me on the shoulder as he passes, before lifting one of the remaining glasses of wine and downing it, 'it's no big deal. Don't worry about it for a second. That's what the rich fuckers who come here are paying for – being able to make a mess and have someone else clear it up.'

I try to give Millie a sympathetic look, but she is already busily tidying and dabbing. I'm not the best at social situations but even I am appalled by Cameron.

While everyone moves from the table to the living room, I go to the front door and step outside for some air, but have to come back in straight away as the wind is now even stronger than it was earlier and it's snowing pretty much horizontally. I go back into the living room where everyone is sprawled out on the fur-throw-covered sofas. Simon is telling some long-winded and no doubt filthy joke to Cameron, and Cass is looking embarrassed. Ria is sitting way closer to Matt than I'd like. She's knocking back yet another massive glass of wine even though, for all she knows, she may be pregnant.

Millie comes in and tops up everyone's wine yet again. 'Cameron, I've had a call from the taxi company – the car they sent is stuck in a drift. Are you OK to wait? I'm not sure what else we can do, to be honest.'

'There must be a spare room here he can crash in, Millie?' Simon booms. 'Shame to break up the party anyway.'

'Cameron, would you like me to make up the bed in the attic room as a contingency?' Millie asks. 'That is, if no one has any objection?'

Cameron waves his hand impatiently. 'I'll wait for the taxi. No great rush to get home. Might even walk – it's not that far. The air'll do me good.'

'Well, it's up to you, but it's pretty bad out there now – I wouldn't be surprised if the taxi can't get through at all,' Millie says. 'I'll make up a bed anyway in the room at the top. Just in case.'

'Thanks, darling,' Cameron says. Millie maintains a fixed grin but I'm sure I see her recoil slightly.

'I'll leave the wine and spirits here, but unless there's anything else, I might call it a night if that's OK?' Millie says. 'What time would you like breakfast in the morning?'

Simon looks at his watch. 'Oof it's late! Breakfast about nine? Then we can still meet our guide at ten if we get a move on.'

Millie nods. 'Of course. See you in the morning.'

Ria is cackling too loudly at something Matt has said. I stand up.

'I hope you'll all excuse me,' I say. 'I'm rather tired and would like to go to bed now. Cameron, it was lovely to meet you.' This is a lie, it wasn't lovely at all. 'I'll give you a call next week when I'm back in the office to discuss how we can move things forward, if that's acceptable to you? Perhaps I can have my PA call your assistant to arrange a suitable time?'

Cameron hauls himself up to shake my hand. 'Yeah, sounds great, mate. I'd like to show you round some of the other chalets later in the week too ideally so you can get a full view of exactly what we offer, why you'll want us on your books.' He's wobbling on his feet and squints as he looks at me, as if he can't quite focus. 'Was good to meet you this evening,' he continues, 'and your lovely wife too, of course.'

Ria smiles sarcastically and slurs, 'And so lovely to make your acquaintance, Cameron.' I am so incensed right now I could almost hit her. Cameron is vile but, even so, how dare she? She knows how important this is for me. For us both.

I go upstairs and flop down on the bed. Despite trying to rein it in, drinking-wise, way more than any of the others seem to be bothering with this week, my head is spinning and I can already feel a headache coming on.

I haul myself up from the bed and go to the bathroom to find some painkillers. There is a burst of raucous laughter from downstairs. I pull a strip of paracetamol from my washbag but it's empty. My head is throbbing now. Ria must have some somewhere, surely? I unzip her make-up bag and rifle through – past the little boxes, brushes, packages, and lipsticks. It smells like her. I wish she'd come up to bed so I could be sure she's not embarrassing me down there. God knows how much she's showing me up. I need Cameron on board. I need Simon to think we're a company worth investing in – though he seemed to be out-drinking even Ria this evening, so perhaps I don't need to worry too much about that at least. My fingers eventually hit something which feels like a blister pack of pills and I pull it out.

It's not paracetamol.

21

January 2020, La Madière, France

Ria

Simon and Cameron are doing shots now. There's a lot of willy-waving going on (metaphorically only, thankfully). I guess this is one of those weird situations where both men stand to benefit from impressing each other. Poor Hugo. He's completely out of his comfort zone here. Still, best that he's gone up to bed rather than staying down here giving me dirty looks. Fuck him.

Millie seems to have retreated for the evening. Does she live in the chalet with us? I guess she must do. I hadn't thought about it until now. You wouldn't want to be going out in this weather. There's talk of Cameron staying the night, so no chance of getting rid of him any time soon, sadly. Matt and I are on a squashy sofa tucked into a corner. The room is spinning slightly. The wine this evening was fabulous. Much as I didn't want to come this week, at least the food and drink are excellent. I pour myself another glass from the bottle Millie left us and sink back into the sofa. I close my eyes and let my head loll towards Matt until it rests on his shoulder. It doesn't matter – Simon and Cameron aren't paying us any attention.

'We still skiing tomorrow?' I murmur.

I move my hand so it rests lightly on his crotch, careful to do it as if I've done it by accident. I feel him harden.

'You sure you want to ski in this weather?' he asks, shifting slightly.

I lift my head to peer out of the huge window at the other end of the chalet. There's a light outside and I can see the snow is coming down even harder than earlier.

'Maybe not,' I sigh. 'What about you?'

'Not if I can help it.' He covers his groin with a cushion and presses himself against my hand. 'I can think of other things I'd rather do.'

I look him in the eyes, unzip him, and place my hand around his straining cock. 'Me too,' I whisper. 'I'll have to see if I can get away.'

With my other hand, I pass him my phone. 'Put your number in and I'll text you. Hugo's planning to go skiing and sucking up to Simon, so we might be able to . . . go for coffee or something.'

I move my hand and see him struggle to concentrate

as he puts his number in my phone. 'OK,' he gasps. 'There you go. I'll look forward to coffee. Or something. I think you'd better stop now or . . .'

I give him a gentle squeeze and he groans softly as I withdraw my hand.

'I'll look forward to seeing you tomorrow. For coffee. Or something. I'd best get to bed.'

I stumble up the stairs and open the door as quietly as I can, not wanting to wake Hugo; he's sure to be cross with me for drinking too much. Matt has left me feeling all horny, but I'm drunk and tired and can do without Hugo slobbering all over me – I'm not *that* horny.

I can see the light is on as I push the door open. Hugo is sitting on the bed with his back to me, staring out at the snow, which is now coming down so hard it looks like diagonal white lines. 'Hugo? You OK?' I ask, trying to make my words sound clear because I can't be bothered with him telling me off for being pissed and not playing the part of the corporate wife well enough. Again. 'I know I drank too much but honestly, listening to those twats banging on, I need something to get me through, and I'm really one hundred per cent sure Cameron will want to work with you – and that's why we're here after all. Simon will invest too, so it will all be . . .'

He stands up slowly and turns to face me. I stop talking. I've never seen him look so angry. 'It's not that,' he hisses. 'Though you did drink too much. Again. It's this.' He throws something down on the bed.

111

The room is spinning and I narrow my eyes to focus on the small object resting on the fur throw on the bed.

It's a packet of contraceptive pills. My packet of pills. Oh shit.

'Why are you going through my things?' I ask, going on the defensive. 'I bet it was you looking at my iPad the other day too, wasn't it!' I add, suddenly feeling sober and trying to deflect attention from myself. I bet it was him. Someone has been checking my emails, I'm sure of it.

'I wasn't going through your things!' he shouts. I put my finger to my lips, wobbling slightly and suppressing a desperate desire to giggle.

'Ssssh. They'll hear us. You wouldn't want to upset Simon, would you?' I stage whisper.

He takes a deep breath. 'I thought you wanted to get pregnant,' he says in a low, measured voice. 'We talked about it. So why are you taking the pill behind my back?'

I take a deep breath. 'We did talk about it. But it's what you want. Not what I want. I'm not ready.'

I flop down onto the bed. I am too drunk for this conversation. I close my eyes, but the room is still spinning. Hugo grabs my hands and hauls me up to a sitting position. I open my eyes again.

'Oh no you don't,' he says. 'We're going to talk about this, now. I don't care how drunk you are. If you're not ready to have children, why didn't you say so?'

'Because I didn't want to let you down,' I lie. 'Because you obviously want children so badly. I didn't want to

112

say no. I thought it would be easier to pretend that I wanted children too.' It's a half-truth. I did think it would be easier. But also I can't afford for him to leave me – to decide I'm not the person for him after all. There is too much at stake. That was the bigger part in my decision. But I can't tell him that.

His face softens. 'Oh, Ria. That's so silly. Of course we can wait. We have time. Not much, but some. You should have said. It's you I want. I want what makes you happy.'

I force a smile. 'And I want what makes you happy. But I don't want a baby. Not yet.'

He strokes my face, but he's guarded. There's something he's not saying. 'OK, my darling. We'll leave it a year or two. But neither of us is getting any younger. Now I'm going to get you some water and I think you should go to bed.'

My mouth is dry and my head is pounding. Hugo isn't there when I wake up. I guess he's already gone for breakfast. Or he's avoiding me after the whole pill thing last night. He'll be annoyed, but he'll get over it. At the end of the day, he loves me – I'm pretty sure of that. I glance at the clock – it's gone nine.

What did I arrange with Matt?

Text. I said I'd text. I haul myself out of bed and open the curtains. There's nothing but white – the snow is so deep now on the small roof below that it's totally blocking the window and I can hear the wind is roaring.

113

I hope Hugo and Simon will go skiing so I don't have Hugo hanging around me all day, but it seems unlikely.

After I've had a way too hot shower I drag myself downstairs. I'm surprised to see that Matt is already here and feel myself blush. Hugo is sitting at the table apparently reading a French newspaper. He doesn't look up, though he definitely heard me come in. I guess I'm not forgiven yet.

I sit down next to Hugo and touch him lightly on the hand. 'Morning,' I say.

He looks up briefly and then back down at his paper. 'Morning.'

'The others not up?'

'Doesn't look that way.'

Millie comes in. 'Morning, Ria,' she says. 'What can I get you? Eggs?'

A wave of nausea passes through me even at the thought of eggs. Hugo clears his throat, still staring at his paper.

'Um, no thanks, Millie,' I reply. 'Maybe pancakes?'

She nods. 'No problem. Maple or golden syrup? Or I could make you a chocolate sauce?'

'Maple, please. Great. Thank you.'

Hugo is still staring pointedly at his paper. As far as I know, his knowledge of French is rudimentary – mine is way better – so he can't actually be reading it. I fiddle with my phone, feeling unusually uncomfortable in the silence. I wish Simon or Cass would get up. Or have they already been and gone? Surely not. Cass won't have got up and gone out this early, especially not in this weather.

'You skiing with Simon today, Hugo?' I venture.

'Not sure,' he replies testily. 'I haven't seen Simon yet and, according to Matt here, the lifts may not be open today.'

I try not to show my disappointment. I'm not going to get my alone time with Matt if Hugo doesn't go out.

'Really? The weather's that bad?'

'Apparently so,' he says, not looking at me. 'Disappointing for you, I'm sure,' he adds snidely, obviously still wildly unimpressed with the idea of me skiing with Matt today.

I'm about to say something in reply – I'm not sure what – when Millie comes back in, placing a massive stack of pancakes in front of me, along with a white jug of syrup. I touch it – it's warm.

'These look amazing, Millie, thank you.'

She smiles. 'It's my pleasure, Ria. Is there anything else I can get for you? Coffee? Tea? Some fresh orange juice?'

'I'd love some peppermint tea, please,' I say neutrally. Hugo tuts – he knows it's what I drink when I'm hungover. I ignore him and turn to Matt. 'Hugo said the lifts are closed today?'

He pulls a face. 'Yes, I'm afraid so. And I don't know if you heard the news?'

Hugo looks up. 'What news?'

'About the body. They found a body.'

PART TWO

22

December 1998, La Madière, France

Louisa

I've never been skiing before. It's not something you generally get to do when you grow up on a council estate, is it? But since I started at Oxford last year, I've got used to keeping quiet about that kind of thing. My vowels have rounded out, I say lunch instead of dinner, dinner instead of tea and try to remember not to say toilet. I didn't do it deliberately, it just happened. Mum teases me about it when I go home, says things like she'll have to get the best china out, but really, I know she doesn't mind. She brought me up single-handed and she's so proud of me. I'm pretty much the first person she knows who's gone to university. And I'm one of those people who always tries to fit in. To pretend they're like everyone else. Always have been.

So the skiing holiday wasn't my idea, obviously, and it wasn't even my boyfriend Will's. It was Will's brother Adam's idea.

'So what do you think?' Will asks. 'Will you come?' We are lying in bed in his room, naked. I sit up and pull a T-shirt over my head.

'With you and Adam? I'm not sure. I don't want to get in the way of your brotherly bonding.'

Will puts his hand up my T-shirt and squeezes my left breast. 'You won't be. Adam's OK, as brothers go, but I like him better when his company is diluted by having other people around. I think we might kill each other if we were on our own together for an entire week. And he's bringing his girlfriend anyway, so having you there would make up the numbers.' He pushes my T-shirt up, moves his head in towards my chest and sucks my nipple for a second before sitting upright and looking me in the eyes. He touches my cheek. 'Please, Louisa. I'd love it if you came.'

Louisa. Before I came to Oxford, I was plain old Louise. I pull a face. 'You know I've never skied?'

He bounces out of bed. 'Doesn't matter! That's fine! Skiing holidays aren't really about the skiing anyway – there's the views, the fondues, the *vin chaud*, all the drinking . . .' He wiggles his hips and I laugh. 'And all the sex, of course.' He dives back on the bed and nuzzles his head against me again, as if he is a puppy. 'But if

120

you can bear to get out of bed while we're there – which, granted, will be difficult with me in it – I'll teach you to ski too, if you like. Please come! It'll be so much fun.'

I stroke his hair. 'OK,' I say, 'I'll come.' Instantly I start wondering how I'm going to afford it, but I push the thought away as Will starts to kiss me again.

I don't know the first thing about skiing, beyond watching *Ski Sunday* now and again, but the chalet isn't at all what I was expecting. It's nice enough, but it's more like a cross between a basic hotel and a university hall of residence than the luxurious mountainside cabin full of fur throws and blond wood I had imagined. When Will told me how much the trip was going to cost I panicked – there was no way I could find that amount of money with my various credit cards almost totally maxed out. I didn't tell him I couldn't afford it – I never tell anyone at uni I can't afford things. But I think he might have guessed. When he caught wind of the fact that I might not be planning to come along after all, he offered to pay for the trip as a Christmas present.

'I won't enjoy it if you're not there,' he said. 'In fact I probably wouldn't even bother going without you – just to pay for the privilege of being ignored by my brother and his girlfriend. So it's as much a present to me as it is to you. You'd be doing me a favour by coming along.'

121

I didn't know if that was true, but it was a very sweet thing to say. Sometimes I think Will really does love me.

When Will said we would be staying in a chalet, I thought it would be just us, Will's brother, and his girlfriend in a little wooden house with someone to cook us our meals, but it's not like that at all. There are about sixty guests, easily, and the rooms are simple doubles with tiny en-suite bathrooms, not that different to the ones in the more modern colleges. Downstairs, there's a lounge with a fireplace and some wooden skis stuck on the wall, and a plain, fairly functional dining room.

Tonight is our first night here. I haven't met Adam's girlfriend Nell before, but she seems to be like Will and Adam: someone who is at ease with skiing holidays and knowing the correct words for everything. Unlike me, she doesn't have to pretend to be something she's not. Although our hotel is far from luxurious, I still feel out of my depth; a fraud. The three of them are talking about the last time they skied in this resort and I am tuning out because I have nothing to contribute. I stroke the back of Will's head, tracing my finger gently along the edge of his ear in the way I know he likes, trying to bring his attention back to me.

It works.

'Louisa has never skied before,' Will says. 'I'm looking forward to teaching her.'

'Gosh, your first time?' Nell says patronizingly. 'How marvellous! I barely remember my first time on skis – I was only three or so. According to family legend, I cried my eyes out.'

'Let's hope it's not that way for Louisa,' Adam says, giving me a wink.

Will squeezes my hand. 'It won't be. I'm sure she'll be a natural. And I'll be there to look after her anyway.'

All of my ski kit is borrowed. I have one friend from home who has been skiing – something to do with being spotted as having potential when she was a child on a dry ski slope and given an EU grant – and she's lent me some things to wear. Even when I was packing I found the amount of stuff bewildering. Why do you need both inner and outer gloves? Why so many layers? Do I really need to wear those things that look like long johns? Why do these padded trousers (salopettes?) have to be quite so padded – aren't I going to look enormous? What is this circular scarf thing? Should I wear a hat or an ear band – isn't that a bit seventies? Goggles and sunglasses – why do I need both? How will I know which to wear and when? I tried it all on at home and looked like I was the size of a house. Then I stripped it all off again as quickly as I could because I was absolutely sweltering. And that's before you even get to the boots, skis, and poles which had to be hired once we got here at seemingly huge expense (I can't let Will pay for everything, so I've got another new credit card especially). I find the ski hire shop utterly bewildering but let myself get swept along as Adam and Will argue about what length of ski I should have and how tight my bindings should be, whatever that means.

So because there is so much gear, it takes ages to get ready in the morning. Breakfast is at eight (why? Aren't we meant to be on holiday?) and served by cheerful young staff in logoed T-shirts – bread, croissants, jam, Nutella, weird butter without salt, cereal in giant plastic containers, rubbery boiled eggs, and more. I hardly eat anything, I am so nervous.

Nell manages to look like a minor royal on their annual ski holiday. Her salopettes are sleeker and way less puffy than mine, and she's carrying a slick black jacket with a gold belt, which makes my colourful geometric-patterned jacket manage to seem both dowdy and gaudy at the same time, as well as even more dated than it actually is.

'Louisa! Look at you!' she says. 'How darling in your retro look!' I smile tightly as she leans down to kiss Will then me on the cheek. My gear is not retro, it's just old, and I'm pretty sure Nell knows that.

'Adam not up yet?' Will asks.

Nell stirs honey and granola into plain yoghurt. 'Yes, he's up. He'll be down in a minute. Then we're going to head out, make the most of the beautiful weather. It's supposed to close in in a couple of days.'

I look out the window where the sky is a dazzling blue. The dining room is stifling and I am too hot. I wonder if I've put too many layers on, but I don't want to ask because Nell is bound to make me feel stupid.

It's boiling and stuffy in here and it's hard to believe it's that cold out there with the sun shining like that.

Will squeezes my hand. 'OK? You ready for the off?'

I nod. 'Ready as I'll ever be.'

We pass Adam coming in as we are leaving the dining room. 'You sure you don't want to get Louisa here an instructor for the morning?' he asks. 'It's pretty difficult teaching a total beginner.'

I see Will's face darken. 'It'll be fine. I want to teach my girlfriend how to ski.'

Adam claps Will on the shoulder. 'Yeah, right. More like you don't want her spending the day with some fit French Jean-Louis and his perfect buns.'

'Don't be so ridiculous,' Will snaps.

Adam pulls a mock-surprised face. 'Ooohhh! I was only joking, for fuck's sake. Now, off you go and have a good time. And you, Louisa, be careful. Make sure Will looks after you properly.'

'I will!' I say, beaming, trying to lighten the mood. Adam can be annoying, but I think Will is over-reacting this time.

Will doesn't say a word as we collect our skis and boots from the dingy underground room which has a concrete floor with broken rubber matting and reeks of smelly feet. Ski boots must be the most uncomfortable things in the world and it takes ages to get them on. Will is ready much faster than me and sits on the wooden bench staring straight ahead as I continue to wrestle my feet into my boots.

125

'You OK?' I ask as I finally manage to jam my heel down into the boot and start trying to work out what to do with the various buckles and straps. 'You're very quiet.'

He turns to look at me and smiles. 'Yeah. Sorry. My brother just winds me up sometimes.'

I puff out my cheeks. 'He seems OK to me – quite funny in his way. I wouldn't really know not having any siblings,' I add, not wanting Will to think I am taking Adam's side, 'but everyone seems to get wound up by their brothers and sisters.'

Will shrugs. 'I guess. He always has to have the last word on everything. Just loves to put me down. Always has done, probably always will do. And . . .'

He tails off.

'What?' I prompt.

'I resent him putting me down in front of you. There's no need for him to do that.'

He looks away from me and bends down, pretending to fiddle with a buckle on his boot. I can see he's gone red.

I touch his knee. 'You don't need to worry about that. I promise I won't take any notice of anything he says about you.' I give his knee a pat. 'Now let's get outside so I can make a fool of myself on these slopes.'

I'm already exhausted and have dropped my skis several times by the time we arrive at the base of a small fenced-off area of slope. We've walked no more than a hundred

126

metres but I am boiling hot and can feel sweat pooling under my armpits and trickling down my skin under my many layers. I knew I'd put too many clothes on.

'Right. Here we are. The magic carpet,' Will says, indicating a conveyor belt running a short distance up the hill. It doesn't look very magic or anything like a carpet. Tiny kids wrapped up like Michelin men are getting on, followed by the occasional man in red. I guess they are the instructors.

'What's magic about it?' I ask, and then force a smile to try to cover my grumpiness. 'Everyone else getting on it seems to be under five – are you sure I won't break it? Am I allowed to use it?'

He smiles. 'Yes, it's fine. I wanted you to get your ski legs on this before I inflict a drag on you.'

I feel a stab of panic. That sounds scary. 'What's that?'

'It's a type of lift, but don't worry – you'll soon get the hang of it. Let's take it one thing at a time, eh?' He cocks his head towards the very unmagic-looking conveyor belt. 'Shall we?'

Will shows me how to get on to the magic carpet. He goes first and actually, it's surprisingly easy. It's like being on a travellator at an airport, as far as I remember from the very few times I've been to an airport, only on a slight incline. I panic as I near the top because I don't know how to get off, but my skis pop off the end and I keep them straight, as Will told me to, he holds my hand to help me shuffle out of the way.

127

After that, things get more difficult. Will explains that what I need to do is go down the hill with my skis in a position called a snowplough 'Look! Keep the tips pointing together and the other ends outwards. Like a snowplough, see?' he says as if I was about six years old. He's saying something about transferring my weight from one side to the other to turn, and trying not to stick my bum out, but I'm not really listening. I've already decided that skiing isn't for me. It's a posh person's sport. You have to have learned when you are tiny, like the little kids around me on this slope, otherwise it's too late. What was I even thinking, coming on this holiday?

But I've come all this way and Will has paid for me to be here, so I can't say that. I force a smile, put my ski tips together and slide down the hill as Will skis backwards in front of me. There is a lot of stopping and two falls, but Will is there with an eager grin and his hand held out each time to help me up. It isn't as bad as I expected it to be.

'Yay!' he cries, applauding and jumping about as we finally make it to the bottom of the tiny slope, to the obvious bemusement of a nearby group of toddlers who are somehow on skis even though they have probably barely learned to walk. By now Will has taken off his skis and is walking alongside me because I am so slow and have fallen so many times. 'You were amazing!' he lies, admittedly enthusiastically. 'Shall we have another go, and then we'll move on to a green?'

A green what? I wonder. Are we playing golf later?

But I don't ask. 'Yes,' I agree. 'Let's do it again. And then we can move on. To a green.'

It turns out a 'green' is a green piste. It's the easiest type of proper slope, but still way bigger than the nursery slope, which was apparently what I was on earlier.

And magic carpets are only for total beginners, no doubt to lull you into a false sense of security.

Initially I am relieved to find out that we are going up the mountain in something called a bubble because that sounds quite fun, but it turns out to be nothing like a bubble at all. It's actually a cable car which, alarmingly, doesn't stop for you to get in like any normal kind of lift. No, instead you have to shuffle along in these impossible-to-walk-in ski boots, carrying your cumbersome skis and poles – ideally without letting them hit someone in the face – then you have to spot a gap while everyone else is doing the same thing, so you end up in the bubble rather than standing on the platform, waiting to get on.

After about three bubbles go past without us, even though we're at the front, I finally manage to hurl myself forward, or rather lurch in as Will shoves me. I fall over as soon as I'm inside, my skis clattering to the floor (why do they have to make so much noise every time?). Will hauls me up while a couple of teenage boys pick up my skis and hand them to me with a brief '*Tenez, Madame*' and disparaging looks.

As the lift rises up, I stare gloomily out of the window

at the beautiful landscape and clear blue sky. This is not going how I hoped it would. I knew we'd be skiing, obviously, but I guess I was imagining getting up late, perhaps some sex, a massive breakfast served by fit French waiters in tuxedos, a couple of runs in the sunshine, which I would somehow be able to accomplish effortlessly, some steak and red wine for lunch, followed by a session of sledging or a sexy snowball fight like in the films, then back for a hot tub and more sex on a bed covered in furs before a dinner of oysters and champagne served by a beautiful Russian woman. Clearly I have watched too many Bond films.

The cable car lurches and adrenaline surges through me as for a second I'm sure the whole thing is about to drop off the wire and crash to the ground. But no, it's just that we've arrived at the top and it's time to get off. I stumble off using my poles for balance – by now Will has realized that it's easier all round if he carries my skis, thankfully. I follow him out of the lift station and squint in the bright light.

It's nothing like the nursery slope up here. People are whizzing past at incredible speeds. Where are they all coming from? Will can't expect me to ski here, surely? I'll get run over.

Will touches my arm. 'OK? I know it's busy here, but don't worry – we're going to head over there where there's a nice quiet slope with a gentle drag lift which is tucked away from the main thoroughfare – it'll be perfect for helping you find your feet.' He points off to the left a little down the hill, where I can indeed see a slope where people do seem to be skiing more slowly (again, mainly children, though bigger than the ones on the magic carpet and, what I now see was a tiny weeny slope at the bottom).

I nod. 'OK. But how do we get there?'

'Um . . . we ski?' A hint of tetchiness there. Although I can understand why he's getting annoyed. I'm not usually so wet; as a rule, I'm up for anything. Magic mushrooms someone found in the forest? Why not? Naked cycling along the Cherwell towpath at midnight? Bring it on! But this is different. Skiing is scary and totally not fun.

Will puts my skis down on the snow right next to me, one by each foot, and then holds out his hand. 'You remember how to clip yourself in? Get your skis on and then we'll go down to the bottom of the drag lift.'

I feel tears forming. 'But there are so many people!' My voice is high and whiny and I hate myself. 'I'm scared they're going to go into me! I'm so slow and they're all so fast!'

He smiles semi-sympathetically and rubs my arm. 'It'll be fine. I'll stay right by you, above you on the hill so no one can mow you down, and it will be much quieter and calmer when we get over there. Look – you don't even have to turn to get there – you go in a straight line, snowploughing all the way so you can control your speed. No one will go into you.'

How do you know? a voice inside me wails, but I force myself to nod and force out a strangled 'OK.' Again, it seems to take forever to get my skis on but, once I'm in, Will clips his on in literally five seconds.

'OK? So remember, tips together, knees bent, look ahead – we're aiming for the bottom of that drag lift, OK? *On y va!*'

'What?' I ask, flustered, trying to remember all the things he said. Tips together, what else?

'Never mind. I just said, "Let's go!" It's French.'

He moves away and I feel a stab of anger – he said he would stay with me! I push with my poles and arrange my skis in a pizza-wedge shape to follow, very slowly.

'Yay! See? You're doing it!' he cries as I slide behind him. I continue in my hunched position, head down, bum stuck out in spite of what Will said, following the sound of his voice until he stops. We've somehow made it to the lift.

But this is unlike any lift I've ever seen. There's a queue of people waiting patiently; I watch as each one takes it in turn to grab hold of a big metal bar which is hanging above them, position it so a disc sits between their legs and then let the thing pull them up the mountain. It's even worse than the bubble.

Will looks at me expectantly. I stare back in horror. 'You're not seriously expecting me to go up on that?'

His face falls. 'Louisa, it will be fine! Look, there are tiny children doing it. All you have to do is keep your skis straight and remember not to try to sit down on the button, just lean on it.'

One of the men in red takes a pole and positions a particularly small child in front of one of his legs, before there is a gentle clang and they start sliding serenely up the hill.

'Can't I go up like that with you?' I ask, attempting to inject a touch of lightness into the situation which I certainly don't feel.

He laughs. I realize it's the first time either of us has laughed all day. 'You'll be fine. You'll see.'

I am not fine. The first time I try, I simply drop the pulley thing. The second time, I manage to jam it between my legs, but it pulls with a jerk I wasn't expecting and I fall over before I've even moved, and then it takes about five humiliating minutes for Will and the lift operator to get me back on my feet and in position to have another go. The next time I go a few metres, but I forget what Will said about not sitting and crash down onto my arse.

It is painful and embarrassing. Everyone can do this apart from me. I feel hot tears threatening and it's clear Will's patience is wearing thin.

And then, just as I am about to throw my poles down on the ground and say I can't do this any more, I finally make it all the way to the top.

But by this time I'm exhausted, so I persuade Will that we should stop for lunch before I attempt any more skiing. Fortunately, there's a café right opposite the little slope we're on.

We leave the skis outside – Will insists on splitting them apart and pairing one of mine with one of his to avoid them being stolen – and we take a table on the terrace. I secretly hope that the skis are indeed stolen so that I don't have to do any more of this. I don't even care if I have to pay for them, they can go on the credit card that I don't know how I'm going to pay off, along with everything else. It would be worth it, not to have to do this any more.

But then, sitting in the sun and looking out over the wooden balustrade, my spirits begin to lift. The sun is out and it is undeniably beautiful here.

Will reaches over the table and squeezes my hand. 'You did really well this morning,' he says.

I smile back. 'That's sweet of you to say, but we both know it's not true.' I pause. 'I'm not sure I'm cut out for skiing.'

He squeezes my hand tighter and lets it fall so that he can sit back in his chair. He sighs.

It's only then that I realize he no doubt had a vision of this holiday too. He probably imagined us whooshing down the slopes like everyone else seems to be, kissing on chair lifts, kicking our skis off in a few seconds to run into a bar for a quick beer or *vin chaud* or whatever, before effortlessly clicking them back on and whizzing off again. He didn't sign up for tears and tantrums.

'I'm sorry,' I say. 'Maybe it will be better this afternoon. I'll try harder.'

He tips his head backwards and stretches luxuriantly, then rights himself and returns my gaze. His face seems more relaxed and I feel a wave of relief.

'Don't be silly. I know you're doing your best. Besides, all I care about is being here with you.'

23

December 1998, La Madière, France

Will

That was a total lie.

I love Louisa, I really do. I haven't told her yet. I thought this trip might be the right time. But fucking hell, she's getting on my tits today.

I get that skiing isn't that easy when you start out. But honestly, I was only four when my parents put me on the slopes, and I managed, so why is she being such a drama queen about it?

Why did I say I'd teach her? Worst idea ever. So far, I've skied two nursery slopes, and that's it. At this rate, I'm not going to get in any actual skiing this week at all.

To be fair, Louisa perked up over lunch at least. A couple of beers, some wine, *steak frites* and an hour sitting in the sun and she was back to her usual self, gushing about the weather and the scenery, even making some saucy promises about what we can get up to later.

I'm looking forward to that, of course, but I was also hoping to do some skiing.

So I've come up with a plan. I'm going to get Louisa down the rest of the slope to the resort – it's an easy green, even she can manage it. By that time I'm pretty sure she'll say she's had enough of skiing for the day, so I can leave her to it and sneak in a few cheeky runs on my own before the lifts close. She gets to go back and relax, I get to ski, it's win-win.

'Right then,' I say as I take my card back from the waiter. 'Ready for the off?'

I feel her good mood instantly evaporate. 'Oh. Yes, I guess so. What are we doing now?'

'Well, I thought we'd ski down – it's a nice, wide, easy run, nothing to be alarmed about, and then we'll see how you feel.' You will go back to the chalet and do whatever the fuck you please as long as you are out of my way, and I will whizz off as high up the mountain as I can go before the lifts close without you holding me back, being the subtext.

She smiles. 'Me, ski all the way down? Yeah right. You're funny. What are we really doing? Another go on the drag?'

For fuck's sake! 'Um, no, I mean it,' I say gently. 'It's not far and it's a very simple slope. We can have another practice on the nursery slope first if you like, but I know you'll be fine. I'll be with you all the way.'

She pulls a face. For a second, I think she's going to cry. 'Will, I'm sorry, but I don't think I can. Is there any other way down?'

Fucking hell.

Be a sympathetic boyfriend, I remind myself. I take a deep breath.

'Well, if you really don't want to ski down, you can walk back up to the bubble and go down that way.' I point at the bubble, which is admittedly quite a hike up the hill from here. 'It's not so far if you get the drag halfway?' I suggest.

She looks at me in despair. 'Seriously? I can't walk that far in these stupid boots, especially not up the hill in the snow.' She looks up at the lift, and then down the slope. 'How long do you think it will take us to ski down? Realistically.'

'Um . . . about fifteen minutes? Twenty, tops.' It would take me about three by myself, I add, silently of course.

She looks at the lift again and sighs. 'OK. We'll give it a go. But you have to promise to stay right by me all the time.'

In the end, it takes almost an hour, not including the ten minutes it takes Louisa to get her skis on, as usual.

139

'Here you go, like this, yes that's it, toe in, lean on me, then push down with your heel . . . just so. No, it's slipped out, let's try again,' I say, calmly and patiently, acting like the ideal boyfriend, while inside I'm screaming. The conditions are so perfect today. I know I should be wanting to spend time with my lovely girlfriend, but right now, I could almost kill her.

Once the skis are finally on, we set off, and almost immediately, she falls over. I can see she's close to tears.

'Hey,' I say. 'Don't cry. You're doing great.'

She shakes her head. 'I'm scared, Will. I can't do it. I'm going to hurt myself. I know I am.'

I touch her arm. 'You're not going to hurt yourself. You're doing fine. By tomorrow you'll be loving it – I promise.'

She smiles weakly, takes her sunglasses off and wipes away a tear. 'Sorry. I'm being ridiculous. I'm going to get this.'

I feel a pang of guilt. She's so beautiful. And she's genuinely scared – I can see that. I vow to be more sympathetic and stop thinking about all the other pistes I could be skiing. I'm here with Louisa, that is what matters. Most men would kill to be here. They wouldn't want to be with Adam and Nell, hooning down the red runs on the glacier before stopping off for a nice cold beer which doesn't have to take an hour because someone takes so long to get their skis on and off.

Really, they wouldn't.

But my resolve doesn't last long.

Louisa eventually manages to snowplough down the top of the almost-flat slope, using the widest traverses I'd ever seen. Then, just as she's performing one of her tortuous turns, a snowboarder clips the end of the ski, and she falls over. Again.

This time, she's more than just a bit tearful. There are huge, heaving sobs and snotty tears – proper ugly crying. 'I can't do it!' she wails between sobs. 'Please, Will, don't make me! I'm too scared!'

We sit at the edge of the slope for about ten minutes, me with one arm around her shoulder and the other stroking her knee, waiting for her to calm down. I encourage her to take deep breaths while I try hard not to think about all the great skiing I am missing out on.

'Thing is, Louisa, now you're up here you have to get down the mountain,' I say. 'That's how skiing works, unfortunately.'

'But what about people like me who really can't do it? Isn't there a rescue service? I saw someone being taken down earlier?'

I laugh, thinking she is joking, but then, looking at her face, see she isn't. 'No. That's only for people who are injured.'

This starts a fresh batch of tears. 'So I have to do it?'

'Yeah. Sorry. But look, once you're down, if you don't want to do any more, that's fine. I'm not going to force you. Obviously.' *Please don't want to do any more, or at least, don't make me come with you*, I plead inwardly.

She nods and bites her lip. 'OK. I guess we'd better

get on with it then. Sooner we go, sooner it's over with. Help me up?'

I haul her up, and we spent another forty-five minutes picking our way down the slope. Fortunately, this time, the snowboarders give us a wide berth.

24

December 1998, La Madière, France

Louisa

'So, Louisa, how was your first day on the slopes?' Adam asks. We're at a table for four in the soulless dining room and have been served a starter of pâté and toast garnished with some limp lettuce leaves.

'It was tricky,' I say, absentmindedly spreading pâté onto a slice of toast as if it was butter. I notice Nell has delicately broken off a small piece of toast to spread the pâté on and feel myself go red. However hard I've been trying to get things right since I went to Oxford, I'm always slipping up. There are so many things to remember.

It's not helped by the fact that I'm already more than

a bit drunk. I'm not generally a big drinker, but by the time we got to the bottom of the horrible endless slope I felt I needed something to steady my nerves. Will took us into a bar and ordered two *vins chauds*. It wasn't really what I wanted – I'd never liked mulled wine on the few occasions I'd tried it, but actually, it was pretty good and went down very nicely.

As I was draining my glass and wondering about having another one, Will glanced at his watch and then reached across the table to take my hand.

'Darling, would you mind terribly if I dashed off and did a run or two before the lifts close? I don't feel like I've skied much today – I haven't been in the snow since last year and the weather's so beautiful, it's meant to change in the next couple of days so . . .'

I smiled tightly. 'Of course,' I said, 'You go,' but my stomach knotted. *He doesn't want to be with me,* I thought to myself. *He'd rather be skiing. I'm spoiling his holiday. I'm not the right type for him, I don't have the right background. He'd rather be with a nice Sloaney girl who grew up with pony lessons and skiing holidays and wouldn't be crying all over the slopes and dropping her skis everywhere like me.*

He leant over and kissed my forehead. 'You're an angel. You should think about what you want to do tomorrow. I'd be happy to take you out again, if you'd like,' he said, which I knew was a lie, 'but if you'd rather not, that's fine. Either way, I'll see you back at the chalet in about an hour. And then perhaps we can . . .'

I stroked his cheek and said, 'Perhaps – if you're a very good boy,' but really I was thinking, absolutely no way. Every part of me hurt and I was exhausted.

It felt like it was going to be a long way from the bar to the chalet so after Will went, I had another *vin chaud* to steel myself. And then another. Then because I was still in these God-awful ski boots and had to carry my own skis back, it took forever to walk to the chalet and I was in such a bad mood by the time I'd arrived, I treated myself to a gin and tonic before my shower to cheer myself up. By the time I was out of the shower, Will was back. He had a quick shower and then we came downstairs and started drinking again.

'So Will didn't turn out to be the excellent teacher he expected he'd be?' Adam guffaws. I see Will's face darken like it did this morning when Adam was goading him but, as far as I can see, what Adam's saying is no big deal. I don't know why Will gets so wound up by him. And to be fair, Adam has a point.

'I don't think I'm exactly a skiing natural, so Will was . . . as patient as could be expected,' I say, pleased with myself for being so diplomatic. The truth is, Will wasn't patient. Almost the whole day I could tell he didn't want to be there. He couldn't wait to dump me in the bar as soon as he could and race off to ski by himself, leaving me to walk back all by myself with my skis and everything. He shouldn't have taken me on that slope on my first day. It was too long and too hard. And the more drinks I have, the more annoyed I'm getting.

145

'So, not very patient then, by the sound of it,' Adam says. 'I did say she'd be better off in a lesson, Will.'

'Louisa did fine,' Will snaps, which is also not true. 'You don't know anything about it, Adam.'

'It can be so difficult when you're learning,' Nell interjects. 'Mummy told me I cried my eyes out on my first trip, with Daddy shouting at me because I was doing it wrong. She insisted on paying for lessons for me for every ski holiday we went on after that and, in all honesty, it was much better being taught by a stranger. Easier for everyone concerned, I think.' She turns to me. 'Perhaps you might want to give that a go tomorrow? Book a lesson?'

I shrug. 'I'm not sure I want to ski tomorrow. I think maybe skiing isn't for me.'

'Oh, but you mustn't give up so quickly!' Nell trills. 'It's so fabulous once you get into it. You'll never look back. The first few times are hard for everyone. Isn't that right, Will?'

Will nods. 'Yep. But it's up to Louisa. If she doesn't want to ski, she doesn't have to.'

He squeezes my knee under the table. Normally I would pat his hand but this time, I don't. It's abundantly clear that the reason he doesn't want to make me ski is because he doesn't want me to ski with him; I'm too slow and he can't do what he wants to do. But I'm not going to let him off that lightly. I don't want to ski tomorrow, but don't want to spend all day on my own either. Will shouldn't have insisted I come along if he wasn't going to make the effort to spend time with me.

Our plates are cleared away and a main course is brought out. It's a chicken and mushroom pie covered in soggy pastry. I pour myself another glass of wine from the unlabelled bottle. It looks like the food is going to be pretty rank this week but, on the plus side, it's as much wine as you can drink during dinner, even if it is pretty rough. We take our time.

Adam and Nell are banging on about their day, referring to things like powder, off-piste, schuss, and other words I don't fully understand. Will says almost nothing. I wonder if I can slope off to bed, I'm really tired. I hope Will won't want to have sex. I'm still annoyed with him. The more reasonable part of me knows he tried to teach me – he can't help it if he'd rather be off skiing properly than standing around trying to help me. But then again, thinking about that only makes the less reasonable side of me more angry.

'Louisa? What do you think?' Adam is asking.

I've absolutely no idea what's been said – my rage towards Will had made me tune out. I know I should admit that I didn't hear, but there's something about Adam that makes me feel like a silly little girl and I'm sure he or Nell will have a put-down ready if I admit I wasn't listening.

'Oh, um,' I bluster, feeling myself turn red.

'Sounds like a plan, hey, Louisa?' Will interjects. He is smiling for about the first time this evening and looking hopeful so, at a loss for anything else to say, I tell him, 'Sure, great, why not?'

'Excellent,' Adam says. 'We'll get you booked in for a lesson tomorrow morning then. You'll be skiing like a pro in no time at all!'

25

December 1998, La Madière, France

Will

I am so excited about today.

The weather isn't as good as yesterday, but it's far from terrible and I'm going to get to ski ALL DAY.

Most of the time I think my brother is nothing more than a pompous twat, but that was a brilliant move getting Louisa to agree to a ski lesson.

I could tell she wasn't listening and didn't know what he'd said. But she should have said so. And yes, I shouldn't have taken advantage – I knew she didn't want a ski lesson. But I really didn't want another day like yesterday.

It's lucky she was so drunk, otherwise I think she'd

have had a bit of a go at me about it. But as it was, all she did was slur: 'You knew I didn't want to ski again. Why did you make me agree to it like that? 'S'not fair,' as she collapsed into bed.

I helped her get undressed and lied that I thought she must have changed her mind. 'It'll be great,' I added, 'I hate to admit that Adam might have been right, but he probably is this time – you're bound to find it much easier being taught by a pro.' And even if you don't, the instructor is being paid to listen to your whining and crying so I don't have to, I thought to myself. I don't even care how good looking he is or how sexy his accent might be. Louisa harmlessly fancying someone else for a day is well worth a good day's skiing for me, I'm sure.

'And I promise, come what may,' I continued, 'I will spend the whole of the afternoon and the next day with you. We can ski at your pace, or we can not ski at all, just stay in bed shagging or something.'

I stroked her face. I was a bit drunk too. 'I love you,' I whispered, but she was already asleep.

26

December 1998, La Madière, France

Louisa

It turns out Adam was right – having an instructor is way better than having Will try to teach me.

To my relief, we are back on the nursery slope we started on yesterday morning. Jean-Marc snakes slowly in front of me as we practise snowploughing – up the magic carpet and down the little slope, again, again, and again.

'I think your boyfriend was too quick to take you to the green slope,' he says after what seems like about ten goes. 'I think you are ready to move on to the green now. But only if you want.'

So we do the green slope again. And by twelve o'clock,

I am exhausted, but I can kind of ski, and can even almost see why people find it fun. My annoyance at Will for rushing me and then abandoning me has almost gone, I'm so delighted with myself. I can't wait to show him what I can do.

Exhausted but exhilarated, I head off to the restaurant where I'm due to meet Will at twelve thirty. I can even carry my skis now without dropping them since Jean-Marc took the time to show me how to do it properly, resting the bindings behind my shoulder and not in front like I was trying to do before. It's all looking good. I'm going to be able to do this after all.

I order myself a celebratory *vin chaud* and look at the menu. I hope Will has had a good morning with Adam and Nell. I hope he's got loads of skiing done because now I want to spend the afternoon skiing with him without him feeling like he's doing me a favour. I'm still very far from fast, but I'm not as slow as I was. It won't be torturous for him like yesterday clearly was. We'll do a few easy runs together, we'll stop for a drink, I'll leave him to go and do a few more slopes on his own because that's the kind of nice, tolerant girlfriend I am today, and then I'll go back to the chalet, not dropping my skis all over the place, so I'll be showered and ready for him when he gets back and we can have amazing sex. Then we will go for dinner and I won't feel intimidated or bored by Adam and Nell because I know how to ski now and I understand what they are talking about and will even be able to join in with the conversation and tell them about the slopes I skied and which lifts I went on and use words like schuss correctly. It will all be perfect.

I glance at my watch: one o'clock. Where is Will? Never mind. I took ages longer getting down the slope yesterday than I thought I would. It's probably just something like that. Or perhaps a chairlift stopped. I order a second *vin chaud* and have another look at the menu.

The door of the restaurant flies open, there's a gust of cold air and Adam crashes in. He looks around wildly, spots me, and plonks himself down at the opposite side of the table. I feel a twinge of unease. Where is Will? Is he injured or something?

'Louisa,' he pants, obviously out of breath. 'So sorry to keep you waiting. Have you ordered yet? How was your lesson?'

'It was great thanks, Adam, but where's Will? Is he OK?'

He whips off his hat, turns and lifts his hand at the waitress in that officious, entitled way that only people from his privileged background can do. She comes scurrying over, of course.

'God, I'm dying for a beer. Absolutely RACED down here. So sorry to be late. *Une bière, s'il vous plaît?*' he says to the waitress, who nods and scuttles off. 'Sorry that was very rude of me – I didn't check if you were sorted. Did you want anything?'

I lift my *vin chaud*. 'No, it's OK, I've got a drink. Where's Will?'

'He sent me to apologize. We were over in the next valley and he broke a binding. Stupid arse is always trying to do these jumps which he can't do properly. Anyway, he landed badly as usual, his skis came off and one of them wouldn't go back on. So he had to walk down, and because we hired them over here he won't be able to exchange them for another pair over there – or at least, not without a huge amount of hassle, finding a shop in the same chain and the like, plus it was going to take ages even for him to walk down on that side, so he asked me to come and tell you and say sorry and be your lunch date today instead. I hope I'm not too poor a substitute.'

I listen to him with growing anger. Is that really what happened, or has Will sent Adam with an excuse so he can get out of having to ski with me this afternoon? I was so excited about showing him my new-found skills and now it's not going to happen.

When Adam's beer arrives, he downs it in one and slams the glass on the table. 'Damn! So thirsty. Are you hungry? Can I have a look at your menu?'

I hand over the menu and he scans it. 'Do you want to share a *pierrade*?'

I don't know what that is but agree anyway – partly because I don't want to admit to my ignorance yet again, but also because now that I know Will isn't going to be here, I feel my day has been ruined and I no longer care what I eat.

'Sounds great,' I say. 'And a bottle of red to go with

154

it?' I want to ask if Will is going to turn up later but don't want to sound too needy.

Adam looks up at me and smiles. 'My kind of girl. Bottle of red it is.'

It turns out a *pierrade* is a hot stone that you cook strips of beef on at the table. It arrives with a massive salad, a huge plate of chips and four bowls of dips, all of which are delicious. Adam orders the wine – I've no idea how much it cost and I'm hoping he's not expecting us to split the bill because I'm guessing it's going to be expensive.

This is the first time I've been with Adam on my own and it turns out he's much better company than I would have expected. When he and Will are together, there's constant sniping – they always seem to be competing, looking for any excuse to put each other down. Without Will here, Adam seems somehow softer.

We talk about his job in the City. Adam says that while he enjoys the money and the lifestyle that comes with it, he doesn't like the job much and doesn't see himself doing it forever.

'Thing is, though,' he adds, dipping an almost-raw piece of meat into the most garlicky sauce and chewing it thoughtfully, 'I don't know what else I could do. Plus it would be hard to give up the money. You get on a treadmill, big mortgage, high-maintenance girlfriend . . .'

'Nell's high maintenance?' I ask innocently as if I hadn't noticed. 'How long have you been together?'

He snorts. 'Couple of years. And yeah, she's high maintenance, but that's OK. She loves the City-boy life-style and all that comes with it.' He sighs. 'But if I'm honest, it goes two ways.'

'How do you mean?'

'Well, she's really fit, so . . . we both benefit. Just in different ways.'

I laugh. 'So she's not "the one"?' I must be a bit drunk. What sort of question is that?

He turns to wave the waitress over again. 'She's more the one for now, I think. No harm in being together for a bit of fun, is there?' There's an awkward pause, broken by the arrival of the waitress. 'Only young once and all that. Dessert?' he asks.

I shake my head.

'Two *genepis* please,' Adam says to the waitress as she clears our plates. I know I should be annoyed about Adam ordering for me without even asking, but what I'd usually see as arrogance, right now I see as admirable confidence.

'What's *genepi*?' I ask.

He turns back to me. 'It's a mountain liqueur. You'll like it, trust me. Don't let the colour put you off. Anyway, enough about me. What about you and Will? Is he your "the one"?'

I blush. 'I can't tell you that. You're his brother.'

He leans in conspiratorially. 'I won't tell, I promise.'

I laugh. 'You might.'

He leans in further and looks directly into my eyes.

'Trust me,' he says. His pupils are large and black. I feel a stab of something I shouldn't and lean back, feeling guilty. The waitress returns with our drinks and we sip from the elaborately decorated shot glasses in silence. Adam is still looking intently at me.

'It's good, huh?' he asks.

I nod as the alcohol burns my throat. It's a weird pale green colour, tastes very strong but it's sugary too. I take another sip, which makes me cough. 'Yeah. It's good. I'm definitely not going to be able to ski after all this though.'

'No matter – take a look out the window,' he says, pointing behind me. I turn to look and notice for the first time that while we have been having lunch, the weather has totally changed. It's snowing hard and a big cloud has come down.

'Wow, that's quite a difference,' I say.

'Yeah,' he agrees, taking another sip. 'You wouldn't want to ski in that. Might as well stay here and get drunk. Or we could go back and use that sauna in the chalet.'

I drink some more of the green liquid which is making my lips tingle pleasantly. 'OK,' I say, unsure of exactly what I'm agreeing to but too fuzzy-headed to care.

Adam leans in again. 'So, you were telling me about Will.'

I smile. 'No, I wasn't. You were trying to get me to tell you about Will. It's not the same thing at all.' I dangle the small shot glass from my fingertips and let it swing.

157

'You seemed pretty cross with him yesterday at dinner.'

I put the glass down. I didn't think anyone would have noticed. Am I that obvious? Apart from anything else, I didn't think anyone at the table was paying me any attention. 'Yeah. Well, I was annoyed about how the skiing had gone; I hadn't had a good day. But it wasn't Will's fault, and today's been much better. I'm not cross with him at all now.'

'Shame he couldn't make it for lunch though,' Adam says, and leans back again.

What did he mean by that? Was the broken ski an excuse?

I'm not going to let him draw me in like this. He's probably just trying to put Will down.

'Yeah. It's a shame. But it doesn't matter, I'll see him later. And he sent you, so . . .'

That came out wrong. I meant he was thinking of me, not that . . .

A grin spreads across his face. 'Yes he did. And it's been nice getting to know each other a little, hasn't it? Shall we have another drink?'

I look out the window. It is snowing even harder now. It's cosy and warm in here with the fire on and I can't face going out into the cold yet.

'One more,' I say. 'And then I'm going to go back to the chalet to warm up in the sauna.'

In the end, we have three more. And two coffees. It is almost half past three by the time we leave the restaurant.

Adam hands me his poles and hoiks my skis onto his shoulder without a word, for which I'm grateful – even though I've almost got the hang of carrying the skis now, I'm going to struggle in driving snow, horrendous wind and after all those drinks.

The wind bites at my face as we trudge back along the short road to the chalet and my hands are absolutely freezing in spite of my thick gloves. I think about how much I'm looking forward to the heat of a sauna. Adam puts the skis in the lockers in the boot room and pulls off his hat.

'Whew! Some kind of weather, hey? Hope Will and Nell are OK and don't get stuck in the other valley or anything. They might be closing lifts soon if it goes on like this.'

'They do that?' I ask.

'Yeah, sometimes. But don't worry – you'll have Will back this evening. Even if they do have to close lifts, they'll lay on buses. Only time he'd get stuck is if he just misses the last lift because of his own stupid fault. So let's hope he got his ski sorted.'

'I'm sure he will. He's pretty resourceful,' I say.

Adam gives me a look. 'If you say so,' he says dismissively. By now we are at the doors to our rooms, which are opposite each other. I've a feeling their room is bigger and smarter than ours, and probably with a better view.

'Right. I don't know about you, but I'm absolutely freezing. I'm going to get changed and then maybe I'll see you in the sauna?' he says.

I blush. Would Will mind me being in the sauna with Adam? I guess not; it's no different to being in a swimming pool with someone.

Or is it? I don't have that much experience of saunas.

'OK,' I say. 'See you down there.'

In our room I strip off my jacket, salopettes, and various layers. Naked, I look at myself in the full-length mirror. My borrowed salopettes are too tight and have left an angry red mark around my waist, and there's a matching mark under my boobs where my bra strap has rubbed. Perhaps I should have invested in a sports bra like my skiing friend had said, but it just felt like one more thing to spend money on.

There's a knock at the door. I grab a towel to put around myself and open it. It's Adam, also wearing a towel which is wrapped round his waist.

'Louisa, hi. Sorry about this, but I seem to have forgotten my trunks. Do you think Will would mind terribly if I borrowed his? If this was Holland, obviously I'd go naked in the sauna, but that's not OK in France, as far as I understand.'

I blush and open the door wider. 'Of course. Come in. I don't think Will would mind – I'll have a look through his stuff and see if I can find them.'

Adam sits down on the bed. 'I remember when we were kids, Will was always really retentive about unpacking whenever we went on holiday, while I'd just shove my suitcase under the bed and take stuff out as and when. Is he still like that?'

160

I turn my back and open the cupboard. Will has indeed stacked all his clothes in tidy piles. Underneath, my shelves are a heap of messy, tangled clothes.

'Yeah,' I say. 'You can probably see which shelves are his and which are mine.' I sort through a pile of folded boxers and find Will's trunks, similarly folded. I turn and wave them at Adam with a flourish.

'*Voila*,' I say, continuing to wave them around, as if I was doing the dance of the seven veils.

Adam smiles and stands. He looks me up and down and suddenly I feel exposed. 'Here,' I say, holding the trunks out to him, but he doesn't take them. Something in his face changes and in that instant, I realize what's about to happen.

I feel a surge of panic and try to back away against the cupboard as he seizes my wrist. His towel falls away and he crushes his mouth onto mine, pushing me back against the wardrobe door. He grabs at one of my breasts and for a second I am too shocked to do anything. He grinds his hips against mine and I feel my towel fall away.

I twist my head away and make a strangled noise. He grips my face and turns it back towards him, forcing his mouth against mine again. He jabs his tongue in and takes my other wrist, pinning it above my head.

I twist my head away. 'What are you doing?' I yelp, panicking. He hauls me round and throws me back onto the bed, still holding my hands above my head. He moves his knee up between my knees, forcing my legs apart.

161

'Don't give me that,' he groans, kissing and biting at my neck and nudging both his knees up further now, edging my legs apart as I try in vain to keep them together. 'You've been coming on to me all afternoon.' He moves himself upwards, thrusts roughly and I cry out as I feel he is inside me. I struggle to lift my arms from where they are still pinned above my head to push him off, but I can't.

'Please, Adam, I don't . . . I wasn't,' I try to shout, but it comes out as a whisper. I'm not sure if he even hears me. 'I didn't,' I force out, but he carries on. His breathing gets faster and more shallow as he grinds into me and he is burrowing his head into my neck. I try to wriggle away but he is too heavy as he thrusts into me, still pinning me down. 'Please . . .' I hear myself beg. I try to move my arms and to twist myself away from him, but it's useless.

He is thrusting faster and harder; then he groans, shudders, and rolls off me.

I lie there where he leaves me, on my back. I feel tears seeping out of my eyes and rolling down the side of my face. Was I coming on to him? Did I want this? I don't know any more.

He sits up and glances at me sideways before leaping up and putting his towel back round his waist, just as it was when he came in. I reach for my towel, which is next to me on the bed, and drape it over myself ineffectually. I've never felt so naked, so vulnerable.

He's probably been in the room less than five minutes,

and the way he looks now, it's almost like nothing has happened at all.

'No need to tell anyone about this, Louisa, is there? No harm done. Anyway, you wanted it as much as I did. And it's not as if anyone would believe otherwise, is it?'

He snatches up the trunks and opens the door.

'I'll see you in the sauna.'

27

December 1998, La Madière, France

Louisa

After Adam leaves the room, I am so stunned I don't know what to do.

Did that even happen?

Did I lead him on?

Did I want it as much as him, like he said?

I start shivering and realize I'm cold. I haul myself up and get into the shower, turning the tap almost all the way round until the water is as hot as I can bear.

I scrub myself with Will's posh soap, and wash my hair, but I'm convinced I can still smell Adam on me.

Should I tell Will what happened?

Would he believe me?

Would he think it was my fault?

Was it my fault?

I wrap myself in a towel again and lie on the bed. My skin feels pink and raw.

Will'll be back soon.

I don't want to be lying here like an invitation. That's what Adam saw. Will isn't like Adam but . . . even so. I don't want to give him the wrong idea.

I haul myself up and dress in jeans and an old hoodie. I'm going to look frumpy compared with Nell in whatever her latest designer outfit will be this evening but right now, I don't care. I can't bear the thought of anything touching my skin. Anyone.

I consider telling Will that I still have a headache and don't want any dinner but in spite of my massive lunch I'm unexpectedly starving and have already played the part of the whiny, annoying girlfriend quite enough this trip – if I'm not careful, Will might dump me. Also – what if Adam tells him what happened and I'm not there to give my version of the story? What if Adam tells Will I was coming on to him all afternoon and that we had sex while he was still out skiing? Would he do that? He's always trying to get one up on Will but . . . would telling him what we – he – did be a step too far?

I don't know.

Would Will believe me if I told him the truth?

I'm not sure about that either.

I change my mind and swap my hoodie for a nicer

top – I don't want Will to be embarrassed by me – but I put on a scarf too, so you can't see my neck. There are grazes and bruises. They're not big – they're ones that I could explain away by saying my ski jacket was rubbing, but I don't want Adam looking at my skin, seeing what he did. I think maybe he'd get a kick out of that.

A couple of hours later the four of us sit down for dinner. I avoid Adam's eye, but the way he is acting this evening, it's as if nothing has happened at all. He pours wine for us all, Nell and me first before himself and Will, as usual. The perfect gent. He winds Will up about breaking his ski, gently teases me about having a crush on my ski instructor, things like that. As if it's an ordinary dinner on an ordinary night on an ordinary ski holiday, where nothing unusual happened and no one has been raped.

And I *was* raped. Wasn't I? Or maybe nothing did happen. I mean, obviously we had sex, but . . . maybe it was like he said? Maybe he didn't force me?

Did I want it? Did I at least make him think I want it?

Is that even the same thing?

I realize in an instant that I definitely can't tell Will. He would never believe me. Right now, I'm not even sure what *I* believe.

'Didn't we, Louisa?' Adam is asking as I tune back into the conversation. 'We had a great lunch at La Taverne? Shame that Will missed it by being such a knob

167

and breaking his ski and Nell by being too slow to keep up with me.'

Nell sniffs. 'I was NOT too slow to keep up with you. I simply wanted to stay on that side of the valley instead of coming back over here – there's more sun there in the afternoon and I like the pistes better on that side.'

I look at Adam, but only for a second because it hurts too much. I can see he's mocking me. Or at least that's how it feels. Does he think we're sharing a secret about what went on between us while Will was out? Or is he simply looking at me with no hidden meaning? I feel like I don't know anything any more.

'Yes. It was a nice lunch. Thank you,' I say mechanically. I only then remember that he settled the bill – it must have been expensive with that posh wine and all those drinks. Was that it? Did he think I owed him? That I wouldn't have accepted all those drinks if I hadn't wanted him?

If we'd have split the bill, would that have avoided all this? Would that have sent the correct message – I am your brother's girlfriend. You and I are just having lunch together. We owe each other nothing.

Stupid, stupid, stupid.

'So what did you do with the rest of the afternoon?' Nell asks, spearing a piece of dry chicken.

'We spent most of it in the restaurant,' Adam continues, 'Louisa telling me her life story, and then we came back here. I had a sauna – I thought Louisa was going to join me, but I guess she changed her mind. This chicken is horrible, isn't it?' he adds, lifting his fork and squinting at a piece of meat.

How can he be so nonchalant?

'I had a shower,' I say, my voice shaking a little, looking up at Adam but he is still concentrating on his chicken, trying to pull it apart with his knife and fork. I'm trying to inject meaning into my voice – *Do you not realize that I had a shower because of what you did to me?* – but he seems entirely oblivious. Is he? Or is he just a convincing actor?

He shoves the chicken in his mouth and chews exaggeratedly, pulling a face. 'Ugh,' he says after he finally swallows his mouthful, 'I think maybe we should go out for dinner tomorrow, the food here is hideous. Anyway, about tomorrow. Who's skiing with who? Or with whom? Can never get that right.'

'Well, I'm going to ski with Louisa,' Will says, 'as I didn't get to today.' He turns to face me. 'Assuming you want to ski tomorrow, that is? Show me what you can do? I'm sorry about today. I was so looking forward to skiing with you, but sorting out my broken ski ate up the entire afternoon.'

Right now I can't imagine wanting to do anything except curl up in bed and pull the covers over my head, but I can't do that without telling Will why, or perhaps him offering to stay in bed with me, which I simply can't face. More than anything, I don't want to risk being left alone with Adam again. Right now, all I want is to not be me.

Adam pulls a face. 'Think the weather's meant to be pretty rank tomorrow. Sure you want to ski, Louisa?'

Not really, I think, but as I open my mouth to speak, Will says: 'We'll take a view tomorrow. How about we all do our own thing in the morning, meet up at lunchtime and see what everyone wants to do from there?'

'Sounds like a plan,' Adam says. 'I'm going to be starving by then – this dinner is almost inedible.'

After forcing down some dessert, I say that I'm tired and would like to go to bed.

Will says he will come with me and I feel a stab of alarm – I want some time on my own. But I guess he thinks all my cries of 'No, no, you stay' are insincere and he follows me up the stairs to our room.

I lie down on the bed and he lies down next to me, putting his head on my chest and his arm across my waist.

I concentrate on not flinching. I don't want to be touched. But I can't tell him why. I've realized that.

'Are you sure you're OK?' he asks, without moving. 'You seem very quiet this evening.' He pauses. 'You don't have to ski tomorrow morning if you don't want to.' He lifts his head and looks up at me. 'Is that what it is? Or are you annoyed that I didn't make it back for lunch? It wasn't my fault, honestly. I really wanted to ski with you this afternoon.'

I force a smile. 'No. Don't be silly. It's nothing you've done. I'm tired, that's all. But of course we can ski tomorrow. I want to show you how much I've come on.'

170

He kisses the end of my nose and lays his head back down on my chest.

'Can I ask you a question?' I say, before I've properly thought through what I'm going to say.

He moves his hand down to my leg and starts to stroke my inner thigh. Normally it would make me want him but right now it makes me feel attacked. I fidget away, pretending that I am adjusting my jeans, as if have an itch or something.

'Ask me anything, my darling,' Will replies.

'Why does Adam put you down all the time?'

He lifts his head to look at me, frowning. 'That's an odd question. Why do you ask?'

'Dunno. I guess, not having any brothers or sisters – or any family, apart from Mum, sometimes I find it difficult to understand these relationships.'

He shifts slightly so that he is lying on his stomach and can look at me more easily. 'I don't know either really. He's always been that way. Obviously, he's older so he's always had the upper hand in some ways, at least when we were kids. I'd never say this to him – and Mum would never admit it in a million years – but I've always been her favourite. I was ill as a child and I think that made her uber-protective of me. I think it's made him jealous.'

'You were ill?'

'Yeah. In and out of hospital for a couple of years – no big deal, got over it, hale and hearty now.'

'I bet it was a big deal at the time.'

'Probably, I don't remember much about it. But I think it's why I'm Mum's favourite, which has its advantages as I've always been able to get away with just about anything at home, so not all bad.'

I smile and touch his face. 'How could you not be anyone's favourite?'

He smiles back. 'That's sweet.' There's a pause and Will looks thoughtful. 'It's an interesting question though. Thing is, I can see Adam's an arse in many ways, and he spends almost the whole time when we're together trying to wind me up, but he's also my brother, whether I like it or not. Always has been, always will be. There's a bond there. It's maybe difficult to understand if you don't have a sibling. Even when I hate him, which quite often I do, I know that . . . well, deep down, I don't hate him really.'

Tears well in my eyes. Will would never believe me. I can't tell him what happened. What Adam did.

A tear falls and Will wipes it away. 'Aww. You're so sweet. Look at me, making you tear up.' He leans in and kisses me. I fight down the rising panic and, after a couple of seconds, manage to relax into it. Nothing has changed between us, after all. I won't let it. I'm not going to let Adam ruin everything.

He pulls back suddenly. 'You smell different,' he says.

The panic returns. 'What?' I stutter. 'No, I don't, it must be . . .'

'You used my soap!' he yelps. 'That's what it is! You smell like me. It's weird.'

172

'Is that OK? You weren't here. It reminded me of you.'

He kisses me again. 'Of course.' There's a pause. 'I love you, Louisa.'

I kiss him back. 'I love you too.'

Adam was right about the weather. When I look out of the window in the morning I can't see a thing – the hotel is totally shrouded in fog.

'Arses,' Will says as he pulls back the bedroom curtain. 'I guess you don't want to go out in this?'

He looks down at me, still in bed, and gets back in, moving close to me and pulling me towards him. 'I've got a better idea . . .'

I feel a lurch of panic. I managed to put him off last night by saying I was tired and had a headache. I can't put him off forever, but right now I can't face the thought of anything like that.

I kiss him chastely on the lips before leaping out of bed practically shouting: 'No, I really do want to ski! I did so well yesterday and I want to show you.' Right now, even skiing in terrible weather is a more appealing option than having sex. I wonder if I will always feel like this. It's somehow difficult to imagine I won't. Has Adam ruined that for me too?

Will laughs. 'Wow, you certainly are full of surprises.' He throws back the covers, stands up, and stretches. 'Let's do this then.'

* * *

173

I start to regret my decision as soon as we step out of the chalet. You can barely see more than two metres. It's starting to snow and the wind is picking up too.

'Any luck and we'll be above the weather by the top,' Will says cheerily as we pull the barrier down onto our knees on the chairlift. I smile weakly.

He's wrong, of course. It is the same at the top, only windier. But that's OK, I tell myself. I'm going to be fine. I know how to ski now. I can do this.

'You all right with this?' he asks. 'If you're not sure, we can get the bubble down. It's just over there. I don't mind, honestly. Whatever you want today.'

Tears spring to my eyes. He is so sweet. If he finds out what happened, he might never forgive me. Or he might never forgive his brother. Or either of us. Or he might think I'm making it up. I can't risk telling him.

He can't see my tears, but they're making my goggles steam up. 'No, I can do it,' I reply. 'I just need to clear my goggles.'

We make it down the slope and I do OK. In fact I do well enough that we go up again and this time try a blue slope, which is apparently slightly harder. There are a few falls, but no tears and no tantrums. Will is sweet, attentive, and patient. I guess he feels bad for not making it back for lunch yesterday. But he can't feel anywhere near as bad as I feel. The more I think about it, the more I think I'm at least partly to blame for what happened with Adam. I shouldn't have had all that wine.

174

I shouldn't have let him order expensive drinks and then pick up the bill. I shouldn't have let him into my room while I was only wearing a towel. I should have fought harder when he pinned me down, shouted, screamed, kicked. I did none of that.

By lunchtime, I am freezing cold and exhausted. We have a much simpler lunch than I ate with Adam; *croque monsieur* and chips with one beer each. That's the kind of lunch I should have had yesterday, I realize now. Not the epicurean and sensual feast with wine and liqueurs I opted for. I am such a fool.

'So, what about this afternoon?' Will asks. 'Do you want to go back up? You did amazingly this morning.'

I look out the window. The snow is sheeting down. Part of me thinks I should go, but a larger part is so exhausted there's no way I can face it.

'Would you mind terribly if I didn't? I'm really tired and a bit cold. But I don't mind at all if you want to go out. I don't want to spoil your fun.'

Will reaches across the table and takes my hand. 'You could never spoil my fun. Tell you what, I'm pretty cold too. Let's go back and have a sauna. I don't think you had one yesterday in the end? Then we could . . .'

He raises an eyebrow and I force a smile. That's the last thing I want to do, but I'll worry about that when it comes to it.

He makes the universal writing in the air sign for 'Can we pay the bill please?' and we both start to gather up our things. Normally I'd be excited about an afternoon with Will on my own with nothing planned, but right now I feel nothing but dread. I don't want him to touch me. I don't want anyone to touch me.

There's a sudden blast of cold air as the door flies open and Adam stamps in, the cold emanating off him as he plonks himself down next to me. I feel myself shrink away from him. He's not particularly big or even that tall, but somehow his presence seems to take up a lot of space at the table.

'Bastardos!' he booms, waving towards the waiter who slouches over so Adam can order a beer. He hasn't brought our bill. Adam turns back to me and Will. 'Did you have a good morning out there?'

'Yep,' Will says. 'Louisa's been showing me what she can do. She's really come on.'

Adam looks me up and down and claps me on the shoulder. I try and fail not to flinch. 'Good girl!' he cries. 'I knew you could do it.'

'Where's Nell?' Will asks.

'Gone back to the chalet. Doesn't like this weather, apparently. But I thought I might find you in here and I wondered if you fancied doing something special this afternoon, Will? Maybe get a guide and do something off-piste?'

There is a brief pause. 'Oh I don't think so, sorry,' Will says, loyally. 'Louisa and I were going to go back and have a sauna.' He sounds like he means it but, much as I love him, I know what the sauna will be leading to in Will's mind and it's absolutely the last thing I feel like doing at the moment.

176

'Don't be silly,' I counter. 'We're only here for a few more days and we can have a sauna any time. You go out with Adam. I'm exhausted – I'll probably just have a nap back at the chalet. I'll be quite happy on my own, honestly.'

Will frowns. 'Hmmm. But I've already abandoned you too much on this trip and I wouldn't want you to think that I—'

'You heard the lady!' Adam interrupts. 'It's FINE. Now get your arse in gear and we'll go and see if we can get a guide. There's a place opposite – I think it's called Skitastic. We'll see if they've got anyone available.'

Will looks at me helplessly.

I smile and nod. This gives me an excuse not to have sex and it will keep Adam out of my way too – all I feel is a wave of relief. 'It's fine, honestly. Go. I want you to.'

He kisses me on the cheek and gets up from the table. 'You're the best girlfriend ever. I'll see you later.'

28

Will

Unsurprisingly, given that the weather this afternoon means almost no one wants to ski, Skitastic has a guide available. The weather has worsened, and even though most people like us who are only out in the snow for a precious week will ski in just about anything, there are limits. Even so, I'm really pleased to be out on the mountain. I meant it when I said I'd go back with Louisa at lunchtime; I wanted to be with her and I still felt bad that I'd left her to her own devices so much this week. But she genuinely seemed to mean it when she said I should go out skiing. It's pretty exhausting, being out on the slopes in this weather, especially if you're a

179

beginner, so it's not surprising she wants to get a few zeds. I'll make it up to her later.

Our guide, Cameron, is English and he's not in the usual ski instructor model – no effusing over working in the 'best office in the world', no taking us to the top of a lift just to point out Mont Blanc (not that we could see it in today's conditions, even if it was right next door), no banging on about the importance of taking time to enjoy the mountains and that it doesn't matter what standard you are or if you don't want to do certain slopes or your parallel turns aren't perfect as long as you're having fun.

No, instead there's some brief form-filling, a curt chat about our levels ('We've been skiing since we were kids and can ski just about anything,' Adam says, the latter half of which is a bit of an exaggeration) and a short conversation about what we want from today (again Adam speaks for us both: 'Something a bit extreme.') I don't disagree. I've spent so much of this week on easy slopes with Louisa, I'm up for something challenging now.

On the way up, Adam jabbers away but Cameron barely responds to any of the usual ski chit-chat – questions about how long he's been here, comments about the weather, etc. In fact, he's abrupt almost to the point of rudeness. But I guess you probably get sick of having the same conversations every day with total strangers who you're unlikely ever to see again. Or maybe he simply doesn't want to be out in this horrible weather.

'Right,' Cameron says, once we're off the top lift. 'We're going to head down off the back here. Couloir Noir.'

By now the wind is blowing so hard it's a struggle to hear. My goggles have steamed up, so I can't see – and we haven't even started yet. I take them off, wipe them and put them back, but if anything it makes them worse.

'The terrain isn't too difficult but in these conditions it's important to take it slowly. I'll lead – to start with, at least. Try to stay close behind me. There's no rush; obviously I will go at your pace,' Cameron says.

'We're not a couple of old ladies!' Adam booms. 'We can keep up. Don't worry about that.'

He nods. 'Fine. Shall we go then?'

We set off. Cameron leads, too slowly, while another guide in the same jacket who has joined us hangs back behind. Adam quickly overtakes so that he is in front of us all. I am happier taking it at a leisurely pace – the snow is deeper than I'm used to and the visibility is almost nil. A couple of minutes later, the second guide whizzes by me, and half a minute later I find Adam and Cameron waiting on a bend.

'So. This next bit's steeper. You'll need to take it easy. I can see you like speed,' Cameron says to Adam as pointedly as you can when you're having to shout to be heard over the wind, 'but there are two things you should know about that: it's dangerous to go faster than is suitable for your ability, and skiing accurately is much more important than skiing fast.'

I smirk – neither of them will be able to see under my various scarves and layers. That little reprimand will have pissed Adam off no end. He can't stand being told what to do or having his skiing ability questioned.

'Got you,' Adam says, not bothering to hide his irritation.

'Right,' says Cameron. 'I'm going to lead – please watch where I go and don't overtake me this time. I know the route very well and it's dangerous for you to race ahead off-piste in these conditions when you don't know the terrain. Understood?'

'Got you, like I said,' Adam repeats, even more irritably. Cameron nods and skis off, slick as anything.

'For fuck's sake, was there really any need for him – whatever his name is – to speak to me like that?' Adam grumbles.

'It's what ski guides do – try to keep you safe. It's their job.'

'Try to patronize me, more like,' Adam retorts. He uses his poles to push himself off, not as fast and not nearly as slick as Cameron, whatever Adam might think. And then, on his second turn, he falls.

I watch in horror as he tumbles down the slope and both skis ping off. It's pretty steep here and it's snowing so hard that soon he is out of sight. Fuck.

'Adam!' I yell. 'You OK?'

Silence. Or rather, not silence, just a howling wind. Would he have even heard me shouting? Would I be able to hear him?

'ADAM!' I yell again. Nothing.

'I'M COMING DOWN!' I holler. 'Stay where you are!'

Fuck. Fuck. I'm never good in these kind of situations. He'll be fine, I tell myself. I push myself away and ski down carefully, slowly. Of the two of us – not that I'd ever admit it – Adam is the better skier and I don't know what made him fall. Ice? A rock? Just bad luck? I don't want the same to happen to me.

Oh God. Oh God. At least his skis came off, so hopefully he won't have hurt his legs.

Shit! His skis! Where are they? I look back up the slope, but the snow is too deep. I can't see them; they could be anywhere. Never mind. I'll worry about that later. More important to find my brother.

'ADAM!' I shout again. 'ADAM!'

This time I think I hear something – though it may just have been the wind. 'Stay there! I'm coming!' I shout, uselessly.

Then I hear it. 'Over here!'

I feel a bolt of relief shoot through me. Thank God! 'Where are you?' I shout.

'Over here, you useless bastard,' he shouts back, making it clear to me in an instant that he's not hurt. 'In the snow.'

'Oh, in the snow! That helps,' I yell back sarcastically. 'Now I know exactly where you are.'

'Over here, you bellend.'

I follow the sound of his voice, though it's difficult

183

to hear him over the sound of the wind. I ski as slowly as I can, making a few slow, gentle turns. I don't want to fall. A little further down, Adam's colourful jacket looms into sight through the whiteness. 'There you are. What happened?' I ask.

'Dunno. Caught an edge, I guess.' He pauses. 'Where are my skis?'

My stomach lurches. I should have picked them up, but I panicked, wanting to get to Adam. Then again, he shouldn't have fallen. 'Where you left them, I would have thought,' I say, evenly.

'For fuck's sake, Will, didn't you think to get them on the way down?'

Nice; he cocks it up and somehow it's all my fault. 'I thought I should come and see if you'd broken your back or fallen off a precipice or something, you ungrateful shit.'

'Right. So how am I meant to get down now?'

We both listen to the wind howl for a few beats.

'I could ski down, find the guides and then we come up again and find your skis on the way down?' I suggest.

'No way,' Adam says, hauling himself to his feet. 'It's bloody freezing, I'm not sitting here on my soaking wet arse while you do that. I can't have fallen that far, let's hike up a bit and find my skis. Can't be that hard.'

I look up the slope. It's barely possible to tell the difference between the ground and the air, and you certainly can't see the sky. Everything is white.

I shake my head. 'I don't think that's going to work.

Your skis could be anywhere – we'll never find them. I think it's better if—'

'Fine,' Adam snaps. 'Do what you like. I'm going up the slope to look for my skis. You carry on down if you want.'

Adam starts trudging up the slope. After a couple of steps, he tips himself forward and puts his hands in the ground and continues to scrabble up that way – it's too steep to go up any further without doing so.

For fuck's sake. I can't leave him here on his own. I click my boots out of my skis and follow Adam up the hill, awkwardly carrying my skis and poles with me. I can't put them down – I might not find them again.

It's hard work, and very soon I can feel myself sweating under my ski jacket in spite of the bitingly cold wind. I stay at a distance from Adam – there's no point in us both covering the same ground. I'm about to shout up to him that this is pointless, that I've changed my mind, that I'm going to go and find the guides, get to a ski shop and bring him back some new skis, anything to get off this fucking freezing cold mountain with no visibility when Adam shouts 'I've got one!'

Thank God for that. I crawl over to where Adam is brandishing his ski like a javelin. 'See!' he crows. 'Told you. It's all going to be fine. Now the other one must be around here somewhere. Let's keep looking.'

We start poking around with our ski poles but, whatever Adam says, there's no guarantee it will be close by and it's impossible to see anything. The snow is really deep here.

'Can't you make it down on one ski?' I ask impatiently. 'Given that you're such a shit-hot skier?'

'Not on this type of terrain, you utter and complete arse,' he replies. 'Come on, help me out, it's got to be here somewhere.'

But the cold is getting to me now. 'Fuck's sake, Adam, this is ridiculous. We could both die out here if we're not careful. I'm going to head off and find the guides. They're probably shitting their pants about where we are anyway. They must have a procedure for this. Maybe they can send a snowcat up to get you or something.'

'Too steep,' Adam barks. 'Just help me look.'

I'm genuinely starting to feel scared now. I think Adam is too, not that he'd ever admit it. But one of us needs to do something.

'No. I'm going down. We could be here forever doing this.'

'Fuck you, Will – help me, won't you? There's no point in having spent this much time looking for it, only for you to—'

'I'm going,' I insist. 'I'm going to get help. It's the sensible thing to do, whether you can see it or not. If you can't make it down on one ski, you'll have to wait here. One way or another, I'll get someone to come for you. They're not just going to leave you here. It'll be fine.'

I carefully place my skis down and try to get them back on but the slope is so steep and there's so much snow in my boots and bindings that it's almost impossible.

'Fuck's sake, Adam!' I explode. 'Why the fuck did I listen to you! I can't get my bloody skis on now!'

'And that's my fault how?' he shouts back. 'Help me look for the other ski and we can both get down off this mountain.'

One ski finally clicks into place. I take a deep breath. 'Adam, I think it's best for both of us if I go and get help. I'm not doing this to prove a point or even because I don't want to help you – which, I have to admit, right at this moment I really fucking don't. But we've no doubt strayed from where we were originally, so even the guides probably wouldn't know how to find us. We're not on a piste – there'll be no patrol. This is properly dangerous, Adam – life-and-death stuff. I need to go, let the guides know that you are here and that you're stuck. OK? Then they can get help. It's the only sensible thing to do.'

Adam doesn't reply but keeps stabbing uselessly at the snow with his pole. Fuck him. I'm getting off this mountain. My second ski finally clicks into place and I push myself away. Adam grabs me.

'You're not going.'

'I am. Let go of me.'

I try to force him off me, but I can't turn because my skis are pointing the wrong way and I'm holding my poles. He pushes me over and we both fall.

My head hits something hard.

29

January 2020, La Madière, France

Hugo

'A body?' I ask. 'What happened?'

'I don't think they know much more than that,' Matt
says. 'A body was discovered early this morning. Until
they've ascertained what happened, no one can ski in the
sector where it was found. They can't open the lifts in
the higher sectors anyway this morning because of the
wind, so . . . There are a few runs open at the bottom,
but not much of any interest to anyone except beginners
I don't think.'

'Oh, how awful!' Ria says. I look at her for the first
time since she came downstairs. She looks pale and
startled, but she's still beautiful. I feel a stirring of lust

189

and am annoyed with myself. I'm still cross with her, I tell myself. I'm not letting her off the hook that easily.

Matt nods solemnly. 'Yes, awful. All I've been told is that a body has been found, the police and mountain rescue are investigating, but it's taking longer than usual because of the terrible weather. The road into the resort is blocked and they can't even fly a helicopter in these high winds so . . .'

'Poor bugger,' I say.

Ria looks at me and then across at Matt and – oh God – she holds his gaze too long for my liking. My face grows hot. I bury my face in my paper and pretend to read the news.

'A terrible thing,' Matt continues. 'The police have sealed off a huge area. As you can imagine in a small resort like this, there's a lot of gossip and speculation going around, but we don't know who it is yet – not even if it's someone local or a visitor – and I doubt we will know for a while.'

'Do they know what happened?' Ria asks. 'Who found him? It. Them. Is it a man?'

Matt pulls a face. 'Like I say, at the moment it's mainly rumour and speculation. As I understand it, one of the piste-basher drivers almost ran over the body on his way back down to the resort in the early hours of this morning. I'm not sure exactly where it was found, but it sounds unlikely it was a skier – the mountain guys would have scooped up any stray people still on the slopes when they did their final rounds at the end of the day. My best guess is someone had a few too many in one of the bars last night, got lost on the way home and tripped over, or simply fell asleep in the snow.' He pauses. 'Not that we should be speculating, of course.'

'Does that kind of thing happen often?' I ask.

'Not too often, thankfully – it's not something I've ever had personal experience of – but you do hear about it now and again, in the press or from other reps. Terrible thing. But people come on holiday, drink too much, and feel invincible. The mountains can be dangerous, and you have to respect them.'

The room falls silent. Matt gives himself a shake and says, 'Anyway. Enough lecturing from me. I assume everyone is present and correct here?'

I look up from my paper, which I can't understand anyway as it's in French; I should have brought my iPad downstairs. 'I haven't seen the others yet. But I imagine they fancied a lie-in – it turned into rather a late night. I'm pretty sure they wouldn't have gone out.'

'Does anyone know if Cameron stayed in the end?' Matt asks.

'No idea,' I say, turning back to the paper. I'm ashamed to find for a fleeting moment that I hope it's Cameron who's been found in the snow. I push the thought away. He's a knob, but no one deserves to freeze to death like that.

'Me neither,' Ria adds.

Matt pauses. 'OK. I guess I'll give him a call later. No need to disturb him unnecessarily.'

We all continue eating breakfast in silence.

PART THREE

PART THREE

30

BEFORE

Mama was crying. I didn't want to eat my dinner – it was Weetabix, like it often was when Mama was too tired to cook. I'd thrown it on the floor. I thought Mama would shout at me because I'd made a mess – but she didn't. She sat down on one of our two rickety kitchen chairs and started crying – not just a bit, but really, really sobbing. Huge hiccupping sobs so big that she could barely catch her breath.

'Mama?' I said, reaching out and touching her hand, which she pulled away to swipe angrily at her eyes. 'Mama? Don't cry . . .' But she carried on, not even saying anything, and soon I started crying too.

Suddenly she jumped up and stood in the corner of the kitchen with her hands over her ears. 'No, no, no!'

she screamed, and then sank down to the floor, still sobbing, but more quietly now.

I got down from my chair, even though I wasn't allowed to get down until I had finished my food, but I thought maybe Mama wouldn't mind this time. Or maybe she would mind even more than usual. I didn't know.

I pushed my chair over to the sink, climbed up on it and picked up a cloth. It was slimy and smelt weird. I climbed down and dabbed at the Weetabix on the floor like I'd seen Mama do when I'd thrown my food before. But it didn't seem to make it better – it spread it out further. I hoped Mama wouldn't shout at me.

'Mama, I clean it,' I said, dabbing at it again and holding up the cloth. 'Look.' I stared down at the mush on the floor. It was still there but I said, 'All gone now,' even so.

Her hands were covering her face and she was still sobbing loudly. I didn't know what to do. 'Mama, I put myself to bed. You have rest. I a big girl now,' I said. I thought that would make her feel better. She was always so tired.

I wandered into the room we shared, took off my clothes and put on my nightie. It was too small and had a rip in it, but I didn't care because it had pictures of bubbles on. It was my favourite thing to wear and sometimes I wore it all day as well as at night. Usually Mama didn't notice.

I got into my little bed with Teddy and opened a

book. I couldn't read but I didn't have many books and I knew all the stories off by heart. I could tell which one this was by the pictures – it was the one about the giant – so I started to read to Teddy. Mama didn't always read me a story, but sometimes when she had had a good day she did. Mostly, she didn't.

It was difficult for me to tell when Teddy was asleep because he didn't move or talk very much, so I read all the way to the end of the book, even though I couldn't remember all the words and I might have got some of them wrong. I didn't think Teddy minded. He and I spent a lot of time together because I didn't know any other children. Then I lay down and shut my eyes tight. I left the light on because that's what I always did when I went to sleep. That way, no monsters could come in before Mama did. When Mama came to bed she would turn off the light, but that was OK, I didn't mind because monsters definitely wouldn't come in while she was there, even if she was asleep. She would protect me.

I squeezed my eyes so tight it started to hurt. I opened them again, but Mama still wasn't there. I held my breath to see if I could hear if she was still crying but I couldn't tell. I sang softly to Teddy – he liked songs. I didn't know many songs, only the ones I'd heard on the TV, but I didn't think Teddy minded.

Teddy danced while I sang. I laughed, but quietly, so as not to disturb Mama. Mama didn't like it if I made any noise once I was in bed. I couldn't tell the time, but sometimes when Mama put me to bed it was still light outside and it would take me ages to get to sleep. But I didn't mind, as long as I had Teddy. Teddy was a good friend to me. My only friend really.

Eventually I fell asleep, but Mama wasn't in bed. And when I woke up in the morning, she still wasn't there.

I took Teddy and got up. 'Mama?' I called. 'Mama?' She wasn't in the living room. Most nights she came to sleep in our room but sometimes she would fall asleep with the TV on and I would find her in the morning on the sofa. But the TV was all black and she wasn't there.

'Mama? Mama?' Normally I was awake first, but sometimes, hardly ever, Mama was already in the kitchen having breakfast when I woke up. But today she wasn't in there either.

Never mind. I was a big girl and I could make my own breakfast. I'd done it before. Sometimes Mama was too tired or too sad to get out of bed and I would look after myself all day. That was what big girls like me did.

The cereal I had thrown the day before was still on the ground. The Weetabix packet was still on the table, so I climbed on the chair to get it. I got a bowl from the cupboard – I couldn't use my favourite one as it was still on the floor, and I chose a spoon from the drawer – my best one with the picture of a princess on the end.

Then I got the milk out of the fridge and sniffed it like I'd seen Mama doing. I poured it into the bowl and sprinkled on some sugar.

The Weetabix tasted nice. Once I had finished I moved my chair so I could stand on it and washed the bowl under the tap like Mama did when the sink would get so full that nothing else would fit. There were lots of other things in the sink already and it smelt funny, but I didn't try to wash any of the other things. There were knives, and I wasn't allowed to touch knives. They were sharp and could hurt me, Mama would say. Sometimes she would show me the cuts on her arms which were from knives. She said she was showing me so that I would know how dangerous knives are, but I didn't like it when she did that and I would say no, no, no I don't want to look.

After I washed up I went back into our room and got dressed. My clothes from the day before were still on the floor so I put those back on. Then I went into the living room and watched TV, but the programmes were not very interesting and there were no cartoons. Sometimes I was not allowed to watch TV because Mama had a headache and she would say the TV was too noisy.

I watched for ages. I was hungry again. Mama was still not back. I had some more Weetabix and watched some more TV. And then some more. Then there was no more milk left so I climbed up on a chair again and put water from the tap on the Weetabix instead. Even *with extra sugar, they weren't very nice but I ate them anyway because I was very hungry.*

Then it was dark, so I changed into my nightie and got back into bed.

Mama still wasn't back. Even with the light on and Teddy with me, I was scared.

My tummy was rumbling when I woke up. Mama still wasn't there. I called out and checked all the rooms but there was no reply.

The Weetabix box was on the table, but it was empty. I opened the fridge and saw a box of cheese triangles. Normally I would have that on some bread, but Mama would spread it because I was not allowed to touch the knives. But I was very hungry now, so I thought that as long as I was really careful maybe this time she wouldn't mind too much. I opened the box where she kept the bread but there was only the end bit, the crust. It was hard but there was nothing else in there. I took a knife from the drawer really, really carefully and spread one triangle cheese onto it. I was not allowed to spread more than one because that would be wasteful and money didn't grow on trees, Mama was always saying. I ate the bread and the cheese triangle and it was nice even though the bread was hard but I was still hungry afterwards. So I peeled the wrappers off the other two cheese triangles and ate them without any bread or anything. I was definitely not allowed to do that but I thought maybe Mama wouldn't mind this time.

'Mama!' I shouted as loud as I could. 'Mama!' But she wasn't there.

I put the TV on again and sat on the sofa, cuddling Teddy.

Mama still wasn't back by bedtime and I had eaten everything in the fridge and cupboards. Some things were very yukky, like the bowl of baked beans which I found in the fridge and ate cold because I was definitely not allowed to use the cooker because it was hot and could burn me. I ate some other cheese which was there and a yoghurt which tasted a bit fizzy like lemonade. I was still hungry but it was dark and probably bedtime so I got into bed and sang to Teddy until I fell asleep.

Next morning Mama still wasn't there. I was so hungry that my tummy hurt and I had eaten all the food. Normally when we had no food, Mama would go to the shop. Because I had no food and Mama wasn't here, I thought I should go to the shop and get some. But to go to the shop I needed money – Mama was always saying that everything in the shops cost too much money. But then I remembered – I did have some money! Sometimes when I was very good Mama would give me some coins to say thank you for being very good. They were small and brown and I kept them in a special jar.

I got dressed and tipped all the money out on to my bed. I didn't know how to count so I didn't know how much money there was, but it looked like a lot, so I thought I would be able to get plenty of food and wouldn't need to be hungry any more. I put the money in my pockets – it took up a lot of room because there were a lot of coins – and then went to the kitchen to get a special shopping bag like Mama did when we went to the shops. I was excited about how proud of me she would be when she got back. She would be really pleased that I had gone to the shop and got some more food so that she wouldn't have to go when she was so tired.

I went to the door but the handle was too high and I couldn't reach it. So I got a chair to stand on and turned the handle. It was hard to turn the handle so I did it with two hands. But the door didn't open. Sometimes there would be a key in a hole in the door which Mama turned to keep us safe at night and I looked to see if it was there so I could turn it but it wasn't there and I didn't know where it was and I couldn't get out.

My tummy rumbled and I started to cry. I couldn't get out and go to the shops and get the food for Mama. She would be sad that I had eaten all the food until there was none left and made a mess on the floor which was still there because the cloth didn't work properly when I tried to clean it.

I started to bang on the door. 'Mama! Mama! Mama!'

31

Daily Mail Online

10 January 2020

A body found in the early hours of the morning in the French Alpine resort La Madière is believed to be that of Will Cassiobury, who went missing in a skiing accident in 1998.

The gruesome discovery was made by the driver of a piste-grooming machine returning from his night's work.

It is believed that the recent bad weather has caused several minor avalanches which may have dislodged the body from its original resting place.

A full post-mortem will be carried out. Mr

Cassiobury's next of kin, his brother who was skiing with the deceased before he disappeared, is travelling to the resort to formally identify the body.

32

Hugo

'Terrible business,' Simon is saying. 'Poor sod. Out there all alone in the snow for all that time. What a way to go.'

'Awful,' Cass agrees.

The atmosphere in the chalet is subdued. Nothing is official yet, but everyone seems pretty sure that the body is this guy Will who died in an accident years ago.

'His brother's on the way over, apparently,' Matt says. 'But his age, sex, and even where he was found, given the recent avalanches compared to where he disappeared, indicate it's him, as far as I understand. Though nothing will be official until he is formally identified.'

'Better for the family to have finally found him,' Cass

adds. 'It doesn't bear thinking about.' She shudders, and then leans down to kiss the top of Inigo's head. He gives a contented sigh of delight and I feel a pang of loss for the baby Ria has so far made sure isn't going to come into being.

Ria is upstairs in our room, lying down; she says she doesn't feel well. I'm all out of sympathy. She shouldn't drink so much. Or lie to me.

33

January 2020, Phuket, Thailand

Adam

It was the last thing I was expecting.

Impressive how they found me so quickly, on the other side of the world and after all these years.

It probably sounds terribly callous of me, but for the last couple of decades, I've barely thought about Will. Or about what happened that day on the mountain, and the things that went on in the run-up to it.

I was in the press a bit at the time, the miracle survivor who'd made it through a stormy night alone on the mountain. I wasn't lying when I told the papers the accident changed me – it did. It made me realize we only have one life. I didn't want to waste it all on a City job

I wasn't that enamoured with – however much money I was making.

So I quit my job and went travelling with my end-of-year bonus – with Nell, to start with. We volunteered in orphanages in Africa, helped pick grapes in France, were part of a yacht crew around the Caribbean for a while. To start with, it was blissful. I couldn't have been happier.

And it was true what I'd said initially; when I woke up, I didn't remember anything about how Will had died. Or the holiday. All I knew was that I had two black fingertips where the snow had frozen them off, and the things that people had told me about that day and my rescue. I'd been found huddled in a snow hole I'd made for myself by a rock. I'd been out there all night – they were amazed I'd survived the storm, so high up on the mountain. Once I was well enough to think about it, I was amazed I'd survived too – Will had always been the practical one, and yet somehow I'd built myself a shelter which had kept me alive, while he had seemingly disappeared into thin air.

But over time, I started to remember more about what had happened. Guilt gnawed away at me. Nell and I split up when my regular black moods, and occasional violent outbursts, became too much for her. Living my free and easy life out in the sunshine while my brother's body was on a frozen mountain became difficult for me to cope with. I ended up in therapy, which was next to useless, but eventually I built a life – not a particularly exceptional one, but a comfortable one. I tried to keep thoughts of Will out of my mind – it was easier that way. Indeed, it was the only way I could deal with it. I've come to terms with what happened – it was over twenty years ago, after all – and I've found that I can live with it.

And now this.

I have to go. I can see that. But I'm not interested in digging up the past. What's gone is gone. I can't see how any good's going to come of this, for anyone.

34

BEFORE

'Hello? Hello? Are you OK in there?' Someone was pushing the letterbox open, looking in.

I was sitting on the floor by the door with Teddy, crying and shouting for Mama. I'd been shouting for so long that my throat hurt. I fell silent as I heard the voice. It sounded kind. But Mama always told me that almost no one was kind, that even people who seemed nice and friendly could change in an instant, and that I had to be very careful about who I trusted.

I stood up. 'I'm hungry,' I wailed. 'And I haven't got any food.'

'Oh dear,' said the voice. It was a lady's voice. 'Is your mummy there?'

'No.'

'Your daddy?'

'A long way away.'

'I see. Where's your mummy?'

'I don't know. Maybe she went to the shops, but she didn't come back.'

'OK, dear. Don't worry, we're going to sort this out. You and me together. How long have you been there on your own?'

'I don't know. Quite long.'

'Can you open the door for me?'

'I'm not allowed. There might be bad people. And it's stuck. I wanted to go to the shops to get some food because I haven't got any left, but I couldn't make the door open and now my tummy hurts and . . .'

It was hard to speak I was crying so much.

'Shhh dear, don't cry. I'm going to help you. We'll get you out and get you some food and find your mummy. I'm going to call someone now who can help us open the door and then I'm going to stay and talk to you until they arrive. Does that sound OK?'

I nodded, forgetting that the nice lady couldn't see me.

'Does that sound OK, dear?'

'Yes.'

'You stay there while I pop back into my house to call someone. I'll be straight back, I promise. Can you do that for me? Be a brave girl for two minutes?'

'Yes.'

'Good girl. I promise I'll be back as quick as I can.'

The lady went away and I sat by the door clutching Teddy tight. I hoped the lady would come back soon. My tummy was really hurting. I didn't have to wait very long though until the letterbox opened again and the lady was back.

'OK, dear, the police are coming. They'll be able to open the door to let you out and help you find your mummy.'

'Can I have something to eat?'

'Of course, poppet. They'll give you some food as soon as they can once they get you out – they said on the phone that they don't want me to give you anything yet. A doctor needs to take a little look at you first. But I'm sure that won't take long. Now, would you like to play a game while we wait?'

'Yes please. Or we could sing a song?'

'That would be lovely. What would you like to sing first?'

It was nice singing with the lady. She knew all the songs I knew, but I didn't know very many. Mama didn't normally sing with me, which is why I always sang with Teddy. Mama said it made her head hurt, so I had to sing quietly. But Sheila (that was the lady's name, she told me) said I should sing nice and loud to keep my spirits up (I didn't know what that meant but thought it sounded fun) so I did. It was nice to sing loud but it felt naughty too. Sheila had propped the letterbox open so that we could hear each other better. I liked Sheila. I didn't often meet

213

new people. Usually it was just me and Mama, and most of the time Mama was too tired or not feeling well enough to play, so it was just me and Teddy.

There were two green bottles left hanging on the wall and I was singing as loud as I could when there was a lot of noise outside and Sheila stopped singing. 'Ah. We'll have to stop singing for now, poppet,' Sheila said. 'The police are here. I'm going to stay right here and wait for you so I can say hello once you're out, but they're going to talk to you now, OK? There's nothing to be scared of and you're not in any trouble. You're being a really brave girl and I've enjoyed singing with you. Perhaps we can do some more singing another time?'

'Yes, please,' I said.

'Hello?' said a voice, another lady. 'My name's Anna. I'm a social worker, here to make sure you're safe. Are you OK at the moment? You're not hurt? And there's no one in there with you?'

'My tummy hurts, I'm hungry and Mama's not here,' I said.

'OK. We're going to get you something to eat very soon. Now what I want you to do is go and stand by the window in the next room – I think it might be your living room – where we can see you. Sheila is standing outside it, so you can wave to her through the window. Can you do that for me? Once you're there, there'll be a big bang as the police are going to have to break the door so we can get you out, get you something to eat, and help you find your mummy.'

'But Mama will be cross if you break the door.'

'Don't worry about that, we will fix it. Now, will you go to the window? I'm going there too so you can wave to me and Sheila. Does that sound OK?'

I nodded.

'Are you there, my darling? Is that OK?'

'Yes,' I said. 'OK. I'm going to bring Teddy and I'm going now.'

I stood up and walked over to the window. I pulled back the curtain and waved at the two ladies there. They smiled and waved back. They looked nice. They didn't look bad or scary at all.

A man shouted something and then there was a bang and the door flew open. It was so loud I put my hands over my ears and started crying. A man and a lady dressed in green clothes came in and the man picked me up and said, 'It's OK, duckie, you're safe now.' He carried me outside and put me on a chair on wheels, which seemed silly because I could walk, but I let him do it because it was comfy and I was hungry and the blanket he put over me was soft and I was suddenly very tired. Teddy was with me and I cuddled him tight.

We went down in the lift and I was carried into the back of a big yellow van which looked like an ambulance but I thought couldn't be because I wasn't ill. Anna stayed with me and asked me things like how long I'd been on my own and had Mama ever left me on my own before. I said I didn't know how long and sometimes she had left me on my own before but never for so long that I had to eat all the food so that was why I had to bang on the door because I couldn't get out to go to the shops.

I was taken to a hospital which was exciting because I'd never been to a hospital before. There was even a blue light and a siren on the ambulance. At the hospital I had my own room which was a treat because I'd never had my own room before and lots of kind people came in and out asking me things and looking at different bits of me. I had to do a wee in a cup which was tricky even though a nurse helped me. They put a bit of paper in my mouth to see if I was too hot, though I told them I was not. The only bit I didn't like was when they put something around the top of my arm which squeezed it, but only for a second so even that wasn't too bad. Anna stayed with me all the time and after lots of people had looked at me and asked me things and I felt like my tummy would turn inside out I was so hungry a nice lady brought me a tray of food – it was mashed potato and fish fingers, which were both my favourite foods.

'Don't eat too fast,' the lady said. 'If you haven't eaten for a while it might make you feel sick.'

She also gave me a cup of purple water which didn't taste nice but Anna said I had to try to be a brave girl and drink it because I was a word that I didn't understand which she told me meant I hadn't drunk enough water.

The lady was wrong because I ate very quickly and it didn't make me feel sick at all. I told Anna I was still hungry so she pulled a string which was hanging from the ceiling and asked if I could have something else to eat as well so the lady said she would see what she could do and brought me in a doughnut with sugar on.

After that I was very tired and told Anna I would like to go to sleep.

'Will Mama come and get me tomorrow?' I asked. 'And will the door be fixed? She will be very cross if the door is broken.' I remembered her sitting on the floor crying and suddenly I felt very sad even though I'd just had fish fingers and a doughnut. If the door was still broken when she got back she would probably cry again.

'The door has already been made secure . . . I mean, made so that no one can get in, and will be fixed properly very soon, hopefully tomorrow. And we're trying hard to find your mummy. You're sure you don't have a granny or grandpa? Or aunties or uncles maybe? Cousins?'

'No. Granny is in heaven. There's only Mama.'

'And no daddy?'

'He lives a long way away, Mama said.'

'You don't see him? Or know where he lives?'

I shook my head.

'I see,' she said. 'Well, we'll do our best to find your mummy.'

'But what if you can't? There's no food at home and the door is broken so I can't go to the shops.' Suddenly I felt scared again.

'You go to the shops by yourself?' Anna asked.

217

'No. Me and Mama go. But this time I wanted to go because there was no food.'

She nodded. 'OK. Well hopefully we will have found your mummy by the time you wake up but if not, you'll go and stay with a nice family until we can find her. There might be other children there for you to play with too. Does that sound OK? You won't be left on your own with no food again either way, I promise.'

'Can I take Teddy if I go to the nice family?'

'Of course. He will be very welcome.'

'OK then. But only until you find Mama.'

I'd never been in an actual house before. I'd seen them on TV and I'd walked past them on the way to the shops with Mama, but I'd never been inside a real house. Our house wasn't called a house, it was called a flat because it was flat – someone else lived on top and someone else lived underneath. Sometimes we could hear music or someone shouting from the other flats. I liked it when we could hear the other people because it felt like they were keeping me company but Mama didn't like it when there were noises and sometimes she would put her hands over her ears and shout shut up shut up shut up so that her shouting was even louder than the noise and then I would go into a different room and sing with Teddy.

Anna brought me to the house because they still hadn't found Mama and she told me I was going to stay there while they looked for Mama. A lady and a man lived *there and Anna said they looked after children like me whose mummy and daddy couldn't look after them for a bit but not to keep them forever. She said it would be just like being at home and I could do all the things I usually did at home, but I could see straight away that it would be nothing like being at home. It was like the houses on the TV where there was a mummy and a daddy and other children, the curtains were open and there was even a bowl of fruit on the table.*

Anna crouched down next to me so her face was level with mine and said, 'Now, if you're feeling OK, I'm going to leave you here with Rhonda and Nick to show you your new room and let you get settled in. You or Rhonda can call me at any time if you have any worries or questions.'

'And when will I see Mama?' I asked. 'If she goes back home and I'm not there she won't know where I am.'

'Don't you worry about that – as soon as we find her we'll let her know that you're safe.'

'And bring me home?'

Anna paused. 'Um – yes. Once we're sure that she's not too . . . tired to look after you properly, we'll bring you home.'

'But until then you're going to have lots of fun here!' Rhonda chirped. 'Why don't I show you your room and then you can meet your new brothers and sisters?'

'I have brothers and sisters?' I asked. I was so excited. I wasn't sure I if wanted a brother but I'd always wanted a sister. Someone else like me to play with.

'Well, *that's what we call you all here,*' Rhonda said. 'While you're here, you're all family.'

I couldn't believe I had my very own room. It was so pretty with pink flowery curtains and a big bed with a fluffy duvet with fairies on it. The bed was a real one which was there all the time, not the kind that could be folded up like my one at home.

There was a wardrobe and a chest of drawers but I hadn't brought anything with me apart from Teddy. I wasn't sure what I was going to wear tomorrow so I asked Rhonda and she said that it was OK because she could lend me a few things, but Anna was going to go to my house and get some of my clothes so that I could have my own things to help me feel at home, which seemed like a weird thing to say because I wasn't at home. I didn't have many clothes but I did want my bubble nightie and my favourite owl T-shirt. Most of my other clothes were too small and Mama always said that I grew very quickly and money didn't grow on trees so sometimes I had to wait for new clothes, and I wondered if the ones that Rhonda might give me would be nicer and fit me better.

We went back downstairs and there were some other children in the kitchen. Rhonda said: 'Would you like to sit down and have some crumpets?'

I said, 'Yes, please!' I didn't know what crumpets were, but it was always nice to have something to eat.

'This is Ben, Ryan, and Layla – your new brothers and sisters.' Layla was very big, almost like a grown-up and the boys were a little bit older than me. 'And there's William,' she added, pointing at a baby sitting in a bouncy chair on the floor.

'Where's your mum?' Ben asked, his mouth full of chocolatey crumpet.

'Ben!' Rhonda cried, louder than I'd heard her speak so far. 'You know we don't ask questions like that in this house. If and when your new sister wants to talk about her family, then she will. In her own time. If not, it's none of our business.'

'My mum's in prison,' Ben said proudly.

'I don't know where my mama is,' I said. 'But she will be back soon.'

'Course she will,' muttered the big girl, 'they all say that.' and Rhonda said, 'Layla! Please!' and I didn't know why because she wasn't asking for anything.

I lived with Rhonda and Nick for almost two years the first time. It was nice there. I was there the longest – other children – or brothers and sisters, as they insisted I called them, came and went. There were always other children around to play with and, once I got used to it, I liked that. I started school and I had friends there too. It was tricky at first as I didn't know how to count or my letters or a lot of things that most other children my age already knew, but it got easier and I got special certificates to show how well I was doing all the time.

It took them two weeks to find Mama. They found her sleeping in the street. But I didn't go straight home with her because she didn't go home herself to start with. Anna explained it all to me. Mama was in a special hospital and Anna would take me to see her every week. I tried to like the visits because she was still my mama, but usually they were a bit scary. Sometimes Mama would just sit in her room and not really say anything and Anna would tell her stuff about me and how I was doing at school and what I'd been doing at home, and then she'd say 'Well, isn't this nice?' every few minutes when it wasn't nice at all and I couldn't wait to leave because it seemed like Mama wasn't even listening.

Other times Mama would cry, and Anna would try to hold her hand and pat her arm and stuff, and usually Mama didn't want her to and she'd back away into a corner – those were the worst visits. And then other times she would hug me too hard and say sorry, sorry, sorry and that I deserved a better Mama than her and I didn't like those visits either because I never knew what to say and sometimes she got snot on my clothes.

Then Mama moved out of the hospital and into a flat which was nicer than the old flat we'd lived in and the visits got better. To start with Anna always came with me when I visited Mama but there was no crying, and often there was homemade cake and the flat was always nice and tidy and the curtains were open. Sometimes Mama would take me out to McDonald's or to the park to feed the ducks. To start with, Anna always came but after a while she stopped coming and it was just me and Mama.

Then one day Anna said that they thought Mama was ready to look after me again and asked how did I feel about that? I didn't know what to say. Mama's flat was OK and I had my own room there, but it also wasn't as nice as it was at Rhonda's and I knew Rhonda wouldn't leave me alone in the house with no food. It had happened a long time ago, but I still remembered it well and it still made my tummy feel weird when I thought about it. But she was my mama and in spite of it all the biggest part of me wanted to be with her, so I said that sounded good as long as Rhonda and Anna could still be my friends and come and see me sometimes. Anna said that that would be fine and she would still be coming to see me a lot and Rhonda said that if it was OK with my mama I could even come back and stay sometimes if I wanted to or if Mama felt like she needed a bit of time by herself, and I said that I would like that very much.

And then I went up to my room and cried. Nobody noticed.

35

Cameron is over again, unfortunately. Sometimes I hate owning a business. Hate having to suck up to people like him.

'So what's with the faces on everyone today?' Cameron asks, looking around the chalet. 'Someone died or something?'

There is an awkward silence. Matt clears his throat. 'Cameron, yes, I'm afraid there's been some bad news. You didn't hear? They found a body.'

'I didn't hear anything – I've only just come up from the valley. A body? Who found a body?'

'A piste-basher. But they think it's a historic death – a

225

guy who died a long time ago and whose body was dislodged by the recent bad weather. Apparently his brother's on the way out here to identify the body and the like.'

'His brother?' Cameron echoes, rubbing his hand across his face. 'Right. Poor guy.'

Matt looks at his clipboard. 'In fact, Didier in the tourist office called me – he said he couldn't get through to you. He wondered if you might be able to offer the brother accommodation. He thinks that, given the circumstances, the bereaved man shouldn't have to pay to stay during his trip. Is that OK? Seems like the least we can do.'

I continue staring at my iPad, wondering if this conversation is for my benefit. Is Matt or this guy Didier trying to make Cameron look like a nice guy so that I'll want to do business with him? I'm never very good at working out this kind of thing. Olivia would probably know, if only she were here.

'Hmm. I'm not sure,' Cameron says. 'It's rather short notice. Do we even have anything spare?'

'It *is* short notice, but I imagine there'll be something,' Matt says. 'I think Chalet Alpaca is free, but I'm heading back to the office in a minute, so I'll double-check then. And it's always good to keep on the right side of the tourist office, wouldn't you say?'

Cameron sighs. 'Yes, I guess so. OK then. We'll do the right thing and help the poor fucker.'

'So shall I suggest Chalet Alpaca, or is there somewhere

226

else you think would be better? Though, like I say, I'd need to check what's free,' Matt says.

'No, no, any of them will be fine, all my places are fantastic,' Cameron says, pompously. 'Whatever we've got that's ready to go, offer him that. But make sure the press people let everyone know that I'm putting myself out for him. Otherwise there's no point, OK?'

'Yup, will do,' Matt says, writing something down on his clipboard.

I wonder if Matt is simply writing 'wanker'. I hope he is. That's what I'd be doing.

Cameron looks out of the window. 'That's assuming the dead man's brother is able to get through to the resort, of course. It's still looking pretty bad out there. They might have to close the road.'

The whole day is dreadful.

I'm relieved to learn that pretty much all the lifts are closed, otherwise Simon would no doubt be trying to drag me out into the snow. Not that sitting around all day in the chalet is exactly fun, given the atmosphere. Ria is staying in her room and I don't want to disturb her too much, the mood she's in. Simon is sitting in the lounge, glumly staring out of the window and complaining about missing a day's skiing. The baby is wailing intermittently, probably picking up on the gloomy atmosphere of the place. Millie checks we have everything we need before going out in an enormous coat to get the only other free chalet ready for the brother's arrival.

227

I'm not sure how I feel about Cameron's offer – is it clever PR? Is there any altruism in the gesture at all? Or is he simply, as I suspect and as it seemed from his conversation with Matt, a callous bastard, bending a tragic situation to his own advantage?

When I go upstairs later, Ria is either asleep or pretending to be. She's been in our room almost all day. I sit on the edge of the bed and look at her. She's so beautiful. With her eyes closed, breathing softly, she looks childlike. Would our daughter look like her? Then I feel a stab of anger, remembering what I found out. There'll be no daughter while she's taking the pill, will there?

I put my hand gently on her ankle and she opens her eyes.

'Sorry, I didn't mean to wake you,' I say.

She sits up. 'That's OK. Listen,' she puts her hand on top of mine. 'I'm sorry. I should have told you about the pill. Talked to you. But I didn't want you to be disappointed in me . . .' Her eyes fill with tears. I touch her face. I've rarely seen her cry before.

'Sshh, darling,' I soothe, all my anger evaporating from me. 'It's OK. If you're not ready, you're not ready. And if you're never ready, that's OK too. You're all I need.' This isn't quite true. I do want children. But if it's a choice between no Ria and no children, I'll take the latter. Also what I just said is the kind of thing I've seen people say in films to make someone stop crying, and I want Ria to stop crying.

228

But it doesn't work – she starts sobbing. 'I'm not good enough for you, Hugo,' she wails. 'I'm so sorry. I'll try to be a better person. I'll drink less. I'll stop taking the pill. I will, honestly. I'll stop taking it now if you like! I'll chuck them in the bin! Or out the window! No, not out the window, animals might eat them and go sterile . . . do animals live in the snow?' She leans in to kiss me and reaches down to undo my trousers. 'Let's have sex now! Let's make a baby! Don't leave me, Hugo!'

Normally I would never say no to Ria if she wants sex – which, let's face it, is hardly ever these days – but I've never seen her like this before and she's scaring me. I gently put my hand over hers and push it away.

'Ria. Don't be silly. Of course I'm not going to leave you. But you seem a bit . . . manic. Why don't you have a sleep and we'll talk again later?'

She flops back on the bed, seemingly calmer now. 'OK. Let's do that.' She turns her head towards me. 'Tell me what's happening downstairs. Is there any more news about the body they found?'

Ah. Perhaps this is why she's behaving so strangely. Perhaps she's more sensitive than I give her credit for.

'They think it's a man who died a long time ago. His brother's coming out to identify the body, apparently.'

She nods, her eyes filling with tears again. 'Right. What a horrible thing to have to do.'

I take her hand. 'Horrible. But perhaps he will be able to take comfort after all these years in having some kind of closure.'

She takes a deep breath and exhales slowly. 'I guess so. Maybe. But I sometimes think it's better that what's in the past stays in the past. Don't you?'

I imagine she's talking about our row over the pills. Wanting to put it in the past. So I squeeze her hand and say, 'Mostly yes. But that's for him to worry about, not you. You should rest. And maybe,' I stroke her breast gently, 'we'll have a go at making babies later. But only if you want to.'

She nods and smiles weakly. 'Yeah. Let's do that.'

36

BEFORE

To start with, it was all OK. Mama had made me a nice room in the new flat – not quite as nice as my room at Rhonda's, but way nicer than the room we'd shared in the old flat which I still remembered a bit. It was tidy at home; there weren't dirty dishes in the sink the whole time and there was always milk in the fridge. Mama wasn't as good at cooking as Rhonda, but she told me she had had some cooking and 'parenting' lessons when she had been in the hospital where I used to visit her and now she was better at cooking than she used to be and she said she was also a lot better at parenting. I didn't understand that – surely you either were a parent or you weren't, but that's what Mama said. Things had changed – I still had Weetabix every morning for breakfast,

231

because I liked it and Mama said it was good for me, but sometimes she would also cut up a banana for me to have with it, and I never had Weetabix for other meals any more. My clothes smelt cleaner and they weren't too small. Mama always got up in the morning and she always slept in her bed. The milk in the fridge smelt like it should do and the yoghurts didn't go fizzy.

The biggest difference was Mama now had a job, so she couldn't stay in bed all day because she was too tired or too sad to get up. She also told me that she was taking special pills the doctor had given her so she could be less sad, and more 'stable', which I didn't understand as it wasn't as if she ever fell over, but they definitely seemed to make her happier. And I was at school every day, so we weren't in the house all day long like before. We had a new alarm clock to wake us up and Mama had to get up to take me to school and she always did and I was almost always on time. I had lots of friends at school and the teachers said I was a good worker. I brought home pictures and other things I'd made at school and Mama would stick them on the fridge with letter magnets, like in houses on the TV. Sometimes I had a friend home to play after school and some days Mama would even make cakes for us, with icing. She was just like the mamas I saw on TV.

Anna came to see me a lot at first, but after a while she came less and less, though she always said that I could call her whenever I liked and made sure that her number was stuck on the fridge. That was the other

232

*thing that was different, now that Mama had a job, she
had enough money for us to have our own phone in
the flat and I didn't need to be scared of getting stuck
inside with no food again even if Mama did go somewhere. But mainly I didn't have to be scared because
Mama didn't leave me on my own anyway.*

*Then Mama got a boyfriend. His name was Dave. He
would bring me sweets and chocolate bars when he came
over but even so, I didn't like him very much. I was
used to it being just me and Mama at home but when
Dave came over he'd give me 50p to go to my room
and even though I liked having the 50p and the sweets
I didn't like having to go to my room, but I didn't want
to say that I didn't want to go in case it made her cry.
I wondered if I should tell Anna about Dave and about
having to go to my room, but I didn't want to get Mama
into trouble or be sad so I didn't say anything.*

*And then one day I came home from school, Dave
had gone and Mama was on the kitchen floor crying.
Then the next morning she wasn't there. I rang Anna.*

*Over the next few years, that was the pattern. Everything
would be OK for a while, Mama acted like a mother
should and held down part-time jobs cleaning or in local
cafés and the like – something that fitted in with when
I started and finished school. Then she'd meet a man
– some of whom were better than others – and she'd
become less interested in me. After a few weeks or months
the man would leave, she'd break down entirely, and I'd*

233

be sent back to Rhonda's until Mama was strong enough to have me back.

Sometimes there would be a few weeks between the start of a breakdown and the time when I (or sometimes Anna) decided it was time for me to move out again, and that's when I started to find out little bits about my dad and what had happened before I was born.

I'd always asked about Dad. When I was little, Mama would tell me he lived on a mountain far, far away. I pictured him in a stone hut, young and good looking, maybe with a small beard, doing stuff like rounding up sheep with a dog who was also his best friend, driving a tractor around fields and perhaps even washing in a stream instead of in a bath or shower. When I asked why he never visited or why he couldn't live with us she just said that he lived too far away. Sometimes she'd play me what she called 'their' song. It had a nice tune, but the words always sounded sad, with the man singing about how everybody hurts. I wondered why they didn't choose a happier song, I think I would have done, but I didn't say that to Mama in case it made her cry.

By the time I was about eight or so, I started to believe that Mama didn't know who my dad was, like some of my friends at school, or that she'd split up with him when I was a baby and didn't want to tell me. I thought perhaps she'd made up the story about the man who lived on the mountain and about the song they listened to together just to make me feel like I had a nice dad somewhere who would like if he met me and who would want to get to know me if only he didn't live so far away.

It never occurred to me that he was dead, until her most recent breakdown.

By then I was fifteen, and things hadn't improved. That week Mama had still been in bed every day when I got home from school, either crying or asleep. I could tell she must have got up at some point during the day to eat by the mess she left in the kitchen, which I tidied away every night when I got home so that it didn't smell too much and to try to give Mama one less thing to be upset about. But it didn't work, of course – she was still always crying.

I was getting back later and later from school because home was so depressing to deal with. Sometimes I went to friends' houses for the night, but I didn't want their parents to start asking too many questions because it got embarrassing. When I was younger I used to ask Anna and the various psychotherapists she used to send me to why Mama was the way she was. All they ever said was variations on the fact that it wasn't my fault or her fault, that it was just the way her brain was wired that sometimes made it difficult for her to cope. Which was no answer at all really, and certainly no help to anyone, least of all me.

As kids go, I was pretty good and not hard to deal with, I thought. I did OK at school, I didn't smoke or drink, I didn't bunk off school. Not that half the time Mama would have noticed if I did do any of those things. Sometimes when Mama had had a particularly bad episode and gone missing or done things like slashed her arms with the kitchen knife and I'd ended up at Rhonda's yet again, I would ask Anna why they kept sending me back to Mama if she couldn't cope. She'd say that it was natural that Mama wanted me home, but they only sent me back when they were sure she could manage and it was Mama's right to have me with her where possible but that they always acted in my best interests.

It was difficult to see how.

By the time I got back from school via Callie's and the park that night it was almost dark outside and there were no lights on in the house. I guessed Mama must still be in bed – I silently prayed that she'd be asleep rather than wailing and crying as sometimes she was when I got home. I was tired and not in the mood for her drama. Asleep, she was easier to deal with.

I went into the kitchen; I was starving. There had been barely any food in the house that week. Mama hadn't been turning up to her cleaning job and had likely been sacked, I thought, though she hadn't told me so. There was only so far a free school meal could last you during the day, so I hoped there'd be something ancient in the freezer I could fish out and bung in the microwave. I flicked the light switch and nearly jumped out of my skin when I saw that Mama was sitting at the table in the dark. There was a glass and a half-empty bottle of vodka in front of her.

'Bloody hell, Mama!' I yelped. 'You terrified me! What are you doing there?'

She looked at me, bleary-eyed and patted the chair beside her. 'Siddown,' she said.

In spite of her failings, Mama was not usually a drinker and so I was wary. I sat down next to her, holding my breath against the waft of staleness emanating from her. She couldn't have had a shower all week.

'You know how you're always asking about your Dad?' she slurred.

'Um . . .' I'd never seen her in this state before and didn't know what to do. I didn't want to provoke her. I didn't ask about my dad that much any more because it always seemed to set her off, but it seemed like now she had decided she wanted to talk about him after all. I figured the best solution would be simply to say as little as possible.

'He's dead,' she said, her voice low and serious. 'DEAD!' she shouted suddenly, banging the table and making me jump.

'Oh.' Tears pricked at my eyes unexpectedly for a man I'd never known. Why was she telling me this now after all these years? Should I even believe her? 'What . . . what happened to him?'

'That BASTARD,' she shouted. 'He . . . he . . .'

'Dad, you mean?'

237

She banged the table again. 'NO! His CUNT of a brother.'

I flinched. I'd barely ever heard her swear, and certainly never use that word.

'His brother? Whose brother?' For a moment I wondered if she was just drunk and rambling, talking total nonsense. When she'd been in the hospital, some of the stuff she'd said made no sense at all. Anna always said it was the drugs they gave her that made her that way, but this time it didn't seem like that. In spite of her drunkenness, she seemed strangely lucid. My skin prickled.

'Will,' she continued. 'Your dad was called Will. His brother . . . his brother made him go out that day. On the mountain. And then he died. His fault. His brother's fault. Adam's fault.'

'What mountain? You said he lived on a mountain before . . . where? I thought you made it up.'

She grabbed my wrist and tried to look at me, but her eyes were all over the place and I could tell she couldn't focus properly. She laughed demonically. 'He DIED on the mountain! DIED! Not lived! We were on holiday. Skiing. He was skiing. His fault. All Adam's fault. And before that . . . before . . . before they went out . . . do you know? Do you know what he did to me?' she hisses. Suddenly she is more lucid. 'I was bright. Clever. At Oxford. Whole life ahead of me. And then Adam ruined it all because he killed Will. And before that, he—'

238

'He killed my dad?' I interrupted hoarsely.

She slumped in her chair. 'They didn't say that. They said it was an accident. But I KNOW!' She was shouting again. 'I KNOW! They both went out and Adam came back and Will didn't. He died. It's all his fault. Adam's. THAT'S WHY I'M THE WAY I AM NOW! THAT'S WHY I'M LIKE THIS! And before that he, he, he . . .'

'What?'

She waved her hand. 'I can't tell you. 'S too awful. You shouldn't know.' She stood up and immediately fell down. I put my hands under her armpits and hauled her upright again.

'C'mon. Let's get you to bed.'

'Will Cassiobury,' she was muttering. 'Will Cassiobury. Only man I ever loved. All the others have been utter bastards. Stay single, my darlin' baby girl,' she slurred, twisting round and waving her finger in my face. 'Stay single. Don't let any men into your life. Waste of time. They ruin everything.'

I hauled her into bed and pulled the covers over her. 'Will Cassiobury? That's my dad's name?'

But she was already asleep.

37

January 2020, Haute Savoie, France

Adam

I'm ashamed to admit that, when I hear the road to La Madière is closed, my first reaction is one of relief. Maybe I won't have to go to the resort after all. Maybe I won't have to go through the gruesome task of identifying my brother's body which has been lying in the snow for more than twenty years.

The world is small now. It never takes long to get anywhere, does it? So even though I was on the other side of the world when they contacted me, one day later, here I am in France. I don't know how the police got hold of me so quickly – I guess it's easy to trace anyone these days. And with only my rudimentary French, I didn't entirely understand what they were saying. Other than that I am Will's only family, so I should come.

After the accident, I took the coward's way out – I left. Couldn't bear the pain in my parents' eyes as they desperately tried not to blame me. Couldn't bear to be inside my own head. I'd like to say I spent my time trying to live the good life Will no doubt would have lived, but I didn't. I've bummed around, taken casual jobs here and there and, for the last five years, since my parents died, lived off my inheritance, as well as what should have been Will's. Which is the only reason I had the money to fly back so quickly when the police asked me to.

I booked a first-class ticket. I could say it's because I was honouring Will by travelling in style. Toasting his memory with my free champagne.

But that would be a lie. I did it because I could.

In spite of my luxurious seat, Michelin chef-designed food and all the alcohol I can drink (which I take advantage of fully) the journey is hellish. We are diverted because of the snow, the likes of which they haven't seen since, ironically, the winter Will died. We eventually land at an airport miles away from the one we were headed to, and it seems that paying thousands of pounds for a posh seat doesn't get you on a coach any faster. Nor does it help when the roads become so blocked that you have to sleep in a school sports hall with dozens of other people, being served hot soup by kindly French ladies from the *Croix Rouge*.

I feel sorry for the couples and families around me – grumbling about losing time out of their precious holidays, griping about the conditions in the hall and about the lack of information while young exhausted-looking reps in colourful jackets force smiles and say again and again platitudes along the lines of: 'I'm sorry, sir, the roads are blocked and there's nothing more we can do. As soon as we have any more information, we'll let you know.' I feel a wave of nausea as I see that some of the reps are from Powder Puff, the company we travelled with on my last ski trip, the one I took with Will.

So while these families are desperate to get to their planned destinations, I'd rather be going anywhere else except the mountains. If travel wasn't already so tricky, I'd be tempted to turn straight round and go back to the airport, back to my beach. Pretend I couldn't get through. Say I tried, but it simply wasn't to be.

Why am I even here? There seems very little doubt that the body they've found is Will. Coming here isn't going to bring him back.

Perhaps it will help me.

Then again, perhaps it won't.

38

January 2020, La Madière, France

Hugo

'God, this is so BORING,' Ria whines, yet again. We've already played Monopoly, Trivial Pursuit, poker and blackjack today. The snow has knocked out the internet and satellite TV. We had sex at least, so that's something, but Ria is now pacing about like a caged animal.

'I've had enough of being here,' she snaps. 'When do you think we can leave? I really want to go home.'

'Darling, you know what Millie said. The roads are closed today. Even if they weren't, there have been loads of flight cancellations and so it's very unlikely we'd be able to get ourselves onto a plane. The weather's due to get better in a couple of days, so we should be able to get our flight as planned and until then—'

'A couple of days!' Ria shrieks. 'There must be something you can do, Hugo.'

I pull a face. 'Um, no. I'm flattered that you think I'm so powerful, but I can't compete with the worst snowstorm they've seen in twenty-odd years.'

I try to take her hand. 'There are worse places to be stuck, my love,' I say. 'It's very comfortable here, everyone is safe and warm, and we have Millie cooking us some great food.'

'And the wine's good,' Simon adds, lifting his glass in a 'cheers' motion. It's only about four o'clock and he's already a good way through a bottle.

Ria pulls away from me and leans her head against the huge window. I can hear Inigo crying upstairs again. 'It's so claustrophobic though,' Ria complains. 'I just want to go home.'

39

BEFORE

When I woke up, Mama was gone. Again. I went to school because I had had enough of dealing with her stuff and now that I was old enough to look after myself I didn't feel I needed to call Anna straight away every time. Mama would probably be back by the time I got home and there would have been a whole lot of fuss and disruption for nothing – as usual.

But later that day when I was in maths there was a message that I was to go and see the head teacher.

Instantly I felt sick. Oh God. What had Mama done now? Had she been sectioned again? The worst time was when they found her in Tesco in her nightie pulling stuff off the shelves and some of the kids from school saw her and knew who she was. I hoped it was nothing like that.

I wasn't surprised to see Anna in the head teacher's office as she always came along when this kind of thing happened but the two police officers – a man and a woman – took me by surprise. I guessed their presence must mean that she'd been arrested.

'Ah, there you are. Thank you for coming. Would you sit down, please?'

I'd never heard Mrs Hardcastle, the head teacher, speak so softly. 'I'm afraid we have some bad news for you.'

'Is it Mama?' I asked, pointlessly, because of course it was. What else could it have been?

'Yes, I'm afraid it is,' Anna answered. Her voice sounded strained, almost as if she was trying to stop herself from crying. This was far from the first time Anna had come to school to give me bad news about Mama, but she was never usually emotional about it.

'What is it?' I asked. My voice cracked. 'What's happened this time?'

Anna came over to me and took my hand. 'There's no easy way to tell you this, but I'm afraid your mother was found dead earlier today.'

I looked at Anna and saw that her eyes were filled with tears. But I must have misheard. 'I'm sorry? You said she's dead? But I saw her last night . . . Dead?' I shook my head. 'You must have got it wrong. I saw her. She was at home. With me.'

Anna looked at the policewoman and then back at me. 'There will be an investigation, of course, but I'm

248

afraid it looks like she may have killed herself deliberately.' She paused. 'She fell from the top of a car park in town. She would have died instantly and wouldn't have suffered.'

I snatched my hand away from Anna and put both hands over my ears. 'No, no, no!' I shouted. 'Don't say that! You're wrong!'

I felt tears rolling down my cheeks. I hadn't noticed I was crying.

Anna pulled my hands gently away from my ears and took me in her arms as I sobbed. 'I'm so sorry,' Anna said softly. 'I've arranged temporary foster care for you for the time being and we'll talk about all the other . . . arrangements later. Would you like to go now?'

I looked up at her and wiped my eyes but the tears wouldn't stop coming. 'To Rhonda's?' I asked.

'I'm afraid Rhonda can't take you this time. It's another family, but you'll be very well looked after.'

And so began the worst few years of my life. It turned out Rhonda had breast cancer and that taking on foster children had become too much for her along with the chemo. And while living with Mama had been unstable and unpredictable, underneath it all, I felt like somewhere deep inside, she loved me. And I loved her. Home was home and she was my mama. With her gone, and without Rhonda, I felt like I had nothing.

My new foster parents were kind enough but they preferred to take in older children, like me. And many older children in the care system have been through some grim things in their lives and are, like me, fairly damaged. Sandra and Terry seemed like good people and did their best to create the family atmosphere I'd grown to love at Rhonda's but when there was so much violence, hatred, and noise from some of my transient foster brothers and sisters, it was often quite frightening to be at home. It was only when one of the boys sexually assaulted me that I managed to get moved to a different foster home. Rhonda was still too ill to take me, though we kept in touch. I moved often, from place to place. Some of my placements were better than others, but I felt permanently dislocated and longed for a home of my own.

I followed Mama's lead and started cutting myself. It was the only way I could make myself feel something. That, or letting men and boys I hardly knew touch me in ways they shouldn't have been doing when I was still basically a child. I enjoyed the power I held over them, even if I felt dirty afterwards. I had weird dreams about hurting people and would wake up strangely excited. I never told my therapists about that. I wasn't sure if it was normal, and I didn't want to be put away like Mama sometimes had been.

Occasionally I felt angry at Mama for what she had done. Why had she abandoned me yet again? Did she give any thought at all to what might happen to me when she left me all alone in the world, aged just fifteen?

But most of the time I felt angry at my father's brother.

Every time I closed my eyes I saw Mama's face when she told me about what he did – so full of hate. But at the same time, so broken and vulnerable. None of this was Mama's fault – she couldn't help the way she was. It was his fault – my dad's brother – the one who was responsible for his death. He made her life turn out the way it did.

If it hadn't been for him, none of this would have happened. Mama would have left university and got a good job. She'd have married my dad. I'd have grown up in a normal family. Maybe we would have lived in the mountains like she'd always said he did and I'd have had an idyllic, rural childhood instead of being shunted around from foster home to foster home. Or we might have lived in a big house with a garden in somewhere like Surrey where he would have a job in a bank and Mama would have a home-based job making jewellery or something which meant she had lots of time for me too. We would do things like bake cakes together and steal each other's make-up. We'd go on holidays some- where sunny and stay in a villa with olive trees and a swimming pool. Now and then we would argue over something silly but we would soon make up and watch something fun on TV together. Mama would have been normal and I would have been normal. There's no way Mama would have been the way she was if my dad hadn't died. If he hadn't been as good as killed by his brother, like Mama said. It was all his fault.

Will Cassiobury. Mama had finally told me the name

of my dad the day before she died. Did she know even then what she was going to do? Is that why she told me? Must have been. She must have planned it that way. She must have wanted me to take my revenge. She couldn't do it herself because she was too messed up by him – but I could do it for her.

Fired up, I hammered my dad's name into Google. I scanned the results quickly but couldn't find anything about a Will Cassiobury who died in a ski accident. But when he died newspapers weren't really online – at least not in the full-on way they are now.

However, there were other ways to research, and I was determined. People still managed to find stuff out before the internet. I was going to do the same.

Mama, I won't let you down.

I spent a lot of time at the library. I told my various foster families that I was studying and because I moved home and even sometimes schools so often those days no one noticed that my marks were dropping. While I still went to school most days, all my spare time was spent trying to find out about my dad, so I pretty much never got my homework done. It seemed unimportant compared to this.

Because I didn't know the exact date of the accident, or even where it happened beyond in a ski resort, it took me a good long while to find any mention of my dad. There are way more ski accidents around the world each year than I would have imagined, had I ever thought about it before. And even when I did finally find the few reports that existed about my dad and his death, the stories were disappointingly small and exact details extremely scant. It seemed that, to everyone but me, my dad was little more than a statistic, one tragic and pointless death among many, and that made me even more angry.

Eventually I found a report in the Daily Mail which mentioned Dad's name, as well as that of his brother Adam. It also mentioned my mama and his brother's girlfriend at the time who was called Nell Herrera. It said that there would be an investigation into the accident, so that gave me something else to look for – wouldn't the investigation have been reported? It said that they were skiing with guides, but didn't name them.

I searched further for several weeks and eventually managed to find a report of the investigation in a skiing magazine on a microfiche. The two guides were British and, in this report, they were actually named. According to the report, although certain 'irregularities' had come to light, they were not found guilty of any crime. That made me very angry. No punishment at all for not adequately protecting a man who was in their care. For killing him.

I put the names of the two ski guides into Google. I managed to find one. And then I started to come up with a plan.

40

Adam

In between crying children, complaining would-be holidaymakers and more and more snow-blocked waifs and strays being brought into the hall throughout the night, I get barely any sleep. That, along with thinking about what I have ahead of me when I get to La Madière. What will be expected of me. And what I need to do.

I regret a lot of things that happened on that holiday. Given my time again, I would have done things very differently. In fact, I wouldn't have gone on that trip at all. Or Nell and I could have gone alone. That would have been much better – we wouldn't have had to stay in that God-awful chalet which Will chose so as not to

255

intimidate his girlfriend too much by taking her somewhere too upmarket.

What was her name? Leah? Lisa? Something like that. She was a minx – a social-climbing minx. I could see she thought she'd done well for herself getting her distinctly lower-middle-class claws into my little brother, with her not-quite-right accent and not knowing how to hold her knife.

Obviously, there was no telling Will that – he was smitten, God knows why. She was pretty enough, I guess, but nothing that special, if you ask me. Which, of course, he didn't.

I realize I didn't cover myself in glory in my, shall we say, *dealings* with her during that trip. I guess now, after all this #MeToo business which I haven't managed to escape even in Thailand, people might say that I'd forced myself on her. Assaulted her. *Raped* her even?

But no. It wasn't like that. Not at all. I saw straight through her act of innocence afterwards in her and Will's room, acting like she hadn't wanted it. She had. She'd made it clearer and clearer the whole of that afternoon. And I know her type anyway. She'd have dropped Will in an instant if someone who'd looked like he might be a better bet for providing her with a big house in the countryside and a huge diamond ring she could show off to her friends had come along.

But I don't want to think about her today. Louisa. That was her name – so she claimed. I bet it was Louise really. She's probably married with two kids by now

256

and still desperately trying to fit in like she was during that holiday. I bet she's with someone like Will, or even like me – of the two of us, I was always going to have the better job and earn more.

I eat my breakfast of surprisingly good *Croix Rouge* croissant and coffee sitting on my camp bed, staring at the irate men and women haranguing the poor reps for more information.

It's different for me than for most of the people in this hall, obviously. There's a large part of me still hoping that the information will be that the roads are remaining closed, we're all going to be put on coaches and taken back to the airport, told sorry for the inconvenience but we're not going to get through to the mountains this time.

I have made my peace with what happened. It might have been my idea to go skiing that afternoon, but beyond that, what happened out on that mountain was not my fault. And I'm not going to let something that happened twenty years ago ruin my life. Whatever it takes.

41

BEFORE

Just before I was due to do my A-levels, I quit school. I was bored of it and my marks had dived by then anyway as I did less and less homework and eventually started bunking off to spend more time on my research. Mama was clever and went to Oxford, and where did that get her? To end up miserable for most of her short life and then dead at the bottom of a car park a few years later. No, no point. Not for me.

I signed up to catering college instead. Anna helped me. She was surprised that I wanted to leave school when my exams were so close and said she thought I had a lot of academic potential. Anna had known me since I was tiny and, as tragic as it was, given that helping to look after me was her paid job, she was the closest thing I had to family, except for Rhonda, who was by now very unwell so I didn't want to bother her with my problems. I knew I was very lucky to have Anna on my side. She was always on about wanting me to follow my dreams, so when I told her that I wanted to be a chef she was more than happy to help set me up.

And while I initially came up with this idea as a means to an end, once I started college I was surprised to find I actually liked cooking – and I was pretty good at it. I'd never done much cooking at my various 'homes', but taking basic ingredients and making them into something else, something tasty, was surprisingly satisfying. Baking was really fun; I loved making elaborate cakes and icing them, and also experimenting with unusual flavours. There was something comforting about it. No doubt my various therapists would have said it was because it evoked the homeliness and nurturing that I largely missed out on as a child. Maybe they would have been right. Then again, maybe I just liked it.

I also enjoyed cooking savoury dishes – finding out which herbs and spices worked with which fish and types of meat, and thinking up inventive vegetarian and vegan dishes.

And as well as cooking, I learned about ingredients and foraging – how to take dandelions and nettles and turn them into tea or soup, how to search for berries in the hedgerows, even in towns, and work out which *ones were safe to eat. How and where to find mushrooms, how to prepare them, how to know which ones were safe. That was my favourite part of the course.*

42

January 2020, La Madière, France

Hugo

We are sitting around after yet another board game. Simon is quite drunk now. Inigo is still crying upstairs. Cass is sitting in an armchair flicking through a magazine she doesn't seem to be reading, in between staring miserably out of the window at the still-falling snow. I am starting to see what Ria means – it is becoming claustrophobic in here.

Millie brings in yet another tray of cake and coffee and sets it down.

'Everything OK?' she asks. Everyone murmurs vaguely in assent.

'It seems unlikely you'll be able to ski tomorrow, I'm

afraid. But the road is due to open later, so hopefully things are improving,' she adds. 'Also, I had something I needed to ask you all.'

Everyone looks up, suddenly interested.

'Do you remember Cameron was keen to offer a room to the brother of the man found in the snow? Well, unfortunately the only chalet we have empty at the moment has suffered a broken window in the storm and there's some water damage. Cameron wanted me to ask you if we could offer him one of the spare rooms here. I know it's quite an ask, but the poor man has already had a terrible journey; at the moment he's stuck in a community hall that's been turned into an emergency refuge for stranded travellers. What with his having come all this way to identify the body of his dead brother, Cameron doesn't want him arriving with nowhere to stay and . . .'

''S fine,' Simon proclaims, taking another large slug of his red wine. 'Poor bastard. Least we can do. Plenty of room for him.'

'No!' Ria shouts. Everyone turns to look at her. 'I mean, sorry, but I'm not comfortable with it,' she adds in more measured tones. I see tears spring to her eyes.

'Why ever not?' Simon barks, looking her up and down with disdain. 'The chalet's plenty big enough. We'll barely notice he's here. And it's only for a day or two anyway, isn't it? Ria, c'mon, show some charity.' He takes another large gulp of his wine. 'Least we can do for the poor sod, surely.'

264

'Darling?' I prompt. 'That's OK, isn't it?' I think she is being weirdly unreasonable and I don't want Simon to think we're the kind of couple who wouldn't help someone in need. Not that he's what I'd call caring, based on what I've seen, but you never know.

Ria turns on her heel, her face red and blotchy, and runs upstairs. I can't tell if she's angry or upset, but neither can I understand why she's behaving this way. I'm embarrassed that she's acting like this in front of Simon and I feel I should make an excuse for her.

'I'll talk to her,' I say. 'I'm sure it's fine. Probably her time of the month or something,' I add and then, noticing Cass's expression, remember that you're not supposed to say stuff like that, especially in front of women. 'I mean, I think she's feeling a bit overwrought about being cooped up in here like this. She keeps saying she wants to go home.' Perhaps I should have kept my mouth shut – it feels like I'm only making things worse.

As I head up the stairs to find Ria, I hear Millie ask Simon: 'So shall I tell Cameron the man's brother can stay here? I'll need to let him know as soon as possible – it's only fair. It's going to be almost impossible for him to find something else at short notice with the resort chock-a-block the way it is.'

'It's fine,' Simon says. 'We're more than happy to help. Ria'll get over it.'

I'm a bit annoyed about Simon speaking for all of us like that but, then again, I can hardly say anything to him. It would help if I understood why Ria is being so strange about it all.

I open our bedroom door, expecting to find Ria lying on the bed, but she bursts past me, jacket and boots on.

'Darling? Where are you going?'

'I can't stay here another second!' she shrieks, eyes wild. I've never seen her like this before. 'I'm going out!'

'Ria, no! Stay here. We can sort this out, I'll talk to the others. You've seen what the weather's like! You can't go out in this snow! It's not safe.'

She pushes past me. 'I'm going. Please, Hugo, let me go. I'll be fine.'

'Let me come with you at least?' I call after her, running into our room, kicking off my slippers and wondering where my salopettes are.

'No!' she shouts up at me. 'I need some time to myself.' She bolts down the stairs and I feel a gust of cold air as she wrenches the heavy chalet door open and I hear it bang closed behind her.

I go downstairs and find Cass sitting alone on the huge sofa.

The sofa gives a *whoompf* as I sit down next to her and say, 'Mind if I join you?' It's quiet in the chalet now so I guess Inigo has finally gone to sleep.

Cass smiles gratefully. She pulls her jumper down over her hands, though the fire is roaring and it isn't even remotely cold in here. 'Of course I don't mind,' she says, 'but please don't feel you have to keep me company.'

Sitting close to her I see again how young she is and feel sorry for her. Why is she with an oaf like Simon?

'How have you found the week?' I ask. 'This isn't your first time skiing, is it?'

She pulls a face. 'No, it's not. I did a season as a chalet girl a few years back, but my employer kept us very busy and I didn't get to ski much at all. So while I have skied, I'm no expert and didn't fancy skiing too much in this weather.' She pauses. 'It's all been a bit weird here, hasn't it?'

I nod. 'Yeah. There's certainly been a lot going on.'

There's another awkward pause.

'To start with I felt stressed about being here because Simon had been with an old girlfriend,' Cass continues, babbling. Maybe she feels she has to fill the silence. 'I've been jealous and insecure about loads of things since Inigo was born. Silly really, especially in light of everything else that's happened since. Things get put into perspective when someone's found dead.'

'I guess they do,' I agree, but I am no longer listening to Cass. Instead, I'm thinking about Simon having been to La Madière before, and trying and failing to remember if Ria also said she'd been here before or not.

I realize, to my shame, I haven't had a proper conversation with Cass this entire week, so I continue, 'Remind me how you and Simon met?'

She blushes. 'Oh. This sounds terrible but . . . I catered a dinner party for him and his ex-wife. Like I said, I was once a chalet girl like Millie, then I set up a small catering company when I got back to the UK. Simon and I kept in touch and I did some business lunches for him and . . . well.' There is a pause. 'They were already pretty much separated by the time we met, and he started confiding in me and . . . one thing led to another. Once they were officially divorced, Simon asked me to marry him.'

But I am still only half-listening to Cass as I am desperately racking my brains to recall if Ria said she had been here before. I'm pretty sure she has. *Was it with Simon?* Was she the girlfriend Cass is referring to, whether Cass knows it or not? Has there been something between them in the past? Is that why Ria's been so strange this week? Has Simon made another pass at her? Is that why she won't come down from her room?

I feel myself growing hot and try to tune back in to what Cass is saying, but it sounds like blah blah blah blah blah.

I remember that it was Ria who booked the chalet, but I can't remember whose idea it was to get Simon along on this particular trip. Was it mine? Olivia's? Or Ria's? I can't think straight with Cass burbling on next to me so I get to my feet and say:

'Oh gosh, Cass, I'm so sorry but I've got to make an urgent call. Let's talk again later, OK?'

She looks startled and says: 'Oh, yes, OK, of course,' and I feel momentarily bad as I realize she was confiding in me but I can't worry about that now. I've got my own problems to think about.

I go back up to our room to try and remember who came up with the idea of this week. And while I'm up there, I might see if I can sneak another look at Ria's iPad. Usually she keeps it well locked down, and she's been exceptionally cagey about it this week. Perhaps there is something in there she doesn't want me to know about. I might have another look.

43

January 2020, La Madière, France

Adam

By late afternoon I am on a coach. It's not a fun journey – you would think people would be cheered by the prospect of getting to their holiday destination at long last. But no – all the talk around me is of how much time they are losing when they should already be on the slopes, with people competing over who has the worst holiday-from-hell story, who has lost the most money, who has had the worst journey, who has spent the longest time awake/on the road/away from a functioning loo, and who has been inconvenienced to the greatest degree. Sometimes I feel like interrupting to ask if anyone here has ever finished a holiday leaving a relative dead on the mountainside and then had to come back years later to deal with the fallout, but of course, I hold my tongue. I don't yet know the logistics of identifying Will's body. I don't even know where it is. Do I *have* to see it? I'm not sure. I don't know if I want to. But the kind-sounding man from the resort who phoned after I'd had the call from the police seemed to think I might like to visit the spot where he was found 'to pay your respects', as he said in his perfect English.

After several hours of a tortuously slow journey, we pass a sign which announces our arrival in La Madière. No doubt the resort will have changed hugely since I was here. I think about Nell. I wonder where she is now? Probably married to someone rich. She was always quite shallow, if fit. I wonder if she's happy? And I think about Will. Lying dead in the snow all that time. Dead, without the privilege of being happy or not.

He didn't deserve to die. But I am not going to be blamed. Whatever it takes, I refuse to let what happened mess up the rest of my life.

44

BEFORE

Not long after finishing catering school, I got a job as a chalet girl. There was a rigorous interview process and I had to cook a three-course meal for a board of tasters. By then I was an excellent cook and had spent hours on social media studying how a chalet girl tends to look and how she is expected to behave. Even though I had never been near a ski resort, let alone a ski chalet, I aced the test and a few weeks later, I left for the Alps.

That was my first time outside the UK. Anna helped me apply for a passport and even paid the fee for me, though I'm sure she's not really allowed to. It was also the first time I'd been on a plane. I felt like I was holding my breath the whole way; it seemed so unreal. Meanwhile my new colleagues, as I guess you'd call them, chatted and joked like it was nothing at all to them. It probably was *nothing at all* to them – I imagined most of them had been on several flash holidays every year since they were tiny.

Nonetheless, there were a few exclamations of 'ooh, look, snow!' as our coach drove in the resort. Only ever having seen short-lived sprinkles of snow at home, I could hardly believe my eyes. There was so much of it! It was like something from a film, or a Christmas card. Everything was white and glistening. Enormous icicles which looked like they could kill someone if they fell hung from the chocolate-box-style buildings.

As well as paying for my passport, Anna also helped me buy a decent pair of walking boots before I left. 'Call it an early Christmas present – can't have you getting cold feet!' she'd said. Thankfully, the chalet company provided not only a uniform but also a logoed ski jacket which we had to wear at all times while outside the chalet, even when we were not officially on duty. This was a huge relief to me, having seen the price of ski jackets.

When we arrived, we were divided up between about six chalets. Many of the girls had put in requests to share rooms with other girls they already knew from school or from previous seasons they'd worked, so I lucked out and got a room all to myself.

It was by far the most beautiful room I had ever been in. The bed was enormous and there were fur throws everywhere. I touched one – it felt like stroking a pedigree cat. I'd never seen towels so white or so thick – each one was monogrammed and had a snowflake embroidered on it. There was both a huge shower and a massive claw-foot tub in my bathroom.

I flung myself back on the bed. It was like lying on a cloud.

Of course, after the training we were moved to our staff accommodation – mine little more than a narrow bed in a windowless cupboard at the top of the chalet I was to work in. I kept my head down, worked hard, and didn't socialize much. The job involved long hours and some of the clients were total wankers, but I loved the cooking and even most of the cleaning so, on the whole, it was pretty OK. Like playing house – something I had never had the chance to do before. Most import-antly, the work was mindless and it gave me plenty of time to think. To plot, to plan, and wonder how I could best make life difficult for the person who had helped to ruin my life.

But then something unexpected happened.

45

January 2020, La Madière, France

Ria

The strength of the wind takes my breath away as I slam the chalet door behind me and step out into the blizzard. I'm wearing my ridiculously expensive furry snow boots and Moncler ski jacket, but I instantly regret not putting my salopettes on. Millie has been coming in and out all day, so it must be possible to get around, I tell myself. But the path from the chalet is uncleared and there are huge drifts of snow, many of which are taller than me.

'It's not safe!' Hugo had been shouting when I stormed out. Maybe he's right. But either way, I need to make this call and I can't do it in the chalet with him or anyone else potentially listening.

I stumble into the first café I come across which is open, imagining I'll be almost the only one in there, thinking no one will venture out of their cosy chalets in this weather, but to my surprise, it's packed. The fire's on, music is blaring, people are drinking, laughing, and chatting as if nothing has happened. As if nothing's changed. I suppose for them, it hasn't. A body in the snow – beyond 'poor guy' and perhaps a silent prayer of thanks that it wasn't them or anyone they know, he's now old news, as far as they're concerned.

But for me, it's all come flooding back. Like it was yesterday. And now that the dead man's brother is on the way out, it's all going to be over. He's bound to recognize us. He'll have questions. He'll want to know what happened – go over the details. And I don't know how much more I can lie about it. Not to his face. Not when his brother's body has been lying in the snow all this time.

Is this what it's all been leading up to? For so many years I've managed to live a normal life, thinking I'd escaped what happened in the past. Though every day I've been scared of someone knocking on my door, telling me that the truth has come out, that I'm going to be arrested, that there's going to be a proper court case, that I'm going to go to prison.

I make my call and Cameron agrees to meet me in the bar. I order a hot chocolate which I don't want to try to make the double whisky I'm ordering to drink alone at my table seem less tragic at this time of day. I wait, my foot tapping under the table, unable to keep still.

46

Adam

'Can I take your name?' asks the cheery girl with a clipboard as I descend from the coach. The weather hasn't improved much. The wind cuts into my face and my feet are soaked as soon as my trainers hit the snow; I don't own snow boots. I should have bought some at the airport.

'Adam Cassiobury,' I tell her. Her expression changes to become more sombre.

'Ah, Mr Cassiobury,' she says. 'We're all so sorry for your loss. Matt is here to meet you personally – he'll be taking you to your accommodation and should be able to answer any questions you have. I'll call him over

281

for you. Matt. Matt!' she yells towards a figure standing a few metres away in yet another logoed jacket, but there's no way he's going to hear her above the noise of the wind.

'It's OK – I see who you mean. You're obviously very busy – I'll go and introduce myself.'

I drag myself through the snow and tap him on the shoulder. This weather is horrible. I feel sorry for all these poor saps who have paid thousands for their holidays and come out to this. 'Uh, Matt? I'm Adam. Adam Cassiobury. The – uh – girl – lady over there said you'd come to find me.'

'Mr Cassiobury!' Matt sticks out a gloved hand, covered in snow. 'Welcome to La Madière. I'm only sorry it's in such sad circumstances.'

I nod. 'Thank you. And call me Adam, please.'

'Adam. Let's go and get your stuff and then I'll take you to your accommodation. I'm afraid the chalet we'd planned to offer you has been water-damaged, so we've found you an en-suite room in another one. It's equally as luxurious, but there are some other occupants too. I hope that's OK for you? They're happy to help, given the – uh – circumstances. There's plenty of room.'

I nod. I don't care – I'm freezing cold and just want to get inside.

'They're very nice people,' he continues, 'and they, um, understand the situation, so I'm sure they'll be – well. I'm sure you'll be comfortable. I've brought a skidoo, so if you're happy to hop on the back, we can

282

get you installed. Just this one, luggage wise, is it?' he asks, glancing at my old and shabby backpack.

'Yeah – I left in a hurry,' I say. 'And I don't have any cold weather clothes anyway, as you can see. I'm living in Thailand at the moment – they don't do snow there.' I am shivering in my thin raincoat and wish we could cut the small talk and get to wherever we're going.

He smiles. 'Well I'm sure we can lend you a jacket or fleece or something for your stay. Best if you put your backpack on and then hop on behind me. We'll get you inside and warmed up in no time.'

I straddle the snow bike self-consciously, noticing that everyone else is having to drag cases through the snow – some aided by porters, some by reps and chalet girls, and others doing it by themselves, in some cases while having also to coerce over-tired and screaming children or precariously balance sleeping babies on their shoulders.

I've never been on a skidoo before and am not quite sure how to hang on – I don't want to put my arms around this guy's waist because, well, it would be weird, wouldn't it? I don't even know him. So I awkwardly hang on to the seat behind me. I don't have gloves and my hands are red raw as soon as we start moving. Matt, probably noting that I'm not fixed on in any way, drives slowly. We travel for a minute or so up a short hill, turn off onto a tree-lined driveway and then stop outside a stone and wood building.

'Oh. It wasn't far then,' I say as we both climb off.

Matt smiles kindly. 'No. But many of our clients don't like to walk through the snow, so it's a service we provide. Normally it's a four by four rather than a snowcat, as it's easier with the luggage, but the snow's too deep today.'

Matt pushes open a heavy wooden door and I'm instantly grateful for the warmth inside. There's a row of hotel-style slippers lined up inside the door, so I follow Matt's lead in slipping off my manky raincoat and sodden shoes (I take off my socks too, which are also soaked), and push my feet into the soft, puffy slippers. They are chocolate brown with a pattern which makes them look like they've been knitted. In that moment they feel like the most comfortable and comforting thing I've ever worn.

'Let's get you inside, show you your room and intro- duce you to the others. I think the – uh – formalities are taking place tomorrow? I'm not sure exactly what you've arranged with the police, and things keep changing anyway on account of the weather. But if you'd like to see where your brother – Will – was found, or any other part of the resort, anything that helps you generally, well, you know, say the word and I'm sure it can be arranged.'

I nod. 'Thank you.' Almost the worst part of all this is everyone else's embarrassment. Why can't anyone treat me normally? It all happened a long time ago. We've all moved on.

Matt opens a heavy door into a beautiful open-plan

living/dining room with a huge window, stone walls, blond wood, and fur throws everywhere.

Matt clears his throat. 'Hello, everyone. This is Adam, our new guest – I believe Millie will have told you . . .'

Everyone looks up. 'Let me in introduce you to everyone,' Matt continues, 'Simon . . .'

A portly man with a flushed face and comb-over gets up out of a leather armchair and comes over and shakes my hand. 'Good to meet you. Sorry for your loss.'

I smile tightly. 'Thank you.'

'This is my wife, Cass,' he adds, indicating a very young, awkward-looking woman sitting with a similar-aged woman on a sheepskin rug half-heartedly dangling a plastic toy above a baby who is intermittently swiping at it, 'our son Inigo and nanny Sarah.'

One of the women gives me a sympathetic smile and raises her hand in greeting. The other doesn't look at me. I've already forgotten which woman is the wife and which the nanny, but I don't imagine it matters.

Another man, younger and fitter-looking than Simon, stands up from the sofa. 'Welcome. I'm Hugo. Good to meet you. Sorry it's in such circumstances.'

I nod. 'Thank you. And thank you all for allowing me to crash your chalet. I'm not sure what I'd have done otherwise.'

A door opens and a young, pretty girl wearing a long-sleeved polo shirt with the same logo as Matt's jacket comes in with a tray of champagne glasses and places them on the table.

285

'And this is Millie, who will be looking after you during your stay,' Matt adds.

She straightens up. 'Hello. I'm so sorry for your loss. And I'm sorry we weren't able to get Chalet Alpaca ready for you in time. But we hope you'll be very comfortable here. Please don't hesitate to ask if there's anything we can do to make your stay . . . well, just don't hesitate.'

She uncorks the champagne – which seems odd to me as the mood is hardly celebratory, but I guess people expect champagne before dinner in a high-end chalet like this. It was the kind of thing I aspired to the last time I was here, after all, but couldn't yet quite afford. Or rather, Will and his little girlfriend couldn't. A few years on, this would probably have been me, if it hadn't been for what happened on the mountain. I haven't skied since.

'Will Ria be joining us for dinner?' Millie asks Hugo.

He sighs loudly. 'I'm not sure. She was . . . she said she wasn't feeling too well earlier. I'll go and check on her in a minute if that's OK?'

She nods. 'Of course. I only wanted to know how many to set the table for. But no rush.'

'No problem. I'll go and see what she says,' Hugo replies.

Millie hands everyone champagne flutes and I sit down. There is an awkward silence.

'So, um, have you had a good week?' I venture. May as well stick to the standard ski holiday chat I just about

286

remember, as no one is going to want to talk about my dead brother. Least of all me.

'Weather hasn't been the best, obviously,' Simon says, 'but we got one day in the sun and then some amazing powder, so can't complain. And anyway, under the circumstances . . . well, there are worse things than bad weather.'

Simon turns a deeper shade of red and takes a large gulp of his champagne. I can't cope with much more of this. I put my glass down on the table and draw my hand across my mouth.

'Look, I appreciate your . . . solicitude and kindness and I'm sorry to be intruding on your holiday like this. But Will, my brother, died a long time ago. I've come to terms with that. Identifying his body is an unpleasant formality and, as I'm sure you will understand, there are many places I'd rather be than here, but there's no need to handle me with kid gloves.'

Silence.

'And now I feel like I'm being incredibly rude.' I stand up. 'Perhaps I should go up to my room, leave you good people to it.'

Simon stands up too. 'You're not being rude. We're being insensitive. Please, you must be tired and ravenous after travelling for however long it's been. Stay and have dinner with us. We'll feel terrible if we've driven you away.'

By now I just want to lie down on my bed and go to sleep but, if I do that, it's going to look like I'm

287

storming off like a toddler having a tantrum. So I force myself to smile and say: 'I'm sorry. It's been a long couple of days and I'm very tired. I think I'll go and have a quick shower – I've been in these same clothes for days – and then I'll join you.'

'We'll eat in about an hour, so plenty of time,' Millie says, placing a plate of exquisite-looking canapés on the table. 'Matt has already taken your bag up, so I'll show you where your room is now, if you're ready.'

I down the rest of my champagne and stand up. 'That would be great, thank you.'

Millie leads me up two flights of stairs and opens a door. It's an eaves room with sloping ceilings and a Velux window. There's a double bed made up with white linen and covered with a fur throw, and a fleece-covered chair. A small door in one wall looks like it probably leads to the bathroom.

'I'm sorry it's rather small,' Millie says, 'but I hope you'll find it comfortable. There are towels and toiletries in the bathroom, and if you need anything else, please don't hesitate to let me know. There's no code for the Wi-Fi – it's open. Though it's not working too well because of the weather, I'm afraid.'

'Thank you,' I say. 'I very much appreciate you putting me up.'

'Cameron – the owner of the chalet – felt that it was the least we can do. He's coming for dinner to pay his respects, so you can thank him then if you like. But there's really no need – he's very happy to have you

288

here.' There is a pause. 'Is there anything else I can do for you?'

She smiles, but it doesn't reach her eyes. I guess she's had enough of having to wait on her guests hand and foot for several days solid since the lifts closed. Having to put me up as well has probably only added to her load.

'No, this looks great, thank you. I hope having me here isn't putting you to any extra trouble?'

'I'll leave you to it then,' she says, diplomatically ignoring my question. 'See you in an hour for dinner?'

'Looking forward to it,' I lie.

47

January 2020, La Madière, France

Ria

'What were you thinking?' I hiss when Cameron plonks himself down at my table, snow falling off his jacket and on to my already-soaked jeans. 'Why are you inviting that guy to our chalet? He's going to recognize us, you know. We were lucky to get away with not going to prison all those years ago, and now you're . . .'

Cameron holds his hand up in that awful patronizing way he does, always has done. 'Stop it. None of this was my idea. The resort's head honcho is apparently fretting about a dead body turning up here, and thinks we all need to be seen as caring and sharing. And as I have the best properties, he asked if I would host. I could hardly say no, could I? How is that going to look? I've got a business to run here and I need to keep key resort people onside.'

I can't believe his tone. Or his expression. How can he be so calm?

'But he doesn't have to stay with us, does he?' I counter, trying to keep my voice low – which is no easy feat when I feel like screaming. 'It's all right for you, you can stay out of the way, but me? "Oh hi, yeah, it was my fault your brother died. Mine and my colleague's. Sorry about that. Hope your short stay in this luxurious chalet while you identify his body makes it all better." Brilliant. That's not going to make for awkward dinner time conversation at all.'

Cameron puts his face up so close to mine I can smell his coffee breath. 'Firstly – he wasn't meant to be in your place, but there's a problem with the only spare chalet I have at the moment so I can't put him there. With some punters unable to leave the resort when they planned to and others miraculously getting through despite the roads being closed – seemingly just to piss me off – everything's full to bursting point apart from your chalet. Which, as an aside, I seem to remember you are staying in this week free of charge while Hugo checks out if it's good enough for his precious company. So, I'm *terribly* sorry if it's inconveniencing you, the dead man's brother turning up and bunking in with you, but you'll have to put up with it.'

I flinch as flecks of Cameron's spit land on my face as he speaks.

292

'Secondly, we spent about ten minutes with this man, two decades ago. Do you remember what the weather was like that day? It was almost as bad as it is now. We were wearing goggles and hats, as was he. We were all twenty years younger. He was in a coma for days afterwards, and apparently remembered nothing about the accident. Do you think you would recognize him now? I certainly wouldn't. So why would you think that he'd recognize us?

'Besides, our names were in the press at the time, as I recall,' Cam continues. 'If the dead man's brother had any interest in pursuing us, he could have done so back then. But he didn't. So why do you think he'd a) recognize us or b) want to do anything about it even if he did? It was a tragic accident that happened a long time ago. He lost his brother. Boo hoo. End of story.'

'Don't you feel any remorse for what we did?' I ask hoarsely.

Cameron sits back. 'No. We didn't *do* anything. Those boys shouldn't have asked to ski that kind of slope in those conditions. They over-estimated their skiing ability. Or, to be more accurate, they *lied* about their skiing ability. They shouldn't have been there at all. If they had been honest about their level or, to give them the benefit of the doubt, hadn't over-rated themselves, we wouldn't have taken them off-piste that afternoon and there wouldn't have been an issue. It was their behaviour that was unsafe, not ours.'

'Simple as that?' I counter. 'Our behaviour was hardly

gold standard. And,' I lower my voice, 'we lied too. It wasn't only them. We lied to rescue, to resort staff, to the police, by extension to the dead man's family, to everybody. If we'd alerted rescue as quickly as we said we did, or even stayed closer to the men so they hadn't got lost instead of us trying to out-ski each other, the brother who died might have been saved. That's *way* worse than someone making out they're a better skier than they are.'

Cameron snorts. 'We hardly lied. We adjusted a few timings in our statements. It doesn't amount to *murdering* someone. It was an accident. The investigation said so. And I'm happy to go with that.' We sit in silence for a few moments.

'Is that it, then?' Cameron asks.

There is a pause. Around us people are laughing, chatting, eating, drinking. Everything carrying on as normal while I feel as though my whole world is falling apart.

'Why did you stay here?' I ask.

Cam shrugs. 'It's my home. It's where I'm happy. I went away for a few years because the tour ops were all steering their clients away from Skitastic and I had to wind it up, but by the time I came back, no one remembered who I was. It was already old news even a few years on. Almost everyone who had been in the resort when we were here had moved on to other places, other lives. No one has been here as long as me now. A lot of people come to the mountains, and once in a while, someone dies. It quickly becomes old news. No one wants to think about it. People come here on holiday

294

or for a season or two, forget about their normal lives, have fun, ski, drink too much, shag a ski instructor maybe. No one wants to think about death. Hardly any of the people here today know about what happened all those years ago, nor would they care, if the body hadn't resurfaced.'

There's another pause.

'Why *didn't* you stay here?' Cam asks.

'You know why,' I hiss. 'I couldn't bear it after what happened. I only came back this week because – well – because you made me.'

He smirks. 'Yeah, handy you working in events like that, sending that mailshot out to all the chalet companies – including mine – when you set up your little enterprise. Been useful for us both over the years, hasn't it? To give you credit where it's due, you've sent some good clients my way.'

'Not out of choice,' I whisper. 'As you know. You blackmailed me. I'd never have contacted Snow Snow if I'd known it was your company.'

Cameron responds with that awful bark of a laugh. 'Ha! Should have done your research then, shouldn't you? It's especially convenient now you're married to Mister big-shot Hugo,' he continues. 'You were always so scared about people finding out about the accident. I'd have been stupid not to use that to my advantage, wouldn't I? You can see that, surely?'

I shake my head. My face feels hot but I'm determined not to let him see me cry.

'But I've been a good boy this week, haven't I?' he continues. 'I've kept to our agreement and haven't let on about your past. Or even that we know each other – that it's down to you and me and our *friendship* that you're all here, enjoying my lovely chalet.'

'We are not friends. You threatened me,' I say in a low voice. 'You said I had to get Hugo to take your chalets on or you'd make it known what happened that day. You'd make sure I took the blame, given your contacts now that you're such a big noise out here.'

He laughs. 'I never said you had to *marry* Hugo – that was up to you.' He looks me up and down. 'You still look all right, in spite of pushing forty. I'm sure the promise of a blow job or something for gormless, grateful little Hugo would have sufficed.'

'I didn't marry Hugo because of you,' I whisper, but even as I say it I know it's only half true. It just seemed easier at the time. I could give Cameron what he wanted – make sure he didn't tell anyone about my past and stop worrying about how to pay the rent every month – all in one fell swoop. I'd even read articles about Hugo before I went to that party at the Natural History Museum, to work out what kind of man he was and what approach would suit him, giving me the best chance of getting Cameron off my back. I didn't go in planning to marry Hugo, far from it, but when that was the way things went, it seemed like the answer to all my problems.

No one wants to work with an events manager who

296

has killed someone, or to be their friend or lover, for that matter. It's bad enough living with what I've done myself – the idea of it becoming common knowledge was, and still is, unbearable.

'None of my business why you got married – I don't give a shit anyway,' Cameron says. 'You can play happy families with Hugo or cut his dick off for all I care, as long as he takes the chalets onto his books. After this business with the body turning up, sales might need an extra push.'

I surreptitiously swipe my hand across my face as, in spite of my efforts, tears brim. Cam rolls his eyes.

'For God's sake, *Andrea*, this happened twenty years ago! No one cares. Move on.'

'I care,' I say hoarsely. 'And don't call me that.'

He snorts. 'Oh yes, it's *Ria* now, isn't it?' he says sarcastically. 'Ria Redbush. No longer ski bum Andy Jones – she's long gone. Classy Ria Redbush married to posh boy Hugo. A whole new life for a whole different person. Well, good for you for caring. I don't. You'll just have to cope with your new house guest being there as best you can. And, for what it's worth, I won't be skulking in the shadows and staying away. I'll be coming to dinner, offering my condolences and all that. I've got nothing to be ashamed of, nothing to be scared of, and neither have you, though obviously it's suited me well over the years for you to feel that you have. Grow some balls. I'll see you later.'

* * *

I can barely face going back to the chalet, but can hardly stay away forever. I sneak in the back door and creep up to our room. Shrugging off my sodden outer clothes, I lie down on the bed and shut my eyes tight.

A while later the bedroom door opens.

'Darling?' Hugo sits down on the bed. 'Thank God you're back. I was worried about you, out in this weather. How're you feeling?'

I open my eyes. 'Not brilliant. I've got a raging migraine and feel totally exhausted.' I sigh. 'Perhaps I'm coming down with something. I'm sorry about earlier. I needed to be . . . by myself.'

Hugo pats my leg absentmindedly. 'That's OK – I'm glad you're back safe and sound. Though I still think you shouldn't have gone out in this weather, especially if you're not feeling well,' he scolds, though good-naturedly. I feel a rare pang of love for him. Poor Hugo. He deserves so much better than me.

'Are you coming down for dinner?' he continues. 'Millie wants to know.'

I'm famished, but there's no way I'm going downstairs and sitting through dinner with the dead man's brother. I may not be able to put off meeting him the whole time I'm here, but there's no way I can face it today.

I've barely been able to think about anything else since I found out he was coming, fretting about what to do. Avoid him? Come clean? Or smile sweetly and hope for the best?

Cameron is right, of course. I don't remember what

298

he looks like. Chances are he won't recognize us. But even if he doesn't, I still know that we killed his brother. I can't just sit at the same table as him, making polite conversation.

I sit myself up, trying to look weak. 'I think I'd rather stay up here, if you don't mind. But perhaps you could ask Millie to send me up some soup or something? I wouldn't mind something simple to eat, but I'm not really up to sitting at the dinner table.'

He kisses my forehead. 'Of course. I'm sure she won't mind. I'll miss you though.'

I squeeze his hand. 'That's sweet, Hugo. I'll miss you too.' I almost mean it.

48

January 2020, La Madière, France

It's a massive shock, my dad's body turning up, and I react the only way I know how, the same way I've always done – I put on a fixed smile and carry on. Though I do go back to cutting myself when I can manage a moment alone, even though I had pretty much weaned myself off the habit. It gives me a momentary release from the horror and awfulness of what is going on around me, and from the memories of my childhood. No one notices – it is easy to hide the scars when you're as used to it as I am.

I never got to meet my dad while he was alive, so I figured the least I could do would be to pay my respects now that he was dead. I would like to see his body and spend some time with him. It's a poor substitute but it feels important.

301

It's very difficult to get time to myself but as soon as I manage a free couple of hours I head down the mountain to the hospital to see if I can see my dad. My French is far from brilliant but, even so, I'm sure the woman understands that I'm saying I am the dead man's daughter. But she says that without my passport and various other bits of paper and ID there's no way I can see his body. Which is ridiculous – do they have random people turning up the whole time to try to look at dead bodies which are nothing to do with them? As far as I can understand, she then says something about his brother, who will be coming out in the next few days. Perhaps I should speak to my uncle if I want to see the body, she tells me.

So I say 'Merci, madame', though really I want to say 'merci pour rien' or 'fuck you, bitch', then I go outside and take some deep breaths. Seeing my dad is not the most important thing now. Taking revenge on my uncle for what he did, avenging my mama – that is what matters. But to carry out my plan – and it comes to me in a flash as if it was destined to happen this way – I need to make sure I have easy access to my dad's killer, the person who ruined Mama's life. So on my way back to the chalet I find Matt and tell him I overheard Cameron on the phone saying he would like to offer the dead man's brother accommodation in one of his chalets. I add that he'd be embarrassed and annoyed if he knew I'd mentioned it and suggest he pretends the tourist office guys had asked him – I know how these things work in ski resorts after all. I look up at Matt through my eyelashes and touch his arm, suggesting maybe he and I could meet for a drink somewhere later. I've seen how he's been salivating over Ria this week – it's obvious he's gagging for anyone he can get. I don't care what I have to do for him – quiet drink, blow job, shag, whatever it takes. I need Uncle Adam close by.

Then later I go to Chalet Alpaca – Matt said he thought it was the only one that was free. It isn't hard to find. I pull my sleeve down over my hand to break a window, let myself in and turn some taps on full blast. I'll pop back later to make it look accidental. Even if Cameron is offering somewhere for free, I can't imagine there's any way he'd want a guest of his staying in a chalet which is less than perfect.

Fortunately, there is a spare room in our chalet, which is apparently the nicest in the resort. It could hardly be better.

49

January 2020, La Madière, France

Hugo

Ria is still claiming to be unwell. I know I'm not exactly the most perceptive of men, but there's definitely something going on. She's refusing to come down to dinner again, claiming a migraine, which isn't a condition she's ever suffered from to my knowledge. And I'd like to know where she went when she stormed off in this weather. Was she meeting someone? Matt, maybe? Simon? Or was he still here in the chalet when she went? I think he was. I can't remember. All this strangeness is making my head hurt.

Then again, perhaps Ria is still annoyed about our argument about children, though I thought that had been resolved. I love her with all my heart, I do, but sometimes she is very difficult to read.

As usual, Millie has gone all out for dinner and the champagne is flowing, but there's a weird atmosphere. Annoyingly, Cameron is here again. He's droning on about how fantastic his chalets are compared to all the other ones in the resort and every time he opens his mouth to speak I'm treated to the sight of red and black fish eggs coating his tongue and even flying out of his mouth now and again. It's disgusting.

Simon is guffawing and nodding at everything Cameron says and Cass is sitting on the sofa with her eyes glazing over.

Poor Cass. Simon has pretty much ignored her on this trip. Again I wonder if he and Ria have a history I don't know about. But I can hardly ask her, the way she is at the moment.

We sit down for dinner. The starter is foie gras, and Cameron is wanging on about its provenance, as if anyone cares. Cass is staring into space. Adam is trying and failing to look interested in what Cameron is saying.

I suddenly envy Ria, alone in our room, not having to listen to Cameron. Maybe I should have ducked out of dinner too.

50

January 2020, La Madière, France

Dinner is risotto. Mushroom risotto. The rice is arborio, and I'm told most of the mushrooms come from a local grower, probably not because his mushrooms are any better than the ones in the supermarket, but so that Snow Snow can use words like 'artisanal', 'hand-picked' 'locally foraged' and the like in their brochures. Such a load of bollocks.

Risotto is a quick and easy dish, with no great magic to it. People act like you have to be an expert to get it right but you don't; you buy the ingredients, tip them in and stir. Any idiot can do it. I fry the 'artisanal' mushrooms with garlic, onion, and few herbs (fresh, obviously) in a pan before tipping in the rice and stock which I made from leftover chicken earlier in the week – no stock cubes allowed here. Then it's just stir, stir, stir.

Meantime, I heat up the now-reconstituted mushrooms which I put on to soak earlier, carefully picked and dried while I was still at catering college. We learned loads of useful stuff there – not only about how to prepare dishes, but also how to forage for food, how to prepare it, what's safe to eat and what isn't. It's amazing the range of edible foods you can find in the wild in the UK, even in cities.

I had to go a little further afield for mushrooms, but there are woods and forests easily accessible even on the London Underground. It became part of my weekend routine, getting up early and going out to the woods before the day really got started. Often I'd see no one at all; at most a dog walker or two.

And depending on the time of year, I'd find all sorts of different varieties you'd have to pay a fortune for in the supermarkets: ceps, morels, and the like. I became adept at identifying the good and the bad, and my various foster mothers and later, flatmates were always delighted with my haul.

You have to be careful, naturally. Poisonous mushrooms don't always look poisonous – they're not red with white spots or anything. Actually – those ones are poisonous, but rarely deadly. They're not nearly as poisonous as something like the Amanita bisporigera, otherwise known as the destroying angel, or its friend Amanita phalloides, commonly known as the death cap. Those two can easily be mistaken for edible mushrooms, even by someone like Cameron's artisanal mushroom grower, I would imagine. Yes, it's important to be very, very, careful, and even experts can make mistakes. I brought quite a range with me, when I came out here; I wasn't 100 per cent sure how far I wanted to go. But now that I have met these two awful men who ruined mine and Mama's lives, I know what I need to do.

Once the risotto is all bubbled down and the liquid is absorbed, I plate it up. I add a sprinkle of parmesan shavings to each of the plates, and my own special mushrooms to two of them.

Then I take them through.

51

January 2020, La Madière, France

Hugo

'And while some of the chalet companies offering lower- and mid-range accommodation are struggling lately on account of the economic climate, because our clients are all high net worth individuals we're finding that during most weeks of the season there is more demand for our chalets than we can cope with, which is why next year we're looking to take on at least one new property in . . .'

I tune out. I can't listen to any more of Cameron's monologue, so I abruptly push back my chair and say, 'I'm sorry, Cameron, you'll have to excuse me. I'm going to go and check on Ria – see if she wants anything.'

'Let me know if you'd like me to take her up anything else?' Millie says, placing the plates carefully on the table. As usual, she serves the ladies first – tonight just Cass – then Adam, I guess because he is the newest arrival and the guest of honour, due to his situation. She then disappears back into the kitchen and returns with two more plates, which she puts in front of Simon, Cameron, and myself.

'Not a problem, Hewg,' Cameron says (no one calls me that) also pushing back his chair, 'I'm going to duck outside to make a call.'

I don't really feel the need to check on Ria and would even go so far as to say I don't especially want to see her at the moment as I still feel she's keeping something from me, but anything will do to get away from Cameron right now. I creep up the stairs, push the door open as gently as I can and whisper, 'Are you awake?', mentally crossing my fingers and hoping that she isn't.

The room is in darkness and there is no reply, so she's either asleep or, more likely, pretending to be. I tiptoe back down the stairs and into the dining room where Simon and Adam are now alone at the table talking about golf.

'Where is everyone?' I ask, sitting down next to Simon in Cass's seat rather than in my original chair, hoping to avoid having to sit next to Cameron any longer listening to him bore on.

'Cam's still on his call, Cass has popped upstairs to check on Inigo – Sarah's having a well-earned night off,'

312

Simon says. 'I think she's got her eye on one of those ski instructors, the minx.'

Cass reappears and I cry: 'Oh sorry, I'm in your seat!' as if I've sat down in the wrong place by accident and only just noticed. She waves her hand dismissively.

'It's fine,' she says, passing over my water glass as I pass hers back. 'I'll sit here,' she says, moving a couple of other glasses around accordingly. 'I like the view from here better anyway,' she adds, pointing at the window. It's dark and stormy and there's no view at all tonight but I guess she's being polite.

Cameron comes back and sits down where I was originally, seemingly not noticing that we've all changed seats, so hopefully not taking in that I've moved specifically to avoid him. 'Sorry about that,' he says, uncharacteristically apologetic. 'Important call. Didn't mean to hold you up.'

He picks up his fork and takes a huge mouthful, chewing noisily with his mouth open.

52

January 2020, La Madière, France

As I come back into the dining room with the decanted red wine, the first thing I notice is that some of them have moved places. For fuck's sake! I can't remember exactly who was sitting where before and who has whose food, but I know that Cass definitely wasn't at the head of the table, Cameron was. Which means she has his food. In a blind panic I pretend to trip, making sure to smash the no-doubt-very-expensive crystal decanter on the edge of the solid granite table.

Everyone leaps up from their seats, grabbing at napkins and frantically dabbing at clothes as I fuss about the table, apologizing profusely. Cameron struggles to contain himself, clearly not wanting to swear at me in front of clients but at the same time, no doubt desperately wanting to yell at me. If it weren't for the guests, he'd probably fire me on the spot.

'I'm so sorry,' I mumble as I rush into the kitchen to fetch paper towels and join the clients in the general dabbing and mopping up. 'I simply can't apologize enough. I think my foot must have caught on the edge of the rug, but that's no excuse at all.'

I take a surreptitious glimpse at the dishes of risotto on the table – I've managed to splash most of them with wine, but not quite all. 'I'm afraid I've entirely ruined the meal – I can't possibly allow you to eat anything from the table in case there are shards of glass – as you can see they've gone absolutely everywhere and they'll be impossible to see.'

Thank GOD for the granite table which sent tiny, sharp pieces of the decanter far and wide.

'And I can only apologize for Millie's clumsiness,' Cameron adds, still barely able to contain his anger. 'Obviously any dry-cleaning will be at our expense, and if anything is ruined beyond repair, we will cover the cost of replacement.' No doubt he means my meagre wages will cover the costs but, whatever, I don't care right now.

People need to pay for what they did to my dad, but that doesn't extend to killing someone innocent in the process, especially not someone as wet and pathetic as Cass.

'But more immediately, Millie,' Cameron continues pompously, 'our guests have had their dinner ruined. It's too late now to find them a table in a decent restaurant

even if they wanted to go out in this atrocious weather,
so do you have anything else you can rustle up quickly
as a replacement meal once you've cleared up this mess?'

'I could do a cheese fondue,' I suggest. 'With salad.
That won't take too long. If you'd all like to retire to
the sofas while I clean up and get organized, I can bring
you a new bottle of wine. Again, I apologize for the
inconvenience.'

'Don't give it another thought,' Adam says, touching
me lightly on the shoulder as he passes.

It's all I can do to repress a shudder.

53

January 2020, La Madière, France

Adam

I don't know how reps like Matt do it – looking so bright and cheerful when I know he was up drinking with us until around 2 a.m. The bags under my eyes are more like suitcases and yet this guy looks like he might have got up at the crack of dawn and already done a full workout at the gym. He's sitting at the breakfast table drinking a coffee when I come down, along with a woman who I haven't yet met.

Matt stands up when he sees me. 'Adam! There you are. I hope you slept well?' He gestures at the table. 'Please, sit down and have some breakfast before we go, there's no rush. Oh, and you haven't met Ria yet, have you? Ria, Adam, Adam, Ria.'

Hugo's wife, must be. Attractive, but older than I'd expected. Probably only a few years younger than Hugo, with a good decade and a half or more on Cass. She looks up and nods at me, before pushing back her chair and dabbing her mouth with a white napkin.

'I hope you're feeling better?' I say.

She smiles briefly. 'I am, thank you. But I hope you'll excuse me, I have a phone call to make.'

I sit down at the table and Millie places a pot of coffee and a small jug of what looks like freshly squeezed orange juice in front of me.

'Good morning, Adam,' she says. Like Matt, she looks immaculate and well-rested, though she can't possibly have got more than a few hours' sleep. 'What can I get you for breakfast?'

'Um . . . I'm not sure, uh . . .'

'I'd like to apologize again for what happened at dinner – I'm so very sorry and hope none of your clothes were stained?'

'No need to apologize, look at me! All my clothes are from market stalls these days. A bit of wine doesn't matter.'

She nods. 'That's very generous of you. I understand you've been travelling for some time so . . . how about a traditional full English? I expect you won't have had one of those for a while?' She puts her head to one side and looks at me expectantly. She really is extraordinarily pretty.

'That sounds lovely, thank you,' I reply, trying to push

320

my lecherous feelings away. I doubt hitting on the chalet girl would go down well in a place like this.

Matt takes a slug of coffee. 'How are you feeling about today?' he asks. 'If it's not a stupid question?'

I sigh, longer and more loudly than I was intending to. 'In all honesty, I'm dreading it.' Is that the right thing to say? I'm not sure. Matt takes another mouthful of coffee and nods sympathetically.

'Must be a hard thing to do after all these years,' he says. 'But good to get some closure too, no?'

I nod. 'Yeah. I guess. I mean, after a day or two of Will being missing there was never any real doubt that he was dead though so . . .' Argh. That doesn't sound like the kind of thing I should be saying.

'Do you remember much about the accident? I understand you were skiing with . . . the deceased . . . your brother at the time?'

Millie puts down a plate of prettily presented full English breakfast in front of me. There are even baked beans, which I haven't had for years. It looks delicious.

'Thank you, that looks wonderful,' I say. Millie gives a brief nod and goes back into the kitchen. I start to eat.

'I don't remember much,' I lie. 'The weather was abysmal that day, the visibility awful. I do recall that it was my idea to go out, though, not his, and I've never got over that.'

Matt puts his hand on my arm. It makes me feel uncomfortable, but it would be weird to pull it away. 'I'm sure it wasn't your fault,' he says.

321

I nod, and for a second I'm surprised to feel tears welling. 'I don't think it was anyone's fault. There was an investigation which concluded that no one was at fault, that it was an accident, pure and simple.' That's my story and that's the one I'm sticking to. I take a mouthful of bacon and force it down. 'Poor Will. It's only now I'm older I realize quite how young he was when he died.'

'Yeah. A terrible thing,' Matt agrees. There is a reflective pause where no one says anything and my chewing sounds extraordinarily loud.

Matt pushes back his chair. 'Right. Well, I'm going to leave you to finish your breakfast in peace while I go and check a few things with Millie. I'll come back at ten thirty to take you to your . . . various appointments. Does that sound OK?'

I nod. 'Great. And thank you for your kindness and hospitality. You and your colleagues are making a difficult situation as easy as possible.'

'Not at all,' says Matt. 'We're a small community here, and something like this affects us all. We all want to do what we can to help.'

He gives me another pat on the arm and a sympathetic smile before heading off to the kitchen.

I get back to my breakfast.

Matt comes back on the dot of ten thirty with a man who introduces himself at Didier Delpont, who is apparently head of the tourist office.

'I am so sorry for your loss, Monsieur Cassiobury,'

he says, his English grammatically perfect but so heavily accented it sounds almost as if he must be doing it deliberately. He shakes my hand in a way that is almost like a clasp, his other hand on the back of mine as he looks directly into my eyes. It feels too intimate and I don't know what to say. It's all happened so quickly, this being the bereaved brother thing.

'Thank you. Your colleagues here at the resort have all been so kind. I am so very grateful for all your help.'

He finally lets go of my hand, thankfully, and gives a little shrug. 'It is the least we can do. Your brother was taken by the mountains and we wish to pay our respects. When one of us is lost, we all feel it.'

Us. We were never an us; Will, me, and the resort. We only visited once. It occurs to me that this sentiment has become a theme since my arrival, and I briefly wonder if all this hero's welcome is to try to prevent me apportioning blame, suing, or similar. The world is so much more litigious than it was two decades ago.

But no. I have no intention of suing, opening the whole thing up again, putting myself under unwanted scrutiny. It would seem my late parents accepted the decision of the investigation at the time, that no one was at fault. As for me, I barely paid any attention to it. As soon as I was out of hospital and well enough to travel, that's what I did, taking as many drugs as I could to forget about it all, enjoying extreme adventures for a while as I didn't care whether I lived or died.

As far as anyone here is concerned, it was an accident.

323

These people love the mountains and are genuinely sorry for me. Sad that something so awful happened in their resort, the place that some of them think of as home. I need to do my death tour, be gracious, confirm it's Will they found, and get out of here as quickly as possible.

'Monsieur? Is that OK for you?' the resort guy is asking.

'Sorry. I was miles away. What was it you said?'

'That is fine. I know it must be a distressing day for you. I said that first we will take you to where your brother was found, then up to the lift where – well, the lift you took that day. I don't know if you remember but the run, it's off-piste and *interdit*, that is to say forbidden, on a day like today, so we would advise not going any further. But if you are very definite that you would prefer to see it and you are a confident skier perhaps we can arrange a guide if the weather is better later—'

'No,' I interrupt. 'Thank you, but that's fine. I haven't skied since the accident and I don't wish to start again now.' It comes out snappier than I intended. 'But I appreciate the offer and I understand that you are trying to make this all as easy as possible for me,' I add.

Didier nods curtly. 'As you wish. And then later we are going to meet Guillaume, the pisteur who found your brother. We thought maybe you might have some questions for him.'

I nod. 'OK. Thank you.'

He nods towards a four by four which is parked nearby and hands me a coat. 'I brought the car – it is not too far, but I think better than walking. Matt told me you didn't have a proper coat as you have come from a hot weather climate, so I have brought one for you. I hope it does not offend you. You are very welcome to keep it if you would like, but I understand if there are too many sad memories here for you to do that, so there is no obligation.'

I shrug it on – it's an enormous coat with the resort's logo emblazoned in red on the back – and feel instantly slightly better. It's comforting – like wearing a duvet. I will definitely keep it. 'Thank you. That's very thoughtful.'

'If you are ready, we will go?' He turns and heads off towards the car. Matt and I follow.

The whole thing feels awkward and wrong. We drive up the hill and out of the village. The road gets snowier and turns into a track. We carry on up until we reach an ancient shepherd's hut, where Didier stops the car and says, 'We get out here.' We are at the edge of a piste just above the village and skiers in colourful gear are whizzing by. I can feel my feet getting wet almost as soon as I step out of the car and the snow soaks through my totally unsuitable shoes. It's still snowing and the wind is fierce. I shove my hands deep into the pockets of the borrowed coat as I don't have any gloves, but then I realize this probably looks too casual for the occasion, so I pull them out again and ball them into fists to try to keep warm.

Didier points up the slope and says softly: 'Your

brother was found there – at the other side of the piste. There was a small avalanche that night and we think he came down from his previous resting place with the snow. I believe there were photos taken by the police before he was moved; I don't know if that's something you would want to see, but if you have any questions about that you can ask later.'

'No, that's fine, thank you.' The three of us stand there in awkward silence, staring at the ground. I clasp my hands in front of me and close my eyes momentarily as if I might be praying, but really I am thinking about how wet my feet are, how cold my hands are, and wondering how long I have to stand here before we can get back into the nice warm car.

I open my eyes and look at Didier. I wonder if he has been having the same thoughts. It is absolutely freezing out here.

'Do you have any questions?' he asks, gently. 'There is no rush, but we can take you to the lift whenever you are ready.'

'No questions. I appreciate you bringing me here, thank you.'

We trudge back to the car, and Didier starts the engine.

I'm already colder than I ever remember being in my life, so am dreading the next part of my death tour, which I am fully expecting to be a chairlift. I can't actually think of anything I would like to do less than take this lift again, but it seems churlish and even borderline

326

disrespectful to say so. However, I am thankful for small mercies when I see that what I remember as a rickety old chairlift has now been replaced by a state-of-the-art bubble.

'Ah. Was this a chairlift . . . when I was here?' I ask. 'Or have I misremembered? As I was telling Matt earlier, my memory of that day isn't so good.'

'It would have been a chairlift. This is one of our newest lifts – it's one of the fastest in the region, in fact. Every hour, it can transport up to . . .' Didier falls silent, perhaps realizing that this isn't the moment to be showing off about the speed of their new lift.

'It was very cold on the lift. And windy. I remember that,' I say.

'I believe so. Having read some of the reports, I think it was so windy they closed the lifts shortly after your . . . the accident.'

There is another awkward silence.

'Are you happy to go up?' Didier asks. 'Perhaps we can get out at the top, if you would like, or we can carry on round in the gondola and come straight back down. It's up to you.'

I don't want to go up at all – what's the point? But I don't feel I can tell him that, so I say: 'Yes, let's go up. Thank you.'

Didier says something I don't understand in French to the lift operator who opens a small gate and lets us through, giving me a small, sympathetic nod as he does. We get into the bubble, which is nothing like the draughty, scratched-Perspex bubbles I remember from my skiing holidays. This is more like a limousine with tinted windows, faux-leather seats, and movement so smooth and silent it barely registers. I bet Didier is dying to point out its best features as he no doubt would to anyone else visiting the resort, but he maintains a respectful silence.

At the top we get out and stand outside the lift station. It is colder and windier up here and I feel the snow seeping into my shoes again. I take a discreet step back so I can stand on the black anti-slip matting of the lift station rather than in the snow.

'So,' Didier says, putting his finger to his lips as if in thought. 'As far as we understand from the reports, you headed off in that direction.' He points towards a sign which reads 'hors piste' and has a somewhat overdramatic and inappropriate picture, given the circumstances, of an upside-down stickman falling down a mountainside. There is an embarrassed silence as we no doubt all take in the sign and decide not to say anything.

'As you know, the weather was not good and you sadly became separated from the guides. After that . . . well, we don't know. You were found at first light the next day in a hole you had dug in the snow, hypothermic and unconscious and poor Will . . . from where he was found we think he must have fallen from the edge. It is not usually a very dangerous path, but it can be tricky to see in bad weather.'

Silence falls again. This is awful. My head suddenly

feels hot. For a second I think I might be sick, but I swallow the intense wave of nausea down.

I have an almost irrepressible urge to scream or, at the very least, bellow at them that I don't understand why they are making me do this as it isn't going to help and it certainly isn't going to bring Will back but instead I keep my voice steady and polite and simply say: 'OK. Thank you. I'd like to go back down now please.'

Matt puts his hand on my arm again and I turn away, pretending I am moving to get back in the bubble but really I don't want anyone touching me.

'Of course,' Didier says. 'We go.'

'And if you don't mind, I don't think I need to meet the pisteur. I don't have any questions for him. This is all quite upsetting and I've already seen enough.'

Didier nods. 'No problem. I understand. Perhaps we can have some lunch, and then we can take you to the hospital to identify the body.'

Lunch is actually OK. They take me to what I imagine is the best restaurant in the resort – according to the blurb on the menu, it's recently been awarded a Michelin star, and we have several tiny courses that look more like works of art than food. To my relief, we move away from the subject of Will and what happened and instead fall into comforting, bland, chit-chat – I talk about my travels and what living in Thailand is like, and Didier talks in general terms about the resort and his career, probably a similar spiel to the one he gives visiting journalists or people who want to invest in the resort.

The oysters are fabulous – I can never remember if you're only supposed to eat them when the month does or doesn't have an 'r' in it, so I don't fret about it. I can't imagine it's something you need to worry about in a restaurant like this. The dessert is particularly impressive – a chocolate concoction served in a balloon made of sugar. But when coffee is served with *petits fours*, in spite of the many glasses of excellent wine I've drunk, I feel my mood dampen. This afternoon I get to see Will's body.

Nobody has said I have to do it, but I get the impression it's expected of me. I don't know how these things work but I imagine they could get all they need from DNA now, couldn't they? Or dental records? Perhaps it's different as he died so long ago.

I don't really know what to expect at all.

After what seems like forever in the car but is probably less than an hour, we pull up at a small hospital.

We go into the reception area and Didier says something to the woman at the desk, who gives me the sympathetic look I am starting to get accustomed to, while explaining something to Didier with plenty of pointing. I guess she is telling him where we need to go.

'OK, they are ready for you,' he says. 'Your brother is in the chapel of rest. It is up to you, you can see him if you want to, but if you feel it would be too distressing, you don't need to. Either way, as long as you give your permission, we would like to take a swab from the inside of your mouth so we can verify the DNA, and that the . . . that it is definitely Will who has been found.'

A wave of panic rises up in me. Do I want to see him? I didn't know there'd be a choice. What is he going to look like after all that time on the mountain?

'Um, ah, I'm not sure, I don't know if . . .' I bluster.

Didier touches my arm and this time I'm surprised to find I'm grateful for the human contact. 'Sorry. We should have explained the procedure. We're going to go and meet the nurse – she has already seen your brother. She will take the swab and perhaps she can tell you about what to expect. Then you can decide if you'd like to see him, or if you'd rather remember him as he was. Does that sound OK?'

I nod and manage to whisper, 'Thank you.' I am suddenly feeling faint and slightly tearful. Perhaps I shouldn't have had all that wine at lunchtime. I stumble and Didier gently guides me by the elbow to a chair.

'Can I get you something? A glass of water maybe?'

I want nothing more than to lie down and go to sleep, but I accept the water, take a few deep breaths, and the dizziness subsides.

'Sorry. Thank you. It's all been a bit emotional today, as you can imagine. I'm OK now. Let's go and see the nurse.'

The nurse is a matronly woman with a kind face who speaks no English whatsoever. Using Didier as translator, she explains that she's going to take a swab from inside my mouth, does so, and then puts the thing that looks like a giant cotton bud in a plastic tube.

She then speaks at length to Didier, before he translates for me.

'So. She says that the DNA result will be back within twenty-four hours because, given the circumstances, they will rush it through. She has read the police and autopsy reports as well as having seen your brother and she wishes to stress that from the state of the – um – well how he is and the clothing that remained, there is very little doubt that it's your brother. That it's Will.'

I nod, which makes my head spin. 'Yes. Yes, I understand that.'

'She also said that you can see him if you would like, and that many relatives find that a comfort. However, in this case, because he has been out on the mountain so long, his appearance is not so good and you might prefer not to. But she would like to stress it is up to you – it is your decision.'

I nod, more slowly this time. I'm still unsure what's best.

'Because the body – Will, I mean, I apologize – had been there so long, it was impossible to finalize a definite cause of death,' Didier continues. 'Would you like me to tell you some of what the autopsy report found, or would you rather I didn't? Or I could let you read it yourself, if you can understand some French?'

'Tell me what the report said, I'd like to know,' I'm

332

surprised to hear myself say, as I'm not sure I do want to know. It's not going to change anything.

Didier nods. 'OK. It seems that he had sustained a fall – there were several broken bones, and a fractured skull. So it is likely that the fall was quite large – which would also explain why he could not be found as he was far from the slope – and that it killed him very quickly and he did not suffer. I hope you will take some comfort in that.'

I nod. 'Thank you. That is good to know.'

'We can also tell you what he was wearing. He wore a blue Spyder ski jacket and black salopettes – these were more degraded so they're not sure of the brand. Do you remember if . . .'

I shake my head. 'I'm sorry. It was a long time ago. I don't remember what he was wearing.' I don't add that I never bothered developing the photos I took on that holiday. I didn't want to be reminded.

'That's OK. The test results will come very soon and confirm everything. Now all that remains is for you to decide if you would like to see your brother.'

Suddenly I am sure. 'No. Thank you. I think I'll take the advice of the nurse and remember him as he was. I think it's what he would have wanted.'

But I know that's not true. He wouldn't give a flying fuck whether I viewed his dead body or not. What he'd have wanted would have been still to be alive.

54

January 2020, La Madière, France

Ria

So far, I have managed to avoid spending any length of time with Adam. He didn't show any sign of recognition when we passed at the breakfast table and, as Cam said, why would he? It was so long ago and it was so cold that day, we were all so wrapped up, he probably never saw my face. And he's had twenty years to get upset about it, to take action, and we've never heard from him. So rationally, I've little to fear.

But that isn't how I feel. All the guilt of the last two decades, all the lies are weighing me down, crushing me. I can't bear to be here any more. I can't spend time with the brother of the man whose death I am at least partially

335

responsible for. I can't do the 'sorry for your loss' thing when his loss is my – our – fault and we've lied about it for so long.

'The roads are open again now,' I say to Hugo. 'Can't we leave? Say it's some emergency at work or something? I'm sure Simon will understand.'

Hugo sighs. 'We're due to leave in a couple of days anyway. Like I've said, I think it will be very tricky to arrange alternative transport, particularly with everything that's been happening, and I also think it would be rude to both Simon and Cameron, both of whom I need onside for the business going forward. So no, I'm sorry, I think we're going to have to stay. After all,' he gestures around the room, 'there are worse places to be stuck, aren't there? Millie's looking after us pretty well and surely the company isn't THAT bad?'

'It's just, I'm finding it very claustrophobic, being cooped up in here, especially now that . . . that other guy is here too. And I think Cam – Cameron is coming for dinner again, isn't he? And he's awful – you agree with me about that at least, don't you? I've had enough of being sociable.'

'You usually like a party.'

'Not today. Can't we go home?'

Hugo narrows his eyes at me. 'What is this about? Is there something you're not telling me?'

I feel myself go red. 'Of course not.' I can't tell him. He wouldn't want me if he knew I was responsible for someone's death and that I'd lied about it all these years.

And then I'd be back out practically on the streets, I'd be no one, penniless again. Just like I was when at Cameron's behest I gatecrashed Hugo's party at the Natural History Museum in the last good dress I had, up to my eyeballs in debt and with bailiffs banging at my door. Hugo might be annoying to live with but, in essence, he's a good man and a life of penury would be way worse. Obviously.

Hugo takes my hand. 'Is it the stuff about not wanting to have children? Is that why you don't want to be here with me? It's OK, I've already forgiven you for the pill thing. We can wait. I'd rather you'd have talked to me than taking your pills without telling me but . . . well, it's you I love. You that I need. The theoretical baby would just be the cherry on the cake.'

I feel myself soften and squeeze his hand. 'It's OK. We don't need to wait. I've already stopped taking the pills. But I would still like to go home.'

He pulls his hand away. 'You're not getting round me that easily. Sorry, Ria, but we're staying.'

55

January 2020, La Madière, France

Hugo

'And this chalet was built in 2016,' Cameron is saying, 'though it looks like it could have been here almost forever. The stone is all local, apart from the granite in the kitchen, which is one of the best types you can buy. As you can see, we have Banksy prints here on the wall – none of this alpine hearts and wooden skis rubbish for our guests. The fur throws are real because that's what most of our guests are impressed by, but if we have any eco-types coming, we can take them away and replace them with fakes – they just have to let us know. Hardly ever happens. The champagne is Bollinger, unless the clients request otherwise, and there are high-end candles in all the rooms – we offer a choice of different brands and scents in an email before they arrive. And pretty much any requests, from helicopter transfers to alligator steaks for dinner, we'll endeavour to fulfil – at a price, of course. It's all very bespoke – high net worth individuals love all that.'

Cameron has been showing me round all his chalets in the resort today. He is still no less of a cock than when we first met but I have to admit, the chalets are impressive and he seems to know the luxury market inside out.

'How many weeks of the year would you typically have bookings?' I ask.

He gives me a withering look, even though I'm sure my question is a perfectly sensible one. 'We're usually as good as fully booked for the winter season, plus we'll get a good few weeks in the summer. But there are enough people out there with more money than sense to make the chalets pay; you can charge absolutely ridiculous money for the peak winter weeks. Sometimes very rich families will book one of the smaller ones like this for most of the season – they'll bring the kids, the nanny, the tutor etcetera and come and go in a private plane or helicopter, since we have an altiport here. They might only end up being here for a total of four weeks or so out of the season and we make a mint on it because they've paid for several months. Some of them who come out don't even ski. It's beyond me why they pay the prices I charge, but they do, so I'm not complaining.'

'Sounds good,' I say, wondering if Cameron's contempt for his clients is really a good fit for Redbush's wholesome and personal service-led image. 'And do you yourself have much, um, contact with the clients?'

He makes a noise which sounds a bit like a bark, which I think is actually what passes for a laugh with him. Not for the first time this week I wish Olivia was here; she's so much better at dealing with people like Cameron than I am. And so much more consistent than Ria, for that matter.

'Fuck no,' he says. 'I've only made an appearance this week because you're the head honcho at Redbush and Simon's wedged. I'm out of here after tonight. I only come up from the valley for skiing or biking usually, or if someone needs a massive bollocking. And speaking of bollocking, I'm still wondering what to do about Millie's display last night. On the whole, she's exactly the kind of girl I like on staff – not fussed about skiing or going out and getting drunk as far as I can tell – but such clumsiness at dinner in front of guests is unforgivable.'

'It was a simple mistake,' I say. 'Could have happened to anyone. Please don't sack her. She's been amazing all week.' It's not my place to say that to Cameron but I get the impression he needs me at least as much as I need him. I hope I'm conveying 'I don't want to do business with you if you're the type who would sack a young girl over something like that', but I'm not sure it's coming across. Poor Millie. I don't want her to lose her job over some broken glass.

'Hmmm,' he says. 'You're a better man than me. And I guess it would be tricky to replace her at short notice at this point in the season anyway – busy period coming up. I'll think about it.' There is a pause. 'Anyway, going back to your question, I'm just here for the mountains. I have as little contact with the punters as possible – I leave that to the experts like Millie and Matt. I'm not a great fan of the general public as you may be able to tell.'

I'm not sure if this is meant to be a joke or not so I smile blandly. I don't want Redbush clients coming into contact with someone like Cameron day to day, but I do think the chalets would be a good addition to our stable.

'Well, they're certainly beautiful properties and I've been very impressed by the level of your service and everything else this week,' I say, adding 'apart from you personally' silently to myself. 'Perhaps you could send through details of your pricing structure for the various chalets and we'll have a look at including you in our luxe range, if we can agree suitable commission and the like. My assistant usually deals with that side of things – I'm not very good with figures.'

Cameron smirks and claps me on the shoulder. I flinch and hope he doesn't notice.

'Gotcha. Yeah, I don't deal with any of that stuff these days either. But I'll get my numbers person to give yours a call and hopefully we can strike a deal. I think we can help each other out.'

'Yes, I think so too,' I reply. Which is true.

'I'm on a three-line whip to come for dinner again tonight,' Cameron adds. 'Matt and Didier think I should put in another appearance for the dead man's brother, and I need to stay in Didier's good books. So I'll see you later. Your lovely wife out of bed yet?'

I wince. It sounds so suggestive when he puts it like that. 'Ria?' I say pointedly. She has a name. 'I think she's feeling better, thank you.'

'It's been great to see her again. We go back a long way.'

'Really?' This is news to me. I feel a lurch of alarm. Ria and Cameron know each other? Since when? Is this something else she hasn't told me about?

He does that weird bark/laugh again and it makes me shudder. 'Ah, silly me – I forgot,' he says, in a sly way which makes it clear he didn't. 'I wasn't supposed to mention it. Not sure why – you'd need to ask her. She's a dark horse, isn't she? Yeah, we worked together. Long time ago. Practically a different lifetime, in fact.'

'Oh yes, that does ring a bell actually,' I lie. It definitely doesn't. I would have remembered something like that. I feel sick. Why wouldn't Ria have told me? I don't want Cameron to know that my wife isn't being honest with me, so I try my hardest to remain nonchalant, but all the while alarms are going off in my head. I'm sure he knew I didn't know – I bet he only told me just now so that he can feel like he has the upper hand here.

Have they slept together? Is that it? Is that why she didn't tell me they know each other? Is that why she asked him not to say anything? Is that why she keeps not wanting to come to dinner? Is that why she's being so weird and strange this week and saying she wants to go home the whole time? Is that even why she doesn't want to have children with me – does she still have a thing for him? My face grows hot and I need to be away from this man. I mumble something about being in touch soon and make a dash for the door.

Ria is in bed reading when I get back. She puts down her iPad and smiles at me. 'Hey. How was the chalet tour?'

'It was . . . illuminating,' I say curtly.

'Oh yes?' She nuzzles against me. 'I imagine they're all pretty much like this one, aren't they? Showy luxury for people who like to feel they deserve only the best?'

I feel a pang of love for her, I can't help it. 'They are. But it wasn't that that was illuminating – the chalets were pretty much as I expected them to be. Cameron says you and he already know each other. Is that true?'

She sits up, looking appalled. 'He promised! I mean . . . what did he say?' she squeaks.

'I want to hear it from you,' I snap. 'How do you know each other?'

344

I didn't realize this actually happened in real life, but the colour drains from her face.

'Hugo . . . why do you need to know?' she whispers. 'It was all so long ago . . .'

I knew it. 'He's an ex!' I shout, my voice coming out much louder than I was expecting. 'Why didn't you tell me? Fuck, I must look like such a twat! He'll have been laughing at me all week! No wonder he has such a smug expression on his face the whole time. God, Ria!'

I turn away and pace to the other side of the room. I can't look at her. And I'm not sure I can bear to look at Cameron again either. Maybe we should get out of here now, like Ria wants to, go home. Maybe Olivia could sort a flight somehow? Perhaps we could get a private jet like those clients of Cameron's he was talking about. Anything, anything to get away from this man who has slept with my wife.

'No!' Ria cries, interrupting my mental fuming. 'Gross. He's not an ex. Nothing like that. I can't stand him. But we . . . we worked together. A long time ago.'

I turn and stare at her. 'That's what he said too. But if that's all it was, why wouldn't you have told me? There must have been more to it than that?'

She shakes her head. 'There wasn't. There isn't. We worked together. That's all. Look, does it matter? It was long before I met you and, before this week, I hadn't seen him in years. I forgot to tell you about it. So what? There are plenty of other people I've worked with who you've never met. It's now that matters.' She throws back the covers and crawls across the bed. 'Look, I've stopped taking those pills now so why don't we . . .'

She starts fiddling with my belt buckle but I push her hands away. 'No. I want to know why you lied.'

'I didn't lie!' she shrieks. 'I never told you I didn't know him!'

'But he was there at dinner,' I say, slow and measured. 'You didn't tell me that you *did* know him. You must see that that's not normal behaviour, Ria? You acted like he was a stranger. You arranged this trip, you didn't mention it then either. He said you'd asked him not to say anything. So if he wasn't an ex then . . .'

She slumps back on the bed.

'There are things . . . something . . . from that time of my life I'm not proud of.'

'We all have things in our past we're not proud of. I'm your husband. You shouldn't be keeping things from me.' I pause. 'Look, if you had a one-night stand with him or something, that's fine, it's not like I think there was no one before me, I'd just rather you'd told me what to expect before we got here, that's all. I feel like he's been laughing at me all week.'

Tears start to roll down her cheeks. 'I never slept with him. I wouldn't ever have wanted to. He's not laughing at you, I promise,' she says hoarsely. 'It's just that he knows stuff about me.' Ria almost never cries. I feel myself soften inside.

'Ria, come on, it can't be that bad,' I say gently. 'What happened? Where were you working when you met him?'

She swipes the tears away. 'Here. We were working here. We were ski instructors. We killed someone.'

56

January 2020, La Madière, France

Adam

Well, that was the worst day ever. Thank God it's over.
The day after tomorrow, I can be on my way back to
Thailand and hopefully things can return to normal.

Poor Will. As soon as I get back in the car I wonder
if I should have visited him in the mortuary after all.
But I can't imagine twenty years on a mountainside is
kind to a body. Seeing him in that state isn't going to
help him, and it certainly isn't going to help me. I don't
believe in an afterlife, so he's not going to know or care
either way.

It's a huge relief to be back at the chalet. I've grown
accustomed to living quite basically in Thailand, in spite

349

of my recent inheritance. It makes a change to have a bit of luxury, especially being waited on so attentively.

When I arrive, Millie is laying out afternoon tea – homemade cakes, biscuits, and plates of fruit. As soon as I enter, she straightens up.

'Good afternoon, Adam,' she says. 'I hope your day went to plan and wasn't too distressing?'

'Thank you. It was upsetting, of course, but Didier and Matt did everything they could to make it as easy as possible.'

'I hope you feel that there's been some . . . closure, if I may?'

'Closure?' I say, taking a beat or two to realize what she means. I hate these new-agey therapy-speak words. 'Yes. I guess so. Though I will still have to arrange a funeral. I haven't decided what to do about that. I haven't really arranged one before.' By 'haven't really', I mean haven't ever. Mum arranged Dad's funeral, and bar a few emails and calls, I left the same funeral house and the family solicitor to arrange Mum's a couple of years later. I simply turned up on the day. It might sound callous, but these people are dead, they're just bodies. They don't care what their casket is like or which flowers people choose. It's all a giant fuss and waste of money as far as I can see.

Will's funeral, though, was something which was brought up at the hospital. It was couched in the nicest possible terms via Didier's translation, but the upshot was that Will couldn't stay in the hospital morgue forever and I needed to let them know as soon as possible what I wanted to have done with the body.

'Oh?' Millie prompts. 'Will you not want to, um, take him home to your family so they can, ah, say a proper goodbye?'

I spoon a few pieces of fresh fruit onto a plate and sit down on one of the lovely plush sofas. 'There's no family, only me,' I explain. 'My parents died some time ago. And I don't have a base as such. I've been travelling for a long time and now I'm mainly in Thailand. But Will had never even been to Thailand, so it would be weird to take him there.' Poor Will. So many things he never had the chance to do.

Millie nods. 'I see. I hope I'm not speaking out of line, but in that case perhaps I wonder if you might like to have him cremated and his ashes scattered here?' There is a pause. 'As I understand it, from what you've said, he was happy here during your last holiday together – perhaps it would be somehow appropriate, if there's no particular home for you as such.' She pauses. 'I'm sorry. I shouldn't have said anything. Obviously, the funeral details have to be your decision and I shouldn't even be expressing an opinion about something like this.'

I see her blush as she starts fussing with the already perfectly arranged tea tray.

'No. No, that's a nice idea – thank you,' I reply, because it is. And what else am I going to do with his body? At least this way I will be seen to have made an effort, rather than having Will cremated somewhere anonymous with no one there at all while it happens. 'Perhaps I could arrange that before I go back. I'm not sure of the formalities, how long it would all take. Obviously, I would find myself somewhere else to stay,' I add hastily, 'I wouldn't want to impose on your and Cameron's hospitality any longer.'

She smiles. 'We are very pleased to have you here. If you do decide to stay on, I can speak to Cameron and see if anything can be arranged. But I'm afraid it's his call, not mine, and I know the chalets are very busy.'

'Of course. I wasn't fishing for an invitation,' I add, embarrassed.

She nods. 'Don't worry, I know you weren't. Now, if you'll excuse me, I need to go and finish the hot chocolate and coffee. Do you have everything you need, or can I get you anything else?'

I suddenly feel very tired. 'Do you have any paracetamol? I've got a crashing headache.'

'I'll bring you some. And perhaps some water – maybe you're dehydrated? Still or sparkling?'

'Still. Thank you.'

57

January 2020, La Madière, France

Adam

I go for a lie-down and fall asleep immediately. When I wake up, I feel worse – groggy and slightly sick. It's dark so it must be evening. I check the time – almost seven. I've been asleep for over two hours.

I feel better after a shower, helped by the lovely thick towels and fabulous-smelling toiletries. The hot water on my skin is invigorating – it's so rarely cold enough in Thailand to warrant using water which is properly hot. I still feel rough and wish I could go straight back to bed, but I think I should put in an appearance at dinner.

By the time I get downstairs the rest of the group is on the various sofas, drinking champagne and eating canapés. My stomach churns.

'Adam!' Simon booms. 'How was your day?'

Simon is red-faced, I'm not sure whether from wind burn from being outside today or from alcohol. Quite possibly both. His young wife (Cath, was it?) gives him a nudge and he pulls an 'oops' face. 'Sorry,' he blusters. 'I mean, I hope your day wasn't too difficult. Can we offer you a drink? Ease the, uh, I mean, well, would you like a drink?'

Millie appears at my side with a tray of champagne glasses and I fight down a wave of nausea. 'Could I have a glass of water for now?' I ask. 'Maybe I'll have some wine with dinner.'

'I hope today went as well as it could have,' Hugo says. It sounds like a line he has learned.

'Thank you. I hope your wife is feeling better?'

He colours slightly. 'Ria's . . . a little better. She said she'd rather stay in her room this evening. But she sends her condolences I'm sure.'

I nod. 'I appreciate that. I'm not feeling too good either. Perhaps there's a bug going round.'

There is an awkward silence which Matt fills by asking Simon about his day. Thankfully he launches into a long and boring story about exactly which pistes he skied and a punch-up he witnessed in a lift queue, so there is no need for me to say anything.

*　　*　　*

We have dinner. There seem to be endless courses. I take a sip of the cold amuse bouche soup, a spoonful or two of the soufflé starter, then a mouthful of *magret de canard* and dauphinoise potatoes. Lunch was enormous and I'm struggling to force anything down. I'm sure the wine is excellent (both red and white, a different one with each course) but I can't even finish a glass. The pre-dessert mint sorbet is the only dish I manage to eat in its entirety – it's refreshing and soothing. I don't even touch dessert, a sickly-looking, oozing slab of something chocolatey. Then there are *petits-fours* – I ask for a mint tea instead of coffee and refuse a digestif.

Dinner starts out as a fairly subdued affair; I'm guessing in deference to my situation. But as more wine is drunk, tongues and inhibitions loosen and now the room feels rowdy. Simon's voice booms above all the others and he and Cameron are unashamedly trying to outdo each other with tales of extravagance, showing off about how much money each of them has. Hugo chips in occasionally. Cass (not Cath, I remember now) and her nanny chat quietly between themselves. I don't have the energy to say anything but nod and smile when someone makes a comment which seems to be aimed at me.

Millie is clearing away the dirty dishes and suggesting we move to the lounge area. I push my chair back and force myself to my feet.

Cass touches my arm. 'Adam? Are you OK? You look really pale.'

355

My head is spinning. I can barely see straight.

'I'm not feeling too good,' I mumble thickly. 'I think I'll head for bed, if you'll excuse me.'

Behind me as I stumble up the stairs as I hear the others mumbling things along the lines of 'poor bugger' and 'must have been a hard day'.

I fling open the door of my room, stagger into my bathroom, and vomit up my entire dinner.

58

December 1998, La Madière, France

Adam

'Ow!!' Will wails, like the girl he is. 'That hurt!' He pushes himself back up on to his feet and rubs his head. He's now covered in snow. The wind is still roaring around us and even though it can't be later than about four o'clock or so, the sky is so dark it looks like it's almost night.

Will glares at me, still rubbing his head. 'Look, Adam, this is getting us nowhere,' he snaps. 'We've lost our guides, you've lost your ski. We're going to have to do something, as the phrase goes, before one of us dies, which in this case, could quite literally happen.'

I clap my hands against my arms, trying to warm up. It really is getting cold now. 'Right then, arse-face – what would you suggest?'

Will makes a big show of turning himself around, picking up each of his skis in an exaggerated way in turn so that he flicks snow all over me. Even as he is all muffled up I see him smirk. I reach down, pick up a huge lump of snow and hurl it at him.

'For fuck's sake!' Will explodes. 'This is hardly the time or place for snowball fights, is it, you moron! Like I said before,' he says, speaking slowly as if addressing a particularly stupid child, 'as you have lost your ski, I will have to go down and get help.'

'No. You're not leaving me here on my own,' I insist. 'We'll wait – the guides know where we are – someone will come eventually.'

Will sighs and looks upwards. There is a pause as we both listen to the wind raging, snow stinging our faces. 'Look, Adam. I know it's not ideal, but I think it's the best plan. The guides don't necessarily know exactly where we are – *we* certainly don't know where we are. We're not on a patrolled piste. For all we know, when you fell we might have come off the path we were meant to take. I'm not saying it's your fault—'

'Well it pretty much sounds to me like you are,' I interrupt.

'Whatever. We probably shouldn't have come out in these conditions. But it's too late to change that now, so we're going to have to be sensible.' His voice softens.

358

'I know it will be scary to be here on your own but I think that, given—'

'I'm not scared, you pompous twat!' I shout. How fucking dare he patronize me like that?

Will sighs. 'Right. Good. Well, in that case, there's no problem, is there? I'll go and get help, you stay here, *not being scared at all*, and before you know it we'll be back in the chalet with the girls.'

The fucker. I'm not having this. 'Yeah. With the girls. Nell and Louisa. Because Louisa only has eyes for you, hey?' I say, snidely.

'For God's sake, Adam, leave it, will you?' Will snaps. 'I'm freezing cold, I can barely feel my face, I'm only in this situation because of *you* to start with, it's down to *you* being such a shit skier and falling over that you've lost your ski and that we're not already down in the warm instead of still stuck on this fucking mountain. I can do without your usual jibes about how you could have had any of my girlfriends you wanted, any of them, any time. Just because you snogged that girl I was kind of seeing when I was thirteen or whatever doesn't make you God's gift.'

He starts fiddling with his poles, putting his hands carefully through the straps the way we were taught in ski school about a thousand years ago and adjusting his various scarves. Why is he wearing so many anyway? What a twat.

Suddenly I really don't want to be left alone here. He is not going to do this to me.

359

'That Louisa,' I say, to stall him. 'I think you could do way better than her.'

He rams his poles violently down into the snow and continues faffing around with his wrist straps. 'Fuck off, Adam. I'm going now, I don't care what you say. You'd better hope that I actually get round to telling anyone you need help, which I have to say, right now, I'm sorely tempted not to bother doing.'

How fucking dare he talk to me like that? 'Right goer Louisa is,' I add. 'What do you think we were doing all yesterday afternoon while you were sorting out your broken ski?'

His head snaps up and he stops fiddling. 'Yeah right, whatever. Seriously, Adam, you can fuck right off. One more word and . . .' He shoves me in the chest, his pole dangling from his wrist but because he's still clipped into his skis he doesn't have much impact.

I step closer to him. 'One more word and what, little brother? We had lunch, we drank a lot. Then we went back to your room, and we fucked. She *loved* it. Couldn't get enough of me.'

I feel a sudden pain in the side of my head and realize Will has punched me. I wasn't expecting that. 'You liar!' Will roars as he tries to come at me again, but he's still fixed into his skis so he can't move much. 'She wouldn't!'

I laugh. 'Oh yes she would,' I sneer. He swings at me again and I shove him hard.

This time, he falls over. By now the wind is even

stronger and it's a virtual whiteout. He scrambles to get up but he can't so he reaches under the snow and clicks his skis off. Stupid, stupid, that was our only way down. Now he will have no option other than to wait with me, the stupid fucker.

Freed from his skis, he launches himself at me with his full weight, pushing me backwards. I grab his jacket, judo style and hurl him behind me. He picks himself up and throws himself at my legs in a kind of rugby tackle which knocks me off my feet. I scramble up at the same time he does and launch my entire weight at his back, giving him an almighty push.

There is a yelp, and for a few seconds I see his bright blue jacket fall through the air, over a precipice neither of us had seen, until he disappears and everything is white again.

And then there is silence.

59

January 2020, La Madière, France

Adam stays in bed the next day. I play the dutiful nurse, taking him water, herbal tea, cold flannels, and hot water bottles, anything he requests, all prettily arranged on trays. He's so grateful that under almost any other circumstances, it would be rather sweet. And by the end of the day, he says he is feeling a little better. Not well enough to come downstairs, but well enough to try some soup. Chicken and mushroom. A thin, nourishing consommé. There's no need for me to include my special mushrooms this time – they will have already done their work when he 'enjoyed' them as part of his full English breakfast. Adam needs to think he's getting better.

It was disappointing when serving Cameron and Adam their special mushroom risotto went awry, but it was easy enough to have a second go at breakfast – for Adam at least. And making Adam ill will damage Snow Snow's reputation and, by extension, Cameron's business if I play things the right way, so it's all good. Two for the price of one.

It was fascinating learning about mushrooms at college. The particularly amazing thing about death cap mushrooms is the way their poison works. You eat the poison, like Adam did at breakfast – and then later that day, as I expected, the diarrhoea and vomiting started. Which is pretty gross – even in a well-insulated chalet like this the other guests would have got a sense of what was going on. But they've all left now, thankfully. It's been pretty unpleasant for Uncle Adam, but nothing more than he deserves. And fairly horrible for me too having to clean up after him, but I can handle that. It will all be worth it.

After the initial sickness which comes shortly after eating the mushrooms, you get better for a couple of days. So, as I thought he would, Adam wrote off his sudden illness as stress around Will's death, or perhaps a bout of food poisoning from something he ate at lunchtime before he didn't visit his brother in the mortuary. There were so many dishes at lunch with so many ingredients, apparently, it wouldn't have been beyond the realms of possibility that one of them poisoned him, Michelin star or not. Perhaps a dodgy oyster. Obviously the food poisoning can't have come from anything I prepared, because no one else in the chalet has been vomiting, have they? It was important Adam didn't decide he wanted to see a doctor or even go to hospital, as the poison needs time to wreak its havoc before he seeks medical attention, by which time it will be too late. It probably already is. So that's why I have been looking after him so well. It's made me shudder, but he's loved it.

A couple of days on, he thinks he's recovering. He's less weak now. And while I've been waiting on him hand and foot, I've also been gently reinforcing the idea of scattering my dad's ashes here. The more I think about it, the more I don't want my dad taken anywhere else. He's been here since he died twenty years ago and moving him to some random place because it might be convenient for Adam seems disrespectful. I'm going to make sure I can take charge of the funeral too, to give my dad the send-off he deserves. The kind of funeral I'm sure Mama would have wanted him to have. I don't think it will be too difficult to get my way.

60

January 2020, La Madière, France

Adam

Millie is an absolute angel, there is no other word for her.

I've spent two days feeling like I was about to die. I've picked up the usual travellers' bugs over the years, even had dysentery and dengue fever, but nothing has compared to this.

It's been a hellish couple of days, made only bearable by Millie bringing me anything I ask for, or anything she thinks might make me feel better.

And finally, I do feel a bit better. Yesterday I managed some of her delicious soup. Today I even got up for a while and ate an exquisite omelette from a tray on my knees while I watched something on Netflix.

The other guests appear to have left while I was in bed. I guess the roads have cleared now – I haven't been outside, but I can see the snow has eased off. I haven't seen Cameron either – I suppose he has other things to get on with and a bed-ridden, vomiting freeloader like me probably isn't much of a draw for him. Millie has new guests arriving the day after tomorrow, so I am going to have to move to a different place and look at booking a flight home. But first, we need to arrange Will's funeral.

Millie has been amazing about this too. I guess she has had the time pressure of her new guests arriving in the back of her mind and needs me out of the way. So along with helping me to get well so I can make my journey back to Thailand, she and Matt sorted out all the paperwork with the hospital so that the body – Will – can be taken to the crematorium and we can have the service, such as it will be, tomorrow. Millie brought the papers here for me to sign – apparently in France you can't do anything without a signature. I didn't entirely understand the forms as they were all in French, but signing them seems to have got the job done.

'Was Will a religious man?' she asks, putting some soup down in front of me on a tray set with silver cutlery and a white napkin.

'I don't think so,' I say. 'At least, we never went to church except for hatch, match, and dispatch type things, even as children. I don't think he'd ever have gone to church of his own accord.'

She nods. 'So no hymns or prayers then tomorrow, do you think?'

I shake my head. 'I don't think so.' I don't *think* Will would have wanted any of that, but more than that, I want to get the whole thing over with as quickly as possible. We don't need hymns and prayers prolonging the agony.

'Perhaps some other music then?' she persists. 'Did Will have any favourite bands? Or maybe we could include a reading? A poem or a book he might have liked?'

My head is fuzzy from lack of food and sleep, and these questions are beyond me. Plus, if I'm honest, I don't care. Will isn't going to know anything about it and my parents aren't around any more, so I don't understand who we're actually doing this for. Don't they say that funerals are for the living rather than the dead? And as it's just me left, it seems like a lot of effort for no reason. But Millie is being very sweet about it all so I don't feel I can say that without showing myself as the callous bastard I arguably am. Plus she really is very pretty and now that I'm starting to feel better and no one else is here, I wonder if I might be in with a chance.

'Um . . . I'm not sure. It was all a very long time ago,' I venture. *And if Will had lived he probably would have liked very different things by now* hangs unsaid in the air.

'You must remember some bands he liked, surely?' she presses.

'He had pretty shit taste in music, as far as I remember. He liked some of that eighties electronic stuff.'

She nods. 'I see. Maybe not so suitable for a funeral.'

Suddenly I think of something which might appease her. 'Oh! I know. He liked REM. He was rather middle of the road like that.'

'OK. Any particular song?'

For God's sake. I appreciate her concern but can't she leave it now? I'm not exactly on top form and I could do without this. I take a sip of my soup. It is scorching hot and delicious. 'I don't remember. I think he liked them all,' I say, hoping she'll leave it at that.

She smiles. 'No problem. Perhaps we can stream some and see if any ring any bells?'

I look at her. She is gorgeous, but I am tired. 'No, that's OK. You choose. I don't think he'd mind which one.'

She gets her iPad anyway and we listen through REM's greatest hits. In the end we settle on 'Everybody Hurts' and a Charlotte Brontë poem which Millie finds in a list of readings suitable for people who died young. What a thing to compile. Honestly, you can find anything on the internet these days.

The only funeral poem I could think of was that 'Stop the Clocks' one from *Four Weddings and a Funeral*, but when I actually read the words, they didn't seem right at all. Will wasn't alive long enough to be anyone's everything and it strikes me that I am probably one of only a few people who remember him much by now.

I might be mistaken, but at times while we are doing this, Millie looks a bit tearful. She's so sweet. After we've chosen the song and reading, she takes my tray away and as good as tucks me in.

It's been a long time since I felt so cared for.

61

January 2020, La Madière, France

'Everybody Hurts' – I remembered it was Mama and Dad's song, the one Mama used to sing to me sometimes during the rare times when she was in a reasonably good place mentally. It took a while, but eventually I managed to steer Adam in the right direction, and that's the song we chose for Dad's funeral. I could tell he was tired and didn't really care, so it wasn't that hard. It's what Dad would have wanted, I'm sure. Mama would be proud.

62

January 2020, La Madière, France

Adam

I wake with a start in the night, awash with nausea again. I stumble to the bathroom, barely making it in time.

Oh God. I thought this had finished? After what feels like hours of my body wringing itself out, I literally crawl back towards my bed. I can't even stand.

At first I think I must be hallucinating, but it looks like someone is there in the darkness, in my room.

'Millie?' I rasp. No one else is still here in the chalet any more, are they? They've all gone home. I know Millie is kind and dutiful – she's left me in no doubt about that over the last few days – but surely that doesn't extend to waiting on me in the middle of the night.

'Why are you here?' I gasp. My throat feels like it's been grated and my head is spinning. Millie lifts the covers back and I haul myself into bed.

'I need to tell you something,' she says. She snaps the bedside light on. Her face is hard and expressionless.

'Now?' I say, but it comes out as a whisper. 'But it's the middle of the night. And I'm not well at all. Can't it wait till morning?'

'No. You'll most likely be dead by morning. Unconscious at least, I'd say.'

I assume this is intended as a joke but, given the state I'm in, it seems uncharacteristically unsympathetic and in extremely poor taste. I lift my head to speak, but she holds her hand up and closes her eyes.

'Don't!' she snaps, opening her eyes again. 'I'm sick to death of hearing your stupid voice. I poisoned you. That's why you're ill. Those mushrooms you had at breakfast the other day? *Amanita phalloides*. Otherwise known as death cap. It's so unfortunate that dear Cameron's *artisanal* mushroom supplier made such a stupid and fatal mistake. *Don't you think?*'

'Not funny,' I rasp. 'Help me, Millie, please.' The room is spinning and lurching. I don't understand why she's still making these unfunny jokes about poison.

She has leaned in close to my ear now. 'Do you still not get it? Don't you know who I am?'

I'm confused. 'You're Millie?' I venture.

She is still staring at me with a look of contempt. 'I'm Will's daughter,' she states, simply.

376

What is she talking about? 'Will? Will's dead,' I force out. 'He doesn't have a daughter.'

She straightens up and steps back away from the bed. 'Yeah he does. Me. I'm his daughter. Do you remember my mama, Louisa, from the ski trip where you killed my dad? She got pregnant that week.'

'Pregnant?' I rasp.

'Yeah. Pregnant. Then she dropped out of uni, ran up debts, never really recovered mentally – not from the pregnancy, not from the poverty, not from the shock of my dad dying. I had a shit childhood, mainly in foster care, because of you. And then Mama killed herself. All because you killed my dad.'

'It was an accident,' I whimper.

'Not according to my mama,' she says briskly. 'She blamed you. And so do I.'

My body heaves again but nothing comes out – there's nothing left. Suddenly I register that perhaps she means it about the poison. She's actually poisoned me?

I realize what I have to do to make her help me. 'Will isn't your father,' I whisper. 'Wasn't your father.'

'Yes, he is,' she snaps. 'Mama told me. And I did my research. There's almost nothing I don't know about his so-called "accident", about him, and about you. That's why I came to work for Snow Snow – I wanted to mess up Cameron's company – he also played his part in this as the ski guide who didn't bother to keep my dad safe. Originally I was going to poison guests randomly – not kill them – perhaps a dodgy prawn

377

here, some undercooked chicken and a bit of salmonella there. I brought the mushrooms with me, dried – some more poisonous than others. I wasn't really planning to use the big guns, though – not initially.'

I try to concentrate on what she's saying but the room is still spinning and I feel like I'm about to pass out.

'But then Dad's body was found, you turned up, and my plans changed,' she continues. 'I was going to kill both you and Cameron that night with the mushroom risotto, because that's what you both deserve, but then you all switched places so I had to spill the wine and smash glass over everything so that no more innocent people got hurt because of you.'

I need to stop her. Need to get her to help me. I need to tell her. It's my only chance.

'You've got it wrong,' I utter. 'Will was infertile. Would never have been able to have children naturally.' My chest is heaving and I can barely breathe. 'Please, Millie, get me some help. I'm begging you.'

There is silence for a few seconds, when all I can hear is my own laboured breathing.

'What?' she says cautiously. 'He wasn't infertile. How could he be?'

'Cancer,' I breathe. 'When he was a child. Made him sterile. He probably hadn't told your mum.'

'But then . . .'

Oh God. This happened. It happened. I need to tell her. Make her stop this. 'I must be your father,' I manage to force out. 'Me and your mum – we had a thing. That

378

holiday. While Will was out skiing one afternoon. Please, Millie, I . . .'

She claps her hand over her mouth. 'But she hated you. The last time I saw her, before she died. She said it was all your fault that my dad – Will – died. She called you a cunt. It was the only time I heard her use that word.'

My body convulses again. 'I'll tell you everything, Millie, please . . .'

'You're not my father!' she yells. I can see tears running down her face. 'I don't want a man like you as my father! You're lying!' She puts her hands over her ears, closes her eyes, and starts shouting. 'No, no, no! Stop saying that! You're not my dad! You killed my dad!'

'Please call an ambulance . . .' I whisper, and then there is nothing.

63

January 2020, La Madière, France

Millie

It's the day of my dad's funeral.

Adam is in hospital. He's unconscious. They're saying he might pull through, but knowing exactly how many mushrooms he ate and when, I'm pretty sure he won't.

Considering how long ago Dad died and his lack of living family, there is quite a good turnout for the service. Matt is here. And Didier. Cameron isn't. He is no doubt busy dealing with the fallout from a man being fatally poisoned in one of his chalets. It's hardly good PR, is it? I sent a few anonymous emails to some newspapers last night to make sure everyone knew about it. I wouldn't want an incident like this to get swept under the carpet. I'm helpful like that.

I've been questioned by the police of course, and will be questioned again, but I'm not worried. I'm just a silly little chalet girl after all – not a mushroom expert. I can't be blamed if I was supplied bad mushrooms. I doubt Cameron can be either, but the publicity certainly won't do him or Snow Snow any good.

There is no one to give a eulogy as such, but Didier from the resort says a few words about how the mountains can give and can take away and how saddened the entire resort is that this man was taken so young. I read the Charlotte Brontë poem – I made a big deal to the funeral director of how I had helped Adam to plan the funeral and lied about how he had asked me to read the poem and to help him scatter the ashes because he didn't want to do it by himself.

'Everybody Hurts' plays and I watch as the curtain closes behind the coffin.

Later, I will collect the ashes. I'm going to take them to the top of the last lift Dad took and let them go. I said that that was what Adam had planned to do and I'd like to pay my respects to both men by doing it for him. No one else can be bothered with it; they're happy to have the job taken off their hands. No one cares about my dad now but me. Everyone else is dead, except Adam, who also doesn't care and will be dead soon too.

And as for Adam saying he was my biological father? It's not true. Mama would have told me. He just said that in a desperate attempt to try to make me call an ambulance. Which I did, eventually, but only because I knew it was already too late for him. And either way, Mama hated him. She blamed him for killing the love of her life. It was what he did that drove her to suicide. It was what he did that ruined my childhood. I did the right thing. He wasn't my father.

Epilogue

Six months later

Ria

I smooth my hand over my bump and feel a small kick. I didn't ever expect to enjoy being pregnant, but actually it's kind of nice. Cosy.

We are having a girl. Hugo is so excited. The house is full of flowers and little gifts for me; he can't help himself.

While Hugo and I will probably never exactly be Romeo and Juliet, since I told him about what happened in the past, we've grown a lot closer. Hugo has made me see a therapist and while I never thought therapy would be my thing, it's made me see things more clearly.

I've never forgiven myself for what happened on the mountain and have been punishing myself ever since, according to my therapist. And although I thought I'd married Hugo purely as a way out from my desperate life and failing business, the couples' counselling we've also been having has made me see that there was more to it than that. More to him than being a source of money and a way to stop Cameron telling the world about what I did. It turns out I do like Hugo after all; he is a good man and he would do anything for me. In time, I'm sure I can grow to love him. I'm determined to, for the sake of our baby.

As for Adam . . . well, that was unfortunate. Mistakes with mushrooms happen now and again even in the smartest of restaurants, apparently, and even to people who are very experienced with funghi. There are some types which can look very like another, so they say. It was lucky we didn't eat the risotto that night, otherwise we could have all been in the same boat. But it was only poor Adam who had the full English the next morning. No one could have predicted the consequences.

In the end, Hugo didn't take on the Snow Snow chalets – the story about the poisoning was in the press on and off for several weeks and no business in their right mind would take on chalets where something like that had happened. I have severed all ties with Cameron – my therapist has made me see that I have nothing to fear from him, plus Hugo now knows about what happened all those years ago anyway. It turns out

Cameron was right about that. Nobody is bothered about it apart from me, and even I'm learning to let it go.

I've read in the press that Snow Snow has had many cancellations this season. It's even possible that Cameron may be prosecuted over Adam's death, but that seems unlikely to me. A man's death will be written off as an accident, like all those years before, and life will move on.

Simon invested in Redbush Holidays after the ski trip nonetheless. Ria Events has now also become an official subsidiary of Redbush and I am events manager for the two companies. And despite several travel companies going to the wall in recent years, Redbush is going from strength to strength, thanks in no small part I would say, to Olivia and me. Hugo is a good man, but he's never really been cut out for business, bless him.

I sent a wreath of flowers to Will's funeral, and another to the one which was held for Adam a few days later. After all, I knew them both once, if briefly. It was the least I could do.

Millie

There was an investigation, of course, and I was sacked, as I'd expected, but no one could prove what happened was anything other than a tragic accident. And just like before, press interest died down after a few weeks. I could probably get another job as a chalet girl next year if I wanted. And I might do that. It would be nice to be out in the mountains again, close to Dad. Perhaps I could even go back to La Madière.

Snow Snow's bookings are well down though, I am delighted to read. I've helped this along with a few fake Twitter accounts and online reviews, complaining about food poisoning in some of Cameron's other chalets. Hopefully the damage to the company is irreparable. Cameron is the type for whom failure is worse than death, so I feel he's got his comeuppance for now. Not to mention that another dead body in the same resort would have aroused too much suspicion anyway. I'm happy with how things have turned out. As far as those two men go, I think I have done what Mama would have wanted.

But there's still the other ski instructor, Andy Jones, to find. I haven't finished yet.

Acknowledgements

Huge thanks to my brilliant agent Gaia Banks at Sheil Land Associates for her always-useful input as well as patiently putting up with reading all my very rough, early and unfinished drafts, and to Phoebe Morgan at HarperCollins for her unbridled enthusiasm for the book and for being the kind of editor any writer would dream of. Thanks also to her colleagues at HarperCollins for their excitement about the book from the very beginning. I couldn't wish for a better home for it.

Thank you to beta-readers Louise Cole, Sarah Dodd, Leila Rasheed, Katrina Riley, Sarah Wells, Jackie Wesley and Laura Wilkins with apologies if I have forgotten anyone - all of you helped shape the book in one way or another.

Thank you to copy editor Anne O'Brien for tidying up my words (and making me realise how much I overuse 'just') and to Claire Ward for the fabulous cover.

Thank you to the WriteWords YA community from a few years back which was always so brilliantly helpful at critiquing my chapters for various books.

Thanks also to the various Facebook groups where I like to waste my time when I'm meant to be writing, especially to the Frisbees, the Manatees (much missed), the Savvies, the Debuts and the brilliant and hilarious Witches.

Thank you to Dad and Liz for sending me on my first ever skiing holiday, putting up with my teenage nonsense and everything else since. I am really grateful even if I don't often say it.

Thank you to Toby and Livi for putting up with the 80s music, slow skiing and much more besides. You make me proud every day.

Finally, special thanks to Alex for pretending not to mind while digging a trench in the rain or chopping wood or whatever while I 'get on with my book', as well as the unending support and belief in me, of course.